MW01228311

BORN OF GHOSTS

Fictive Kin book two

BORN of GHOSTS

Nicole Silver

WHITE RAVEN PRESS

Second Edition, 2023.
ISBN: 978-0-9879363-6-3
This book was previously published as *Hexen* by Nic Silver.

White Raven Press
North Cowichan, British Columbia, Canada
www.whiteravenpress.com

Cover design and digital alterations by Nik Sylvan
Model stock © Neo-Stock via www.neostock.com
Animal stock © Mircea Costina via Shutterstock.com
Background stock (moon) © Dary423 via Dreamstime.com
Background stock (forest) © Shukaylova Zinaida via Shutterstock.com
Background stock (city) © Songquan Deng via Dreamstime.com
Fog brushes © Krist A via brusheezy.com
Title typefaces: Eva Antiqua Heavy by Spiece Graphics, and Snell Roundhand by Linotype

Content warning: This book contains material that is not suitable for all audiences. It is recommended for readers 18+. Some content that may be triggering for readers includes explicit sex, violence, and sexual violence.

For Nicole D.
who copyedited

Chapter One

I'VE NEVER BEEN addicted to anything stronger than caffeine – not that I remember, anyway, and since my memory's not much longer than a year past, I guess that doesn't count for much. But that I recall, I've never been addicted to anything stronger than caffeine, and I've never tried to kick that habit, so I have no idea what withdrawal is like.

I suspect, though, that the kind of withdrawal most people go through when they clean up from booze or heroin or whatever their self-destructive substance of choice was, is nowhere near what Evgeny felt when he stopped drinking *hexen*.

Hexen's not a drug, though, it's a kind of person, a witch. And Evgeny's a vampire.

Yeah, I'm Su, and my boyfriend's a vampire. And let me tell you, before you decide to go looking for a pretty vampire lover of your own, you don't want one.

Not all vamps are gorgeous, like Evgeny – I got lucky there – though most of them are in pretty good health. Except the ones that aren't. Because vamps – they call themselves "Reborn," by the way – are pretty much like humans. They come in a variety of shapes and sizes (though the vamp symbiont keeps them on the lean side), colors and temperaments. Except they're stronger and faster, they hear and see better, and in general they're more *powerful* than the humans from which they're made. And that makes a lot of them much bigger pricks.

You know that saying about power and corruption, absolute power and absolute corruption? Yeah, that's vamps. Well, a lot of them. To be fair, aside from Evgeny, who's not exactly a normal bloodsucker, I met a bad crowd. It is possible for someone who's a decent human to remain decent on becoming a vamp. It's just really, really unlikely. First thing, vamps don't tend to choose decent people when they select their offspring. Second, if they *did* choose someone nice, that person isn't likely to survive very long, because vamps are not at all against cannibalism, so it takes a distinct lack of niceness to make it through the re-birth process. And third, give a hundred nice young men (or nice young women, though female vamps are rarer for some reason I never discovered) a taste of super-strength, and how many nice young men do you suppose you'd have left? Probably not many.

But like I said, Evgeny's different from other vamps. Hell, he was different from other humans. But I'm biased, 'cause he's mine.

Right now, I'm wishing he was someone else's problem. And how's that for being a great girlfriend? But as soon as he started showing signs of the DTs (that stands for detox, right, because if not, I have no idea what it means), he decided to stay at my place until it passed. Because I live on the top floor of a converted warehouse, and my only close neighbors are the werewolf downstairs and a guy on the first floor who's so seldom home I can't even remember what he looks like.

Yeah, weres are real, too. And good thing, because when things started getting real bad, I thought Evgeny might try to drink *my* blood, and that's one place I will not go, no matter how pretty the bloodsucker. So Magne – he's the werewolf neighbor – helped me tie Evgeny to a metal roof-support pillar in my loft.

You know how a shark's jaws kind of unhinge when it chomps on something? Or a snake's? Well, a vamp's jaws can do that, too. Both upper and lower, till their mouth is like a gaping red hole in their face. And their fangs are like a snake's, too. A cobra's maybe, or a cottonmouth. They fold out of the way when they're not needed, with only little gaps between the other teeth to show where they fit. But they can fold down like a venomous serpent's, and they're curved and needle-sharp like that, too. And when the symbiont's foremost, a vamp's eyes catch the light and appear to glow — blue-orange in incandescent light, purple in fluorescent.

It's pants-pissing scary, even when you know the vamp, when he shares your bed and brings you flowers (night-blooming jasmine), and helps you build the stupid cheap bookcase you bought at the discount department store so you'll have somewhere to keep the boxes of books he helped you carry home. Even when he starts building you a real bookcase out of real wood the next day, and then cooks spicy noodles for supper and gives you a backrub and…

Well, I'm looking at this vamped-out *beast* tied to a pole in my loft and it's only because I'm stubborn and it's my damned apartment that I don't turn and walk out. And also because, fucking bloody hell, I fell in love with him, hard and completely. I'm pretty sure Evgeny wouldn't hurt me, even like he is now, but I'm not *certain*.

I crouch down on the floor in front of him, talking quiet, like you do to a frightened animal, but making sure I'm out of his reach. His mouth's reach, that is.

"Evgeny," I say, and I try to put all my feelings for him into his name, though it's hard to bring those feelings to mind looking at him, jaws gaping and fangs straining like they could almost shoot out of his mouth and fasten onto my neck like the proboscis of some huge, horror-movie insect.

"I know you feel like shit," I say. "But you're stronger than this." I say a bunch of other stuff that doesn't really make sense, but that sounds nice, and somewhere in the middle of it, he actually starts to listen.

I shift my weight a little, to reach behind me for the bloodbag I've warmed up in a pot of hot water on the hotplate – I bought a microwave specifically so Ev could heat up blood without having to use the hot-plate, but you can't microwave blood in a bag unless you want an explosion, and he can't deal with a cup right now. A little drool escapes the corner of Evgeny's mouth and splats onto the floor. His hands are tied behind his back, secured to the pole, and he sits with his legs tucked under him, leaning forward, straining his shoulders.

"Hungry," he says.

"I know," I say. "This'll help." I had to buy the blood from Liam, who runs a vamp market not far away. I don't trust Liam – I trust him even less now that I know some of the things he's involved in – but since I sort of… disrupted the running of a big vamp corporation that supplied a lot of "sustenance" as the PC term is, there aren't so many choices of vendors around. Though I have noticed a lot more vamps being nice to me.

I don't trust Liam not to try drugging Evgeny, so I asked Magne to test the blood before I gave it to Ev. See, werewolves are created by a close relative of the symbiotic organism that creates vamps, so a lot of the things that affect vamps will affect weres, too. Of course, Magne reminded me that if something's undetectable to vamps, it probably would be to him, too. But at least he could tell me it wasn't *obviously* tainted.

I cut open the sticky-out bit on the bloodbag where the IV attaches – Liam's goods are strictly black market and stolen, or so he'd have us believe, but the IV thing makes a handy straw – and edge closer to Evgeny.

His nostrils flare and he says, "You smell good."

"So you always say," I tell him. It was the first thing he ever said to me, when he was a newborn vamp and I saved him from becoming a snack for his own kind. All vamps like the way I smell. To them, I smell delicious, but the joke's on them, because my blood tastes foul, and it's probably toxic for them, too.

Because I'm not human. I'm not exactly *other*, either. Not yet. I'm in the process of becoming something, though. I was healed once, and given a sort of gift by three old Asian ladies – fox demons, though realize that I use "demon" metaphorically. A better term might be "spirits" or even "fairies," though the supernatural connotations aren't quite right. But it turns out I already had an inheritance of my own, something that came with the German half of my DNA and my German surname, Fuchs. It means "fox."

And there's a reason a powerful, sexy woman is called "foxy" and "vixen." Whatever it is I'm becoming exudes a strong, you could almost say supernatural, sex appeal. And for vamps, that means I must taste good, because bloodsuckers like to feast and get laid at the same time. "Fuck 'n' feed," they call it. Elegant, no? But sex and blood are the two things that keep them from shriveling up like Count Orlok over their very long lives.

"Hungry," Evgeny says again.

"I know, Ev," I say. "But I have to make sure you drink the bloodbag, and not me." I scoot closer, and get the tube into his mouth, but he's still vamped out and can't suck. I squeeze the bag and a little blood squirts into his mouth and it surprises him.

He jerks his head back and looks at me, eyes flaring in the lamplight. Then he licks his lips and the action makes his jaws fold up into their human configuration. He sucks on the bloodbag until it's flat and empty. Then he sits back, eyes closed, head resting against the pole he's tied to.

For a moment, I think he's fallen asleep, but then he says, "Thank you."

"Sure," I say.

He opens his eyes and there's no vamp glow. Just crazy bright blue that looks even brighter because of the black hair falling over them.

"I'm sorry," he says. "It's getting harder to stay in control."

I relax. The symbiont's dormant, as it should be, and the sweet man I love is back.

"You scared the shit out of me," I say. I crawl the rest of the way to him, and start to untie him.

"Maybe you should leave me tied up," he says. When his hands are free, he looks at the rope burns on his wrists. His fingers tremble and he folds them into fists. "Or find a cell to lock me in. If I get really crazy, these ropes won't hold me."

I lean against him. "It'll be morning soon," I say. "It hasn't been so bad when you're asleep."

He turns his head to kiss my cheek. "It's getting worse."

"I could ask Liam – "

"You know how much I trust Liam," he says. Yeah, no more than I do. Less, probably, because it was Liam's drug cocktail, fed to a handful of minions who Evgeny then fed off after they attacked us, that led us to where we are now, sitting on the floor trying to figure out how to get through the worst withdrawal in the universe.

But that's not quite true. Evgeny's papa vamp, the bloodsucker who made him, had been experimenting on his progeny by feeding them witch blood all along. Evgeny's been fed it since he was a newborn – he was the only vamp ever discovered to be able to consume it without dying. It *had* almost killed him, but he lived and it made him stronger, so strong he broke his chains, fed on the old vamp's other progeny, and wandered out into the street. And then I found him.

If things had stopped there, he might have been free of *hexen* relatively easily. But there were others, including the shadowy Reborn council, who wanted a vamp able to metabolize *hexen*, because they could then feed on *him*, and gain some of the abilities that witches have genetically. And Liam helped the council capture Evgeny. And they force fed him so much *hexen* it really *should* have killed him. But it didn't, and I rescued him. And then we should have had our happily ever after, but things never turn out that way. Not in real life. Not even when your real life is full of fairy-tale creatures.

Evgeny touches my face and I startle out of my thoughts.

"Su?" he says gently, his voice making my name sound so much more beautiful than it is.

"Mm?" I say. I'm tired, but he must be exhausted.

"If it gets too bad, if I try to drink you – "

"It won't," I say. "It's just withdrawal. You'll get over it, and you'll be fine."

His fingers slide over my cheekbone, behind my neck, and he kisses me. He tastes like blood and it makes me hungry. Whatever I am – fox woman, *fuchs*, demon – it doesn't drink blood, but it sure doesn't mind the taste. I open my mouth to his tongue, ready to start shedding clothes.

Because not only does this fox attract anyone who likes sex with women, but she also likes to *have* sex. Lots of it.

Evgeny pulls away, tilts his head so our foreheads rest together. "If I try to feed on you," he says. "Kill me. I don't want to live if I become that kind of monster."

"It won't come to that," I say. I *hope*.

Late in the day, I wake up next to him and lie in the darkness of the heavily-curtained bed, trying to figure out why I woke. I listen, I breathe in the loft's smells. Nothing's out of the ordinary, but there's a nagging feeling of not-quite-rightness.

I roll over and look at Evgeny. Unlike a vampire, who actually needs a fair bit of light to see, I can see in almost total black. Just a little faint light and my vision's good, if only in black and white. Foxes have eyes like cats, slit pupils and reflective retinas and all.

His breathing is rough and he's shaking, even in sleep. No doubt I'll be tying him to the pole again when he wakes, but for now he doesn't seem too bad. No worse than yesterday, anyway.

I crawl out of bed, between the curtains, and into the brightness of daylight. I prowl around, but nothing is out of place, so I sit on the couch in a pool of sunlight and brood. Whatever woke me up is in my own head, and it annoys me that I can't figure out what it is. It makes my tail thrash, which feels really odd because I'm sitting on it.

Did I mention I have a tail? A big, red, fluffy, completely ridiculous fox tail? I didn't always have it. In fact, it's so new I'm still surprised every time I feel it twitch or catch sight of it in the mirror.

Something happened when I went to rescue Evgeny. Something I don't understand, and that I only remember in a sort of slideshow of snippets. But Evgeny was watching, and he says that just for a moment I turned into a fox. Not in the way weres seem to become wolves, by reconfiguring the way their joints bend and their bones articulate so they appear to have transformed without actually shapeshifting, but really, actually turned into a fox. And when I turned back, I had a tail stuck to my ass. A for-real, living tail properly connected to the end of my spine, that hurts when you tweak it and goes all pins-and-needles when I sit on it too long.

And while it's pretty cool to have a tail, it pisses me off that I have to cut holes in the seats of all my jeans, and I have to wear long coats when I go out. So much for my favourite motorcycle jacket.

So that's another thing that makes me brood, that I still haven't figured out how to call on my fox-woman powers – or whatever you want to call them – at will. Never mind that it's only been a couple of weeks since I sprouted this furry appendage. I can still only use that extra strength and speed, it seems, whenever I'm about to be killed.

But Evgeny's the bigger problem now. I resisted falling for him because he's a vamp, and even though I've had to kill a few (so I know I *can*), he's more powerful than any of them. Because of what the witch blood did to him. And because he's got witch ancestry himself. It made him scary strong, scary fast. Hell, scary *everything*. Except he's also sweet and gentle and nice. But right now he's really scary again.

When the sun moves away from my spot on the couch, I get up, put the kettle on, and rummage in a drawer in the kitchen. At the very back, under a box of emergency candles, I find it. A tattered slip of paper with a name and phone number on it.

Alex.

It's a name irrevocably associated in my memory with terrible things, and wonderful things.

I lost my memory a little over a year ago when the fox women saved my life. I'd been raped and beaten and left for dead, and they'd healed me, taken the worst of my memories of the attack so I'd be able to function like a normal person, and left me to my own devices. Except they didn't just block the few memories they'd intended to, they erased them all. And later, they had no way to give them back, except for that one night, the night they found me and started to awaken the fox in me. So the only memories I have from before are of being raped by a werewolf – and he's had his punishment, care of Magne – and of falling in love with a red-haired gardener's apprentice named Alex.

I trace the letters of her name with one finger. I've dug this bit of paper out of the drawer so many times, but never called. I made my choice, and I chose Evgeny.

Alex, as it turned out, was a witch – as much a surprise to her as it was to me – and she was one of the ones captured by the council to feed to Evgeny. I'd freed her, and the rest of the witches, along with a bunch of vamps and weres and less identifiable *others* when I broke Ev out.

She remembers all our past together, when we worked at the same tourist-trap formal gardens, and I slowly worked up the courage to ask her out. I only remember that one night. The night she sent away a creep who'd been hitting on me, and then we'd walked around the garden when we should've been working, and made love next to the koi pond.

I can feel the damp between my legs, remembering her. The smell of her skin, the feel of her nipple in my mouth, the way she kissed me hard as she slid her fingers through the folds between my legs and made me come, kissed me so no one would hear me cry out in pleasure and find us there.

Evgeny moans and I glance towards the bed. Soon I'll have to tie him up again. And hope he doesn't break the rope. I should ask Magne if he has any chains. If this goes on much longer, I might go mad.

I look back at the paper in my hand. I don't have a phone, never saw the need, but I could borrow Magne's. Alex is a witch. She might not know much about being a witch yet, but she'll be in contact with the other witches. Witches are rare, and it seems to me they'd want to keep in touch. For safety from vamps, if nothing else, in case any of them try to rebuild what Samuel Charleston, self-appointed head of the vamp council, had lost. When I let his imprisoned minions kill him.

I don't know what I think the witches can do. Donate a little blood, maybe, to take the edge off for Evgeny? Does that even work? Taking the edge off? Or is it best to just quit flat?

Even if they *could* help me, it doesn't mean they would. Not even if Alex doesn't hate me for choosing Evgeny. To the *hexen*, Evgeny is an abomination. Not because he's a vampire, but because he's a witch – and male witches are vanishingly rare – who was *made* a vampire. Just a witch is great, just a vampire's okay, too, but both – that's apparently the worst thing anyone can be, to a witch, never mind that he didn't choose to be made a vampire, and didn't know he was a witch.

I stare at Alex's number until the sky starts to dim, and then I put it back in the drawer, under the box of candles, and reach out to shut off the madly boiling kettle.

Not yet. I might call her, if Evgeny gets worse. But not yet.

Chapter Two

EVGENY'S SO CLUMSY with his breakfast that I have to take the bloodbag from him, empty it into a big mug, and microwave it. I'm wondering if it wouldn't be a better idea to leave it in the bag and heat it up by pouring water from the kettle over it, or using the pot and the hot plate again. That way, he couldn't spill it.

I remember when he first tried to drink from a bloodbag, he didn't know what to do with it, and tried to bite it. Liam had to show him the straw trick. Later, we learned that sucking from the bag is like drinking from a baby bottle or a sippy cup. It's what baby vamps do so that can't make a mess. Feeding him from the bag, like I had to do last night, would be too much like admitting he's incapable of feeding himself like a grownup.

He sits at the table, shoulders rounded, like he's curling in on himself, like somehow he can stop shaking if he keeps himself contained in a smaller space. His hand trembles violently as he reaches to take the mug. I hold onto it until he'd got a secure grip with both hands.

I turn away to make bacon and eggs and fried potatoes for myself. I didn't use to be a big breakfast eater, but lately it seems I never get a chance to eat during the night, or else I forget to. When you start living nocturnally, you realize how inconvenient the world is for non-daytime-dwellers. So now I feed up first thing just in case. Plus, Evgeny likes to nibble at whatever I'm having. Vamps don't need to consume anything but blood and water, but they *can* eat, and Evgeny enjoys food. He doesn't eat a lot, but he refuses to give up the pleasure all the different flavors bring.

Tonight, he refuses my offer of a slice of bacon. "What's wrong?" I say. He usually loves bacon.

He shakes his head. "I feel nauseated," he says. And, right on cue, his face goes faintly green and he slaps a hand over his mouth. He only makes it halfway to the bathroom before he falls to his knees and vomits a flood of half-congealed blood onto the hardwood floor.

I grab the mop in one hand and a hand towel in the other and rush over to him. He's shaking even more, and I drop the mop to crouch and wipe his face. Beads of sweat stand out from every pore and his nose is running.

"Jesus, Ev," I say. "Do you think the blood was tainted?"

He opens his mouth to speak and vomits again, ribs heaving. This time he keeps going, retch after retch, until only thin dribbles of foam come up.

I put my arm across his shoulders and every muscle is tense, like he's straining to hold himself together. And maybe he is. His hands clench, fingers digging into the wood.

"Evgeny?"

He shakes his head, gasps, heaves, and nothing comes up.

I hold him close, feel him shaking, and hope like hell this is just a temporary – very temporary – phase of the detox. Because if he doesn't feed, the symbiont will devour him from within and he'll start to shrivel until he's little more than a barely-breathing corpse.

Vamps aren't dead, really. They die and get revived – like CPR only with mystical trappings – as part of becoming a vamp. It's why they call themselves Reborn (aside from it sounding suitably pretentious). In the brief time they're dead, and continuing after they're reborn, the symbiont makes all sorts of changes to their physiology. It slows down most of the bodily processes, including aging, but makes them stronger, faster, and more agile. But in order to remain properly *vital*, shall we say, they need to speed things up once in a while. Get the blood pumping, quite literally. Feeding does that, and provides nourishment besides. And sex does it. Somehow, I don't think Evgeny's in any more mood to get laid than he is to share my breakfast.

After a long moment, he takes the towel from my hand and wipes his face. He reaches for the mop, but I snag it before he does.

"I got it," I say. "You just sit somewhere for a bit."

He crawls to the nearest wall and leans against it, head between his bent knees. "I feel like shit," he says. "Worse than shit. Like shit hollowed out and infested with maggots."

"That's lovely," I say, and I drag a bucket of water out of the bathroom and dunk the mop into it.

"I don't feel lovely," he says, and his voice in uncharacteristically harsh, like I've said something really stupid. I can understand why, but it still stings.

He drops the towel in the floor and scrubs his face with both hands. I can see the muscles standing out on his arms as he tries to hide the shudders that have started.

"I'm sorry, Su," he says. "For everything. For all of this." Then he looks up and there's something odd on his face. Sorrow, maybe, or dismay. "You should have gone with your witch lover. Alex. Was that her name? She would never hurt you."

For a moment I wonder if he's seen me looking at the paper with her phone number, or if he's shared my dreams – which is something that's happened a couple of times before, only it was me sharing *his* dreams. If he's been looking in, so to speak, when I fall asleep and remember the koi pond, and the feel of her skin.

But there's nothing on his face to show he feels betrayed. And I should be clear. I may have an overactive sex drive, but I'm *loyal*, and I'm too honest for my own good. I may remember Alex fondly, and I may think about calling her, but I'd never cheat on Evgeny. Hell, I don't even *think* about cheating on him. It's only sometimes when I dream that my memories bring back Alex, and I can't help that, can I?

"You're not going to hurt me," I say. I make a last few passes over the floor, jam the mop back into the bucket, and shove the whole thing into the bathroom. "When Charleston had you captive," I say, sitting next to him and lacing my fingers in his, "you didn't hurt me." He grips my hand so hard it aches, but I don't complain. "You were so drugged that you didn't know who I was. Or who you were. The vamp was all you were. And you didn't hurt me then. In fact," I say, leaning closer and bumping my nose against his cheekbone, "I believe you kissed me."

He smiles at that. "I remembered that I loved you before I remembered my own name."

"So I'm not worried about you hurting me." Okay, so I said I'm too honest, and I am, usually. But sometimes you have to lie. Not often, and it never feels good, but once in a while it's necessary. Because I *was* afraid of him. Or of what he might become. But if I told him that, it might weaken his confidence, and that could make all the difference.

"Thanks," he says. He's breathing a little easier, shaking a little less, so I slide around him on the floor until I'm in front of him, kneeling between his thighs. I lean over and nudge his face with my nose until he tilts his head up enough that I can kiss him.

He tastes like blood again, and vomit, and gross as that is, the fox in me doesn't mind. Mostly he just tastes like Evgeny. I kiss him until I can smell that he wants me – did I mention I have a super-sensitive nose? And then I hunker down until my face is just about in his crotch and tug at the waistband of his jeans. He relaxes a little, unfolds his body enough that I can undo his fly and reach inside, where he's hard and hot and throbbing slightly.

"Are you sure?' he says, and each word is as much panting as it is coherent sound.

I don't say anything, I just flick my tongue over the tip of his erection and he moans and buries his hands in my hair. Usually I like to take my time, to tease him and draw out our lovemaking as long as possible, but I know we probably don't have much time until the next horrible phase of withdrawal hits.

So I suck fast and hard. But I stop before he finishes, because I want some, too. I fish a condom out of my pocket – a girl's got to be prepared and even though vamps can't reproduce sexually, there are other things to be cautious about – and unroll it over him.

He looks at me, and he's still got that look of wonder he gets, like he can't quite believe I love him, want him. But I do. Then I stand up, strip my jeans off (and doesn't *that* feel good for my tail), and kneel down again, over his lap.

He pulls my face to his, kisses me, cups by breasts in his hands and tweaks my nipples between his fingers. He's good at touching me, but he's hurrying too, and from that I know he's as worried as I am. So I slide myself over him faster and faster until I'm about to climax, and then I take him inside me.

His moan is short, bitten off, and it's over quickly. It's not the best sex we've had. Not by a long shot. Hell, it may even be the worst. But it feels good, if only for the release. A bit of intimacy I wasn't sure we'd get for a while, and that we might not get again for another while.

I stay on his lap until he goes soft inside me, which is about the same time he starts trembling again.

"I think," he says, pausing in doing up his fly to clench his fists against the floor, bracing against the tremors. "I think you'd better tie me up again, before you need Magne's help to hold me still."

It's worse this time, but he's weaker, and he rages until he exhausts himself, and then falls asleep on the floor.

His wrists are bloody where the ropes cut into them and I wish we'd thought to bandage them ahead of time. There's a pool of saliva next to Evgeny's face, but I don't dare get close enough to wipe it up. He didn't try to attack me or anything; he didn't even seem to know I was there once the symbiont took over, but I'd rather keep my distance just the same.

I'm making it sound like the symbiont is another personality within a vamp that replaces the vamp's original self sometimes, but that's not really it. I'm no expert, but back when I was still trying to figure out what I was, I thought my long canines and reflective eyes might mean I was some sort of vamp hybrid. So I read a lot – turns out old folklore is… well, not so much wrong as… frequently a misinterpretation of the facts. I also asked a lot of questions that probably would have got me killed if I'd asked them of anyone but Liam, who's a dodgy personality at best, but can be counted on not to do anything unless he can gain by it. And he stood to gain more – mostly cash – by helping me.

So I learned that the vamp symbiont is not a single separate entity, but a colony of symbiotic organisms. But while the new vamp's body is still adjusting to its presence, it kind of… represses the vamp's own memories and personality, leaving the newborn a creature of base instinct. In times of extreme stress, like when a vamp's heavily drugged or badly wounded, the symbiont is so busy trying to put the vamp's body to rights that it can overwhelm their brain again, just as if they were newborn.

And that's what's happening to Evgeny. Once he was used to metabolizing *hexen*, his body came to expect it, his symbiont could deal with it. But take the *hexen* away, and the symbiont has to work overtime to compensate again, so periodically it blocks Evgeny from himself.

Maybe. That's my hypothesis, anyway. I just hope the symbiont can adjust as quickly to *not* having witch blood as it did to having it.

That's not the only thing I'm worried about, though. The *hexen* made Evgeny even stronger and faster than other vamps. He is as far beyond even the older vamps as those vamps are beyond humans. All except Charleston, and Charleston had been feeding off Evgeny and getting all the benefits of witch blood with most of the toxicity filtered out. With no more witch blood, was Evgeny going to be just an ordinary vamp?

It makes no difference to me if he is a super vamp. In fact, I'd be more comfortable with him at normal vamp level, because then I'd know I'm his equal. You know, just in case he goes crazy and I have to kill him. Not that I think he would. I just don't like being weaker than my lovers. But supposing someone, one of the real vamp elders maybe, who even Charleston's so-called "council" is afraid of, decides they want a vamp who can drink witch blood and act as a sort of living filter for it, enabling them to gain its benefits by feeding on him? Without the extra oomph that *hexen* gives him, Evgeny won't be able to protect himself. Even *with* the extra power, they'd captured him, though it took underhandedness and a lot of drugs. And Liam. I will not forget the part Liam played.

I stand up, finally, tired of brooding, tired of worrying, needing to be in stillness. For me, the quickest way to stillness of the mind is through movement of the body. I find peace in kung fu. I have vague, shadowy memories that start to surface now and then, of being an angry teenager and discovering calm in the lessons of a diminutive Chinese man who moved like a hurricane. I never remember much more than that, except he was the only one back then who used my middle name, Su. Maybe it was because "Su" is Chinese and so was he. He called me "Angry Su" until I learned how not to be angry.

I can't practice here in the loft, even though there's room. Not now, not with Evgeny tied up and asleep on the floor. But I can't exactly leave him alone, either. Magne's not home when I knock, though, so I compromise and prop open the loft door and the door onto the roof with bricks. If I stay close to the door I'll be able to hear down the stairs, along the hall, and into the apartment if Evgeny wakes and starts moving around again. Yeah, I have really good hearing, too.

It's cold on the roof, and no doubt my landlord would be pissed at all the open doors in December. I'm not wearing a coat, just yoga pants and a thermal undershirt with a snug t-shirt over it, but pretty soon I'll be warm enough that it won't matter. I've got on a pair of highland dancing slippers that I found at a thrift store and wear around the flat – they're thin enough it's almost like being barefoot, but thick enough to protect my feet from the odd stray pebble or bump in the tarred roof.

I stretch a bit, and then start on a routine that fits my amorphous almost-memory of teenaged Angry Su. Strike and block and kick. Spin and kick and strike and leap. I'm good at kung fu. Good enough it saved my life from vamps once or twice. And a werewolf once. I'm better at it now that I'm something a little more than human. Faster. Much faster. As I am now, I'd leave my teacher in the dust.

But my tail… That's something else. I didn't have a tail when I learned kung fu. It's only been, what, a couple of weeks since it sprouted? It seems longer. But even though it weighs almost nothing, it changes my balance. How I move my tail changes everything. I've been so busy with Evgeny since I got this tail – yes, mostly with making love with Evgeny, fucking Evgeny, and making love some more – that I haven't really practiced properly. And my tail keeps throwing me off. I'm getting frustrated.

So I stop, spend some time just breathing, and then start again. Instead of running through the whole series, I go with basic moves. Newbie moves. Simple strikes and blocks and steps, one at a time. I try holding my tail one way, then a different way. Then I try moving it. And slowly, I find that I'm relearning everything. Slowly, I begin to feel more comfortable with an extra appendage. I feel less like I have a weird growth stuck to my ass, and more like it's a natural part of me. Just when I'm feeling like I've pushed myself as far beyond tired as I can go without hurting myself, I realize I've forgotten my tail is there. Well, not forgotten, but I'm only as aware of it as I am of my arms or legs. It just goes where it needs to be without me having to think about it, and not only doesn't it throw me off, but it actually makes the strikes more effective.

I've only managed the simplest moves when I stop, but I feel like I've accomplished a lot. I can even imagine living the rest of my life with this bushy tail, because it feels less foreign, and more a proper part of my body. It feels *good*.

I turn and look at the eastern horizon – or what passes for a horizon here in the city – looking for any hint of sunrise. The city's glow could mask some of it, but it doesn't look like day has arrived just yet. I realize I lost track of time while working out. I have no idea how long Evgeny's been down there by himself. So after a good stretch I go back in, pull the doors shut behind me, and start to think about cooking myself some supper. It still feels odd to have breakfast at nightfall and dinner just before dawn, but I'd rather not watch my boyfriend scorch in the sun. Besides, foxes are creatures of twilight, so day time and night time don't feel that different, except night's quieter, and I like quiet.

Evgeny's awake and sitting up, leaning against the post. He watches me come in.

"You hungry?" I ask, and he just stares. "Ev?"

A look of disgust twists his mouth into a scowl, so intense I feel it like a jab in the gut. Then Evgeny shakes his head sharply and it's gone. He looks confused.

"Su?" he says. "Did you go out?"

"Just to the roof," I say. I don't know what to think of that look. It's not like anything I've experienced before, not even from bigots who can't see beyond my slanted amber eyes and round Asian face. I may be half Euro, but to Chinese-haters, I'm all Chinese, and to Korean-haters, I'm all Korean. Hell, all Asian-haters seem to think I'm whatever flavor of Asian they least like. None of them ever see *me*. But I've never noticed any anti-Asian sentiment from Evgeny at all. In fact, I get the strong impression that ethnicity is irrelevant to him, except that it produces interesting variations in culture and folklore. Recently we've discovered that for some *others*, at least, there are genetic differences, too, but those things aren't any more significant, really, than eye color or the particular shape of a person's nostrils. Interesting details, sure, but not important to who a person really *is*.

"Did you… Was something wrong just then? Just before you spoke?"

There's that look of confusion again. It's familiar from when he was recovering from being reborn, but I'd hoped it was gone for good. His eyes are ringed with dark circles and his killer high cheekbones make him look gaunt rather than beautiful.

"No, I – " But he pauses. "My head's muddled," he says. "I'm having difficulty remembering."

I crouch in front of him. "You want me to untie you?"

He shakes his head. "I'm afraid, Su." His voice is quiet, and even my ears can't catch any tremble in it. He's simply stating the facts.

"It'll be over soon."

"It's not just that," he says. "I feel like something's happening to me beyond just withdrawal from witch blood and Charleston's drugs."

Of course. Charleston's drugs. I'd forgotten to factor them in, but they *would* make everything worse.

"Something like what?" I say. "Maybe the witches were wrong and being made a vamp didn't destroy any chance you have of developing witch abilities."

"Maybe," he says. "But wouldn't that feel… right? This just feels all wrong. All – " he stops abruptly and leans forward with a jerk, all the disgust and more back on his face. I almost fall over backwards trying to get away from him.

"*Lisa*," he says, hissing the word at me. "Filthy animal." Then he spits at me, draws breath to say something else and suddenly faints. His head makes a painful "thunk" when it hits the floor, but I can't even move to see if he's still breathing. I can't even make myself listen that closely.

It's not even the repulsion on his face, in his voice, in his very posture. It's the fact that he said those words in a voice completely unlike his own, like someone else stepped in and took over his body, just for a moment.

Chapter Three

I'M HALFWAY to Magne's door before I remember he's not home. I walk the rest of the way there, anyway, just for some distance. Tears are building behind my eyes, hot and salt-prickly. I refuse to cry.

What the hell was that? Was something... Is possession even a real thing? Sure, a lot of things I'd never have believed in when I was (or thought I was) human turned out to be real, but not everything. And the things that are real aren't ever actually *magic*, just weird. (I very carefully am *not* thinking about turning into a fox, about suddenly being a hundred pounds lighter, not to mention a different shape and covered in fur.)

But either something – someone – else was speaking through Evgeny, or else he's not remotely the person I thought he was, and he's real good at faking it.

I lean against Magne's door and listen. I came down the stairs, too freaked out to wait for the elevator, and it's only one floor anyway. There are two steel doors and a lot of space between me and Evgeny. And even though my loft is directly overhead, this place used to be an industrial warehouse and it's got steel and concrete and thick planks of wood between each floor – enough to hold up many tons of machinery and goods.

So it's not surprising that I can't hear anything. Usually the only thing I *can* hear is the whir of the elevator, unless something loud happens near a window. It's why Evgeny wanted to detox here instead of at his place, which is a nice genteel apartment on the top floor of a Victorian house in a pleasant neighborhood with lots of people. *Human* people.

It's kind of inconvenient for a vamp, since it's nowhere near a blood supply, either black market or fresh (since the only living donors are ones that won't be missed – but Ev doesn't kill people, anyway, unless they try to kill him first, or unless they threaten me). But a nice apartment is another thing Evgeny refuses to give up. He doesn't figure he should have to change his *whole* life, just because he has a new diet and can't go out in the sun anymore.

I should go back upstairs, make sure Evgeny's okay. That he hasn't escaped. But all that kung fu calm has evaporated. So I sit next to Magne's door on the prickly mat he's got out for wiping his feet on, and I listen. I still don't hear anything, but paying attention at least makes me feel like I'll be prepared if someone comes down or up to this floor.

I don't want to dwell on the idea that someone's possessing Evgeny, but I also know that ignoring the issue won't make it go away. That's true in the human world, and it's even more true for *others*. Weres and vamps and fairies – yeah fairies are real, too. Some kinds, anyway. Selkies are a kind of were, and I'm not sure what Jinny Greenteeth are, but I know they exist. Others too, though I haven't met them all. But if we ignore our issues, they only get worse.

So I close my eyes and very carefully picture the scene again. How Evgeny watched me come through the door. Whatever it was was already present, I think, lurking behind Ev's own personality unti it realized… well, whatever it realized about me that disgusted it. What had it said? "Filthy animal." And it had called me "Lisa." Had it mistaken me for someone else? I focus my thoughts, trying to hear that voice again.

It was deep, almost guttural, growling. It was a voice that would be pleasant to listen to reading a story, maybe, if it hadn't been so full of loathing. It had an accent. Eastern European? No, it hadn't been the accent that had sounded wrong coming from Evgeny, but the voice itself. Russian, then. I've heard Evgeny pronounce Russian words with a proper Russian accent.

Lisa. The syllabic emphasis was wrong for a name, at least as it's pronounced in English.

One thing I've learned about myself over the last year is that I know a lot about languages. I think I must have studied linguistics, and I know a little grammar and vocabulary from quite few different tongues, though I only seem to be completely fluent in English.

Lisa. Russian. Then I remember, and it's obvious. Fox. *Lisa* means "fox" in Russian. He, it, whatever was using Evgeny's throat recognized what I was, and found me repulsive. It isn't much, but I have a little more information than I had before. Now, do I have any books on Russian folklore that might be useful?

What seems like ages ago, but isn't even two months past yet, before Evgeny was captured by Charleston, but after he was made a vampire and escaped his fate as dinner for his sire, we raided the lair of his dead Papa Vamp and found a whole library of folklore books in numerous languages, each volume full of bookmarks and notes. Papa had been studying *others*, trying to discover which ones, when consumed by a Reborn, gave the drinker extra abilities.

Now I have that library, shelved on two large bookcases – one cheap and flimsy, and one beautifully handmade in oak. They're only loosely arranged by geography, and I've mostly only looked through the ones on Asian folklore, specifically the chapters on foxes. So much has happened that I haven't even had time to start on the German ones, where I might find clues about the other half of my heritage.

But surely Papa Vamp had looked at Russian sources, too. He must have. And I should have looked for them once I realized Ev wasn't a normal vamp. Papa Vamp's notebooks indicated that Evgeny was chosen specifically for his Russian ancestry.

We'd learned that while witches are almost invariably female – the genes are passed on from both sides, but the abilities are only expressed with the double X chromosomes – there was one Russian family in which sometimes boys expressed witch abilities too. It just happened to be the royal family and despite being slaughtered by revolutionaries, one boy escaped and lived long enough to pass on his DNA. And Evgeny is his descendant.

I was determined to put off calling Alex until there's no other choice,

I don't want to ask for her help for the lover I chose instead of her. If it was for me, maybe, but how could I ask her to help Evgeny, who not only stole me away (never mind that he hadn't known she existed, and I hadn't remembered because she was part of the life and memories I'd lost), but who was an abomination to witch-kind?

If I could have thought of another way to contact the witches, I might have done it, except *that* would probably hurt her feelings, too. And yeah, I'll admit it, it wasn't just that I didn't want to hurt her. I was also *afraid* to see her. Afraid that one good memory might tempt me to betray Evgeny – and I've got an overactive sex drive to deal with, too, remember? And afraid, too, that maybe I *wouldn't* feel the same about her, and all I'd have left of our relationship would be memories. One memory. Which would probably be a good thing, really. But sometimes the best things are the most terrifying.

Now, things have changed. If something *is* trying to take over Evgeny, and that something has to do with witchery – and it might not, but I didn't have any other trails to follow – then I don't seem to have any choice but to consult the *hexen*.

Maybe they'll refuse to help because Evgeny's an abomination, but I don't think they'd keep any vital information from me, especially if whatever's happening to him is a threat to them as well. And maybe, just maybe, they'll help because of Alex. Because she's my...

But what is she? She *was* my lover. Maybe even my girlfriend, briefly. Can I call her my friend? And there's the other reason I haven't called her. I don't know how to act around her. How to *be*.

I'm not the quiet, soon-to-be manager of public programs at the formal gardens anymore. From the scant hours I remember of that me, I wore smart skirts and probably only did kung fu for the exercise and the mental peace. I was *nice*.

Not that I'm not nice now, or quiet and contemplative. Hell, I even wear skirts sometimes, especially when I'm working, because a pair of curvy long legs is a great way to distract someone from the fact that you're picking their pocket. But I don't wear *business* skirts, and I rarely wear skirts at all since I sprouted a tail.

I still do kung fu to quiet my mind, but I also do it to kick the ass of anyone who tries to hurt me. I've even killed people. Okay, vampires, and only a few, but they were still thinking, sentient beings and I ended their lives. They were scum and they would have killed me if I hadn't killed them first. But it still makes me sick to think about it too closely.

What I'm saying is, I've changed since she knew me, and not necessarily for the better. And maybe that's why I chose a blood-sucking killing machine as my life partner instead of a strong-but-nurturing gardener, a cultivator of life. But that's not fair to Evgeny. Whatever state he's in now, the man I fell for is sweet and kind. And yeah, an efficient and sometimes remorseless killer. When it comes to other vamps, anyway.

So, I'm Su, and I'm getting more fucked up psychologically every day.

Finally, just when I'm thinking I'd better get back upstairs before the sun comes up and fries Evgeny, I hear the whir of the elevator. It's never occurred to me before to ask Magne why he takes the elevator instead of the stairs. I mean, I assume it's to let me know when he's around. But he's a big, strapping werewolf in the peak of fitness and he only lives on the second floor. But maybe at the end of a long day – or night, as the case may be – of whatever he does for a living, he's too tired to take the stairs. Or maybe he *does* do it for my benefit, so I'll know when he goes out and when he gets home. And that's an odd thought – someone doing something like that just for my comfort.

He's startled when he sees me sitting there, but he recovers immediately. "Hey, Su," he says. "What's up?"

"I need to borrow your phone," I say.

"You know it's barely seven in the morning?"

"This can't wait."

"Okay, but when you're done, you can tell me what the big rush is."

I don't know if I should be surprised or not when there's no answer. It just rings and I'm about to hang up when Magne holds up his cell phone – why does a werewolf need a cell phone? Why does anyone? – and it's got a number displayed on the screen. He points to himself and then to the phone.

So I say to Alex's voicemail, "Hey, it's Su. Panya." I forgot she calls me

Panya, which is my actual first name and I guess the one I used to go by, before. "I… I need your help, but I can't really talk about it on the phone. It's… It's a witch thing, I think. And I don't know what to do." Then I leave Magne's cell number. I can't quite bring myself to mention Evgeny.

When I hang up, Magne says, "A witch thing?"

So I give him the condensed version.

"I'll let you know if she calls," he says. "I'd just lend you the phone, but I seem to be in charge of all sorts of organizing for those wolves you sprang from Charleston."

Samuel Charleston was feeding werewolves to Evgeny. And to other vamps. And each other. He had a whole industry of special "sustenance" blends for the discerning Reborn.

Then Magne nods towards the window. "Sun'll be up soon. What've you done with Ev?"

For a while, Magne would only call Evgeny things like "your bloodsucker boyfriend," but they seem to have made friends since. I think Magne likes that Liam's afraid of Evgeny. Magne and Liam don't get along, mostly because Liam's a dick, but also because Magne's a tad prejudiced against vamps. Most sane people are.

"Still tied up," I say. I *hope*. "I should go make sure he's himself again, or else I'll be rigging up curtains around that post."

"I'll tag along," Magne says. He doesn't say "just in case," but I suspect he's thinking it.

He lets me go first up the stairs, and I know it's only partly because we're heading for my apartment. It's also so he can check out my ass. He's a bit of a dog, like a lot of men are, but at least he's honest about it, and he's not creepy. I don't think he'd ever try anything with me unless I made the first advance. Not since I fell for Ev. But I know he still likes to look, and I think he likes me even more with a tail. Maybe it's a werewolf thing.

Evgeny's still unconscious on the floor, but I approach cautiously, in case he's faking.

Magne gives a low whistle when he sees Evgeny's wrists. "Poor bastard," he says. "Next time come see me before you tie him up. I've got bandages you can wrap his arms in."

We both crouch next to Evgeny and I turn his head carefully. He doesn't stir, and his temple is faintly bruised where it hit the floor, but he's breathing normally. Vamp-slow and smooth.

"Ev?" I say, and pat his cheek gently, then a little more sharply. "Time to get out of the sun."

For a while I get no response and I have terrible thoughts about concussions and comas. But then his eyelids flutter and he moans softly.

"Why does my head feel like it's about to crack open and spill my brains on the floor?"

"Maybe because it already has," says Magne.

At that, Evgeny's eyes snap open, and then quickly shut again. "I wonder if I have a migraine," he says. "I've never had one before, so how would I know?"

"You're way too philosophical for me," says Magne. "You have any beer?"

I shake my head. "There's some cheap Scotch in the cupboard. I didn't have the cash for the good stuff." I'm also not a big drinker. I get hangovers that make me wish I was dead. Quite literally. In fact, from the look on Evgeny's face, he's probably feeling a lot like I do after a night of too much booze. And that's why you'll never see me drunk, or even buzzed. It's just not worth it.

"Is it safe to untie you?"

"I don't think I could move if I wanted to," he says. "Not without excruciating pain behind my eyes."

So I untie him. After a bit, he does move, but just enough to crawl into the bed.

"Do you want some food?" We never call it blood unless it's absolutely necessary to be specific. I'm not sure why, and it's not something we ever talked about or agreed on. We just both do it.

"I'm so hungry I might be sick," he says. "But yeah, I better try to eat." He makes a feeble attempt to get up, but Magne's already getting a bloodbag out of the fridge. He has an annoying habit of treating my apartment like an extension of his own, instead of as my private space. Annoying, but also kind of nice sometimes.

"Why are you here, anyway?" Evgeny asks when Magne hands him the warmed cup. He sips cautiously, swallows, and pauses with his eyes closed. His next sip is quicker and deeper and he swallows more rapidly. By then time he's drained the cup, Magne's getting more out of the fridge.

I'm going to have to make another trip to Liam's soon. I hope Ev has cash, because I'm almost out, except for the rent stash, and I haven't had time to go to work lately. If you can call picking the pockets of rich bankers "work." Yes, I'm a pickpocket. There's not a lot of demand for not-quite-humans who don't remember who they are and consequently have no valid ID (an expired driver's license doesn't get one very far) or work references.

Or maybe I'm just making excuses, because picking pockets is easier and I don't have to work well with others.

"Just being neighborly," says Magne, but he looks at me, dark eyebrows raised. He's really got quite amazing brown eyes and he'd be dead sexy if he wasn't so heavily muscled. And hairy. But such is the curse of the werewolf. I've often wondered if werewolf women are the same, but I haven't met one yet.

I glance out the window. The sky's not even starting to turn grey, so we have time to talk. Though it's not like vamps suddenly go dormant during the day, like in the movies. They just get sleepy, like humans do at night. But right now, sleep's the only thing Evgeny seems to be able to do without feeling crappy, and he probably needs it more than anything, so I don't want to keep him up too late. If you can call early morning "late."

"You…" I stop. I have no idea how to explain what happened. So I start with walking in from the roof. I tell Evgeny in plain words what I saw and how he seemed. I leave out my hurt feelings, but I have no doubt he'll realize they happened. There's no reason to make him feel worse than he already does.

"Lisa?" he says, and it comes out in a crisp Russian accent. For a tiny moment it chills me right through, but he's not speaking in the stranger's voice. It's just Evgeny with an accent, so I relax. It's not even the first time I've heard him use it. Once, when we were talking about our names he said his, Evgeny Kostas Alexeyevich, in perfect Russian. Even his Greek middle name, because that's how his parents said it. His mother, too – though she was born in Greece, she grew up in Russia.

Evgeny laughs. It's not a full belly laugh, but it's more than a chuckle. He sounds beyond tired, but genuinely amused. "Fox," he says. "Maybe I was just reverting to my childhood language in my delirium."

I shake my head. "It was more than that," I say. "It wasn't your voice at all. And you… he… it… You were disgusted. Repulsed. You called me a filthy animal." Again, I'm careful to keep my voice even and calm, but he still reaches for my hand and kisses my fingers.

"You're not filthy," he says. "Well, you are, but only in the best way." He waggles his eyebrows at me, and if Magne wasn't there, if Evgeny was feeling himself…. Hell, just if Magne wasn't there… I'd be in the bed with him in seconds, with my mouth on his naked skin.

Then we sit there, the three of us, just thinking, I guess, each in our private thoughts.

"I don't remember any stories about foxes, when I was a kid," Evgeny says, finally. "Witches, sure. Baba Yaga and her chicken-legged house. Vasalisa the Wise." He shrugs and scrubs his face with his hands.

"Vasalisa has '*lisa*' in it," I say.

"Different derivation," he says, his voice muffled by his hands. "It's the feminine version of 'Vasily'."

"Well, you should get some sleep," I say and he nods. "Will you be okay if I crash on the couch? I'm restless and I don't want to disturb you."

"More likely I'd disturb you," he says.

I don't say – can't say – that I'm also afraid to sleep so close to him when he could turn into that other person at any time. I think he knows.

"You want me to stick around?" Magne asks.

I shake my head and I'm about to say "no" when Evgeny says, "Yes." There's something peculiar in his voice, and for a moment I remember that he's attracted to men as well as women. But I don't think that's it. Besides, Ev's not any more likely to cheat on me than I am to cheat on him. And as far as I know, Magne's dead straight.

"If I…" Evgeny says. "If I do something, if something happens, would you look after Su?"

"You know I would," says Magne.

"Hey," I say, suddenly pissed at both of them. "I'm not some damsel in distress. I do not, nor have I ever, needed looking after." I glare at them each in turn, and they both laugh.

"From the noise I hear drifting down into my windows some days, I'd say Evgeny does a lot of looking after you." Magne's grin is wide enough to show his heavy wolf teeth and it's a bit unsettling, or would be if I didn't have too-long canines myself.

I'm about to reply with exactly what I think of sex-starved men who listen in on other couples' pleasure when there's a knock on the door.

We three exchange glances and I realize none of us heard the elevator. Was the sound covered by our conversation and laughter?

I walk slowly to the door, and Magne follows, almost as quiet for all his great size. The sun's starting to peek in at the windows, so Evgeny stays in the shelter of the bed curtains, but I can almost feel his watchfulness on my back.

Magne stands to one side of the door, and I grab the handle and cautiously ease it open. The only person I can think of who might come knocking, who has an idea of where I live, and who *might* (and this one's the most unlikely of three unlikely ideas) be able to come quietly up the stairs, is Liam. But what the hell would he want from me?

As the door swings open and I see who it is I realize that of course it couldn't be Liam, because he's a vamp and it's sunrise.

So it's not him. It's Alex.

Chapter Four

MY HEAD IS SUDDENLY so full of different things I don't know what to say and just stare at her. Joy, terror, love, disappointment, lust, uncertainty – they swirl through my brain like loose debris in a tornado.

Then, without either of us seeming to move, she's in my arms and my mind is still.

"Alex," I say, and I know I don't need to say anything else.

"Panya," she says. Then, "But I guess you go by Su now." She steps away but keeps her hands on my shoulders. They're warm and strong and I want to look away from her eyes – they're even darker brown than Magne's, so dark they're almost black, but touched with warmth.

"Yeah," I say, "But you can call me Panya. I know who you're talking to." I grin, feeling at ease, all my worries and confusion gone. I rest my hands on her forearms and for a moment we just grin at each other.

Then Evgeny hisses softly from his perch on the bed and my first thought is he's jealous. My second thought is that the… whatever took over his mind is back. But then a pressure in my head I didn't even notice was there eases off and the doubts and anxieties about seeing Alex again flood back.

I step away from her and I can tell by the look on her face, as much as I can tell from the return of chaos to my head, that the stillness and ease were her doing.

Witches can't do magic, but they often have an affinity with living things – flowering plants in Alex's case – and they can subtly influence perception and probability. When we were escaping from Charleston the witches banded together to take over the will of some of the vamp minions. Charleston, who had gained some witch abilities third-hand by feeding off Evgeny, had tried to mess up my thinking. Evgeny had blocked his influence then, as he must be blocking Alex now.

"Panya," she says, reaching out a hand as if to calm me. "Su, I didn't mean – "

I take another step away and shake my head.

"Do not do that again," says Evgeny. His voice is fully his own, but it chills me nonetheless. Not counting when the symbiont has overwhelmed his thinking brain, he's at his scariest when he's defending me. I once watched him snap another vamp's neck just for *threatening* to feed on me.

Alex drops her hand and her focus flicks over to the bed. Her eyes widen and I realize she didn't know he was there until he spoke. He's got only a slit of bed curtain open, so he can see out without letting any sunlight in, and all that's visible is a pale blur of face and a glint where the overhead lamp reflects off one eye.

"I didn't mean to," she says. "She was confused. I only wanted to still her turmoil. I – "

"Do not do that to her again."

"I am right here," I say. "And I can speak for myself."

Alex looks at me. She's uncertain now, I think, like she realizes she's messed up, but isn't quite sure why it's a big deal. She starts to talk, but I wave my hand and she stops.

"Never mind," I say. "I forgive you. Just don't do it again."

I really need to consult the fox women who live in the formal garden where I used to work, and find out if there's something I can learn to block witchy mind-meddling tricks. I know the *kitsune*'s fox mask blocked the efforts of all Charleston's captive witches at once, but the Japanese fox woman's mask was broken weeks ago, and I wasn't even able to recover the pieces.

"I won't," she says. "I'm sorry."

I sit on the couch, and Magne sprawls beside me, an amused smile quirking at the corner of his mouth. Alex perches on the edge of a chair, clasping and unclasping her hands.

"You could have just called me back," I say, and when she looks confused I realize she hasn't got my phone message yet, that she found my place on her own, not because I asked for her help.

Magne suddenly leans forward and extends his hand. "I'm Magne," he says, and I'm pretty sure he's making a jab at me for being a lame hostess and not performing the introductions, as much as he's just being polite.

"Alex," she says, taking his hand and shaking.

"I'm a werewolf," he says, grinning to show off his teeth. If he'd extended them to their full length, I'd have kicked him in the shin.

"Yes," says Alex. "I know." She looks at him consideringly for a moment, then says, "I'm a witch. And a lesbian."

Magne laughs, not in surprise at her bluntness, but in genuine delight. "Very nice to meet you," he says. I can tell he likes her, though he's also a little disappointed, I suspect, that she's not a potential bedmate. She's tough, but also lovely, which I'd think is just what a werewolf would want in a lover. And she's got red hair. Who doesn't love redheads?

"The voice behind the curtain is Evgeny," I say, not wanting him to feel left out. I *need* him to be included, here where my ex-lover is sitting closer to me than he is. I'm glad, now, that Magne took the other end of the couch, taking away the option to sit next to me. I wonder if he did it on purpose, so Evgeny wouldn't need to feel jealous.

"I am more than a voice, I assure you," Evgeny says.

"You've met," I say. "In Charleston's… facility."

"Yes," says Evgeny. "I'm the one you call an abomination."

Magne's eyebrows go up at this. I guess maybe I left that detail out when I told him about the events of that night.

"Not me," says Alex. "I'm still new at this witch thing. I don't really see what the big deal is." Then she turns to me. "You said something about calling you back?"

"Why are you here, if you didn't get my message?"

"You first."

I consider arguing, but I could hear the strain in Evgeny's voice and I know he needs help. *Her* help, or at least that of her fellow witches. So I go over the story one more time, and she listens attentively.

When I'm done, she shakes her head. "I don't know," she says. "Like I told you, I don't know much about being a witch yet and apparently part of the whole deal is you have to figure a lot out on your own." She frowns. "It's tradition. And I guess if you manage to learn enough, then find the other witches again, *then* they'll teach you. I don't know why they can't just help out a new witch right from the start. You'd think they'd want to give each of us the best chance they could, since there are so few of us."

"Be glad it's just your abilities to you have to figure out," says Magne. "New wolves have to survive being attacked first. Then we have to adjust to some pretty freaky physical changes." He flexes his left hand and the bones rearrange so it looks more like a paw than anything human. Another flex and it's back to being a hairy man-hand. "It's a rite of passage. If you get help, you're considered weak. A lot of new wolves die that probably don't need to."

He sounds pretty matter-of-fact, but there's enough bite behind his words that I wonder if he's trying to change were traditions from within.

"Well, suddenly manifesting the ability to guess what people are thinking with frightening accuracy may not be life-threatening, but it's scary just the same," says Alex. Her chin goes up and she looks fierce. I once compared her to a Celtic goddess, and I think the comparison still fits. Then, finally, she leans back in the chair and relaxes, like she's realized she doesn't have to put up a front here.

"Sometimes I can get in touch with a few of the others," she says. "I guess I've made enough progress in the past couple of weeks that they'll let me ask questions. Though they don't always answer them. I'll try. I'll see what I can find out. If they decide it's a Reborn problem, then I don't know how I can help."

"Maybe you can – " I hesitate. Evgeny won't like what I have in mind. Hell, I don't like it. But I forge ahead. "Maybe you can look into his mind. Evgeny's. When – "

"No!" Ev's voice is so vehement we all turn and stare. He's swept the curtains aside, and fortunately the sun's not very strong yet, or he'd be suffering from a hell of a sunburn.

Magne jumps up and pulls the curtain back into place before I even think to move. Good thing he's thinking straight, because I'm sure not.

"Dumbass," he says. "Do you think Su went though all that trouble to rescue you so you can barbeque yourself at the first opportunity?"

Evgeny ignores him. "I will not have my thoughts probed," he says. "I will not be experimented on. I will not put myself under another's power."

I guess those days in Charleston's care affected him more than I thought. But then, would anyone remain unchanged after being strapped naked to a metal table and force-fed drugs and other toxic substances until one's own mind was driven into hiding? I'd probably be way more messed up after that than Evgeny is.

"I didn't mean she should force her mind on yours," I say. I'm not big on forcing anyone to do anything. It comes of having been forced myself, I guess. "I meant that when... *if*... the... presence comes back, takes over you again, she could sort of listen in and see if there's any clue about who – or what – he is, and what he wants."

Evgeny's quiet then. I think maybe it's sunk in that he *has* been under another's power, and that maybe letting Alex read him, or whatever she does, will help.

"I don't know how much I could get, anyway," she says. "I'm better at letting others see my thoughts than the other way around. Comes from being a loudmouth, I guess."

"I will allow you to try," Evgeny says. I can tell he's stressed just from the way his speech patterns get more formal, but his voice is tired, too. It makes me angry, hearing him so weary. It makes me want to fight something to protect him, but how can I fight an intangible foe?

Alex nods. "I'll try," she says. "And I'll see if I can contact the other *hexen*."

"So why did you come, if not because I called?" I ask. "How did you find me?"

She smiles and looks a bit embarrassed. "I found you the day after we escaped," she says. "A lot of... of Reborn were thankful you helped them. I guess some of them talk to each other, and a few of them talked to me. Eventually I met a guy named Liam. He told me which building to try."

"Liam?"

She nods.

"He didn't tell you for free. He never does anything for free."

She smiles. "It cost me a week's pay. Or what would be a week's pay if I still had a job."

I can only stare at her. She spent a week's wages just to find out where I lived? And she never visited till now?

"I wanted to be able to know you were safe," she says. She glances towards the curtain, then away. "I know you don't need protecting, not anymore, but – "

"You feel guilty," says Magne. "I know that feeling. It was a wolf who…" He trails off.

"And I'm the one who left her alone after he was creeping around," she says.

They're talking about the rape. *My* rape. Personally, I'd like to forget it again. It happened to a different me. It happened to the woman Alex loved, not to the woman I am now.

"Su is safe," says Evgeny. His voice is low and edgy, and I'm pretty sure the sharpness is because he's actually not sure I *am* safe. Not from him, once that other presence takes over. And maybe not even when he's vulnerable and the withdrawal gets too bad and his mind blanks, leaving only his vamp survival instincts in charge.

"As for why I'm here," Alex says, staring at her hands, which she's suddenly balled up in her lap. "Can I tell you that privately? Over coffee maybe?" She looks up and smiles, but it's a thin, uncertain smile.

Having coffee was a sort of personal joke. After she gave me a breathtaking kiss, all I'd been able to think to say was, "Maybe we can have coffee sometime." Biggest date cliché ever. Since then, not that we've had a lot of time to talk since then, coffee was a little teasing reminder.

"Ev?" I say. I'm not asking his permission – that would be way out of character – I'm making sure he'll be okay if I go out for a few hours, though really I'd like to be in bed too.

"I'll be fine," he says. "I'm about to fall asleep with my eyes open."

"I'll stay, just in case," says Magne. This time, he doesn't leave the "just in case" unspoken.

So I get my coat – a long, heavy one, to hide my tail – and put on proper footwear, and Alex and I head out into the cold morning. Once, I would have taken her hand, but now I shove my hands deep into my pockets and hunch my face into my collar so I don't have to look at her.

We don't talk, at first. We just walk, side by side. I'm not sure I'm ready to hear something she can't say in front of the others.

We pass by several coffee shops – I don't have to look up to know they're there. The smell of hot drinks and pastries is almost overwhelming and my stomach rumbles. Good smells make me hungry. Not so good smells sometimes do, too.

Finally Alex says, "Here," and steers me into a café that's not too crowded with the morning before-work rush. Or else it's just too early in the morning for the crowds to have assembled yet. I get decaf mocha, no milk, because I've yet to find a place that makes a decent cup of tea in this city. I wonder if I knew of one before. When I still had all my memories. I don't want caffeine because I plan to sleep when I get home.

Alex gets a huge cup of something coffee-based with foam and cinnamon on top, and asks for no sugar.

Then we sit and sit. Minutes pass and I wonder if she's waiting for me to ask before she'll tell me anything.

But then she starts to talk. "When I first found out I was a witch," she says, "it was the night a vampire grabbed me on my way home from work. Though I didn't know it was a vampire at the time. I didn't know any of those things existed." She pauses, sips her drink, and then stares down at it.

"I thought you were dead." She looks up at me, her eyes bright, but if it's tears that make them shine, she doesn't let them fall. "We found your clothes, and blood. A blood trail leading up the hill, into the Japanese garden, but no body. The police searched, and they never found a body, so you were officially missing but presumed dead."

I want to reach out, to touch her hand, but for me that time is over. Even though the fox women gave me back that memory, it's done with. It has to be. I can't be that weak human girl who was so vulnerable. I'll fall apart if I'm her.

Nicole Silver

"So I applied for a new job. A better position, actually, so no one was surprised when I resigned. But it was really because I couldn't keep going there day after day. Not after what happened to you. What I let happen."

"You didn't let it happen," I say, suddenly angry. She must hear it in my voice, or maybe her witch senses let her get it directly from my mind. "And you couldn't have stopped it even if you had been there. He'd have raped both of us. Left *both* of us for dead."

She looks around at the other people in the café, like maybe I'm making a scene. But I've kept my voice low. Vehement enough, I guess, that a few people are giving us curious glances, but I don't think they can hear what we're saying.

Finally I reach out and put my hand over hers. "It's over and done, Alex," I say squeezing her fingers. "I have no memories from before that night, and I the ones *of* that night are... they're kind of detached, like they happened to someone else."

"I though maybe you chose... you chose Evgeny because I failed you," she says, and I snort in exasperation. "But... you don't remember?"

There wasn't time before to explain what happened to me the night the werewolf almost killed me. I realize, when I see the look on her face, that I never told her any of that. Never said that the reason I chose Evgeny over her wasn't so much that I liked him better, or that I was more attracted to him. Or that she failed me somehow that night, which is something that's never even occurred to me. It was because, from my point of view, with only the memory of a single night with Alex, I had more *history* with Evgeny.

"How can you not remember? Was it... Did he somehow – ?"

I shake my head and take a long gulp of mocha. The bitter chocolate feels good in my throat, even though the heat is a little too intense.

I put the cup down precisely in the wet ring it left on the table. "No," I say. "I did almost die. Almost. But the fox women found me." I can't really explain what happened then, because the fox women didn't tell me, and I spent a lot of time blacked out. I didn't remember *them*, either, until I followed a vague remembrance – brought on by a troubled dream – back to the garden and found them waiting for me. But I tell her about the fox heritage and she nods.

"The other *hexen*, they explained a little bit, though even they didn't really know exactly what to call you."

"Anyway," I say. "My attacker was a werewolf, and the weres exercised their own kind of justice."

"So he's – " She can't seem to bring herself to finish the sentence, so I finish it for her.

"Dead," I say. "Probably. Almost certainly. I asked Magne to make sure he could never hurt anyone again, and Magne's word is good."

She nods, but there's a sort of shadow in her look. "You asked for his punishment?" I can tell she's uncomfortable with the idea. I told you I've changed. But I won't feel guilty.

"The weres said it was my right to execute his punishment. They expected me to kill him myself." I make my voice hard.

She nods again, then steers the conversation away from the topic, which I'm happy to leave behind.

"Anyway, I was walking home on my last day at the garden. No one was expecting to see me again, there. My car was packed and ready to go. And a guy – he was skinny, you know? Not very big. But strong. Way too strong. I should have been able to take him, easy. But I couldn't. And he dumped me in a van and another guy stuck me with a needle. When I came to I was in a cell and there were other women. Well, you saw."

"Yeah," I say. "But that was … How long were you there?"

"I'm not sure. It took a long time to build up some resistance to the drugs they used on us, and there was no way to tell from the sun how many days passed, because we were underground. Going by the date we escaped… a couple of months. I keep meaning to look at my journal, to see which day was my last day at the garden and do the math. But I keep avoiding it. I guess it's not that important." She pokes at a bit of foam on the lip of her cup. "Or else I don't want to know. Like knowing the exact number of days will make it more real."

"A couple of months!" Evgeny was only in there a matter of days. But the witches hadn't been experimented on that I knew of, just kept drugged so they'd be docile, and had their blood drained regularly.

"It was mostly just boring, aside from the terror."

"I'm so sorry. I should have – "

"You wouldn't have remembered me yet, if you only went to see the fox people just before you sprang us. You could hardly have helped me if you didn't even know I existed. Don't *you* go feeling bad for something you had no control over."

I sigh, but she's right. And in a way, I guess we're even. I realize I'm still holding her hand, so I give it a squeeze, and then withdraw mine.

"Okay," I say. "So you found out you're a witch."

"Right. And that freaked me out almost as much as being nabbed off the street. But once I got over *that* shock, the others, the *hexen*, they started to help me figure out how to awaken my abilities. Or strengthen them, I guess, because it turns out I was using some of them without knowing it. But since I got out of there, since it's not an emergency situation anymore… Well, they check in on me now and then, but I'm supposed to figure out a lot on my own."

"So why didn't you go to your new job?"

"Aside from the fact that I was months late?"

I raise my eyebrows. I've never acquired the trick of just raising one, much as I've tried.

"I couldn't," she says. "I couldn't leave you."

I stare at her. "But – " I say.

"I know. You have your vamp – Evgeny. I know. But it's not just that I still… that I still care. I've also been having dreams about you."

She must sense my doubts. I have dreams about her, too, and all they mean is that I remember her and the great sex we had, that night by the koi pond.

She holds up her hand. "These are not ordinary dreams," she says. "They're *hexen* dreams. It's hard to explain the difference, but they are different."

I kind of do know what she means, though. I've looked in, so to speak, on Ev's dreams a time or two. Purely by accident, and I think it was his developing witch abilities and not some power of mine that made it happen. But they really aren't the same as normal dreams.

"What happens in these *hexen* dreams?"

She leans back in her chair, and looks out the window. "They're never really clear, but there are trees. Lots of big trees, like an old hardwood forest. And fear, and blood. And you. Wolves. Witches. Then you alone, and more blood." She shakes her head and looks at me, and one tear has escaped and trickled down her cheek. I resist the urge to lean over and wipe it away.

"It's hard to put into words. I just know that something bad's about to happen to you, and I need to protect you."

Chapter Five

WE PART AWKWARDLY, and Alex promises to come by the loft after sundown, to see if she can read anything from Evgeny, or whatever is trying to take him over. I consider inviting her to hang out all day, but it doesn't seem like a good idea. And I'm too confused about the whole situation to feel comfortable with it.

I'm not really ready to head back myself, anyway, tired as I am. Let Magne babysit while Evgeny sleeps. Instead, I walk around for a bit, then doze sitting up on a park bench, trusting my fox instincts to wake me if necessary. Most of the dangerous things come out after dark, anyway.

I only manage an hour or so before the uncomfortable seat gets to be too much. I think about picking some pockets – I could use to replenish my cash stores – but I'm tired enough to be clumsy, and a clumsy pickpocket is as good as nicked.

Finally, I decide to talk to Liam and pick up some more groceries for Evgeny while I'm at it. Except, of course, it's still daytime, and Liam's a vamp. I must be *really* tired if it takes me until I'm standing in front of the market staring at the "closed" sign to remember that. It's the second time I've expected to see Liam in daylight. If I don't get some sleep, I'm going to end up making a much worse mistake.

When I walk in the loft door, it's about as dark as it gets in a room of giant windows in daylight. Magne's closed the few blinds I have, so there's no direct sun, but there's enough that a vamp would still be extremely uncomfortable in it. Magne's nowhere to be seen, though his scent is strong and there's a head-shaped dent in one of the couch cushions. I forgot he was out all night, too.

Two sets of breathing sounds come from the curtained bed. One is quicker and harsher than it should be – that's Evgeny, who should be breathing so slow in sleep that even I have difficulty hearing it. But it's been a while since he breathed the way he should. The other is deep and slow – Magne. Then I hear him stirring and a moment later his shaggy dark head pops between the curtains.

"You're back," he says.

"Yeah."

"What was so secret?" He wiggles his eyebrows suggestively, and I scowl.

As I tell him about Alex's dream – I leave the rest of the conversation out as personal and irrelevant – Magne climbs the rest of the way out of bed. Behind him, Evgeny makes a feeble sound, but doesn't wake.

I stare at Magne. He's stripped to his boxers, his hairy, muscular splendor all on view. That would explain the tidy pile of denim and cotton on the end of the couch. He notices me staring and grins, spreads his arms, and does a slow turn in front of me.

"Why were you in bed naked with my boyfriend?" I say, wishing again that I could do the one-raised-eyebrow thing.

"Almost naked," he says. "And wouldn't you like to know?" He sprawls on the couch – I don't know if sprawling is an inherent werewolf skill, but Magne's the best I've ever seen at it. I try very hard not to savor the view. While he's really not my preferred physical type, he is still fine to look at. I mostly succeed.

"He was cold," Magne says. "Which is an understatement, I'd like to add. He was shaking and his teeth were chattering, and I decided I'd rather have you tease me for this than have to explain why I let him expire from hypothermia."

I sit down abruptly. "He's okay now?"

Magne shrugs one shoulder. "I wouldn't say he's okay, but his lips aren't blue anymore."

I doubt Magne could actually see the color of Evgeny's lips in the curtained bed. Even though they're nocturnal, neither weres nor vamps have perfect night vision. It's better than human, of course. Much better. Mine is better still.

Magne leans forward, his muscles bunching and sliding smoothly under his skin. In the filtered light, the tracery of scars that seems to form a web, a map of old fights across his body, is almost luminous. Not for the first time, I have to suppress the desire to trace them. I don't want to be attracted to Magne, but there it is. Fox women like sex.

"You need sleep, too," he says. Then he stands up and pulls me to my feet, steering me towards the bed. I pause to strip out of my coat and jeans and climb behind the curtain. I don't even care if Magne's gawking at my tailed ass as I do.

I crawl over next to Evgeny, who doesn't wake, but curls close to me, tucking his head against my collarbone. His skin is clammy. Vamps tend to be on the cold side most of the time, because of their slowed-down circulation, but this is colder-than-corpse-cold.

Magne's footsteps retreat across the room and I hear a jingle of belt-buckle as he picks up his jeans.

"Magne?"

Another jingle as he puts them down.

"Yeah?"

"He's freezing."

There's a pause, then his footsteps come closer. "You want me to help warm him?"

"Do you mind?'

"I'd rather get you in bed alone, but if I have to put up with Vampire Boyfriend to do it, I guess it's still worth it." I can hear the teasing in his voice, and I know I should reply in kind, but it's too much effort, and I'm too afraid for Evgeny.

"Please," I say.

So he gets into bed and lies along Ev's other side, curling his body to get as much skin in contact as possible. Then he pulls the quilt up over all of us.

"Jesus," he says. "He wasn't this cold when I left him."

I'm worried, too, that Evgeny hasn't woken. He's usually a light sleeper, and would at least respond to being talked about.

After a moment, Magne reaches across Evgeny and touches my cheek. Maybe he *can* see better in the dark than I thought. But no, his thumb strokes next to my eye as if searching for tears. If he could see me he'd know I'm not crying. I feel like it, a bit, but I won't.

"You know I'm always here if you need me, right?" he says. "You know I'm your friend?" He pauses, then adds, "And Ev's too."

I nod against his hand.

"Good," he says. His hand leaves my face and settles in the curve of my waist, holding the three of us snug together. To the fox in me, it's comforting; though foxes are largely solitary, they sometimes spend time in small family groups.

To the human in me, it feels weird to be in bed with two men at once, and exciting.

Fortunately, I'm too tired to think about excitement, and as soon as I feel Evgeny lose the chill and begin to warm up, I relax and sleep.

I'm in a forest of huge old hardwood trees, so tall their lower branches are far above my head, and I'm running on all fours, black paws flashing as I pelt, flat out, toward a shadow that might be undergrowth.

A horn sounds behind me, and hounds bay, and I try to run faster. I'm far from familiar territory, but I can smell another fox somewhere up ahead.

Shouting behind me, but the shadow under the trees has resolved into a clear image – not brush, but a house on stilts with a garden of shade-loving herbs. In front of the house are two women, tall and straight, white-haired. One holds a staff with a skull on top of it – it seems to lean on her rather than the other way around. A human skull? No, too small. A monkey, perhaps.

The other woman looks too young for white hair. But I see as I stumble to a halt at her feet that her hair is not white, after all, but such a pale blonde it shines like silver. In her arms is the fox I scented. He is bright red, hardly any black on his legs at all, and he grins at me, leaps from the woman's arms, and bounds up the ladder into the house.

"Go on," says the old woman to me, gesturing to the ladder with her skull-staff. Then to the younger woman, she says, "Rose-Perle, you know what to do."

I don't know what it is she does, or what becomes of the hunters who chased me, because I follow the other fox into the house, wondering if this is the proverbial fire I've escaped to, fleeing the frying pan of the hunt.

Hexen, those women. The fox is their familiar.

Time passes in the house on stilts deep in the gloomy forest. The witch-wood. *Hexenwald*. I learn from Rose-Perle and her familiar – the older witch is often gone and I never learn her name, because Rose calls her Grandmama. I learn how to hide in plain sight, how to trick the eye into looking elsewhere. And I learn how to appear human. I remain a fox, but I can walk on two legs and wear clothes and seem taller. I can look to anyone not magical, not *other*, to be a human woman.

More time passes, and I become Rose-Perle's familiar, too. There is a handsome young man, human I suppose, or mostly human. There is love. And then he is dead at my feet, his skin grey and splotchy with illness, his eyes open and staring, and sad. Then my kits are born and the last one tears me open, she is so big.

"Her name is Sigrún," I tell the witches, as my vision goes grey.

Then, for a while, darkness. Then a soft touch on my skin, a heat between my legs. My own moan wakes me.

Evgeny's mouth is on mine, insistent and warm. He takes my hand, guides it to his erection and pulls my leg over him.

My calf slides up his leg and over his thigh, and rests on another thigh beyond. Magne. I try to pull away, but Evgeny's hand is behind my head, holding me firmly as he kisses me.

"Mmph," I say.

"I should probably go," says Magne. "As much as I enjoy the smell of you aroused." He starts to sit up, but Evgeny rolls over and puts his arm over Magne, pulls him down again.

He kisses Magne and I'm surprised that Magne doesn't pull away. Hell, I'm surprised at Evgeny, too, but I was so sure Magne's straight.

I'm still half asleep, or I'd be more freaked out, but instead I prop myself up on one elbow and enjoy the sight of two attractive men kissing. Evgeny slides one hand into Magne's boxers and Magne tilts his head back to moan.

Then Evgeny rolls over top of Magne, onto his other side, and pushes us together. Magne reaches for me, pulls me to him, kisses my neck, my breast.

I want to just relax into this, let it happen, fuck two sexy men at once and watch them fuck each other – just the idea has me aching and wet. But something's niggling at my brain. There's a pressure behind my eyes that doesn't feel right and suddenly I realize what it is and I shove Magne away so hard he fetches up against Evgeny.

"Fuck!" I say. "Get the fuck out of my head!"

Evgeny looms over me suddenly, eyes flaring. I hear a pounding from somewhere, but Evgeny's on top of me, pinning me down, rubbing his hardness against me, and sneering in my face.

"Filthy *lisa*," he says – or whatever's inside him says. "I will play with all of you as I see fit. This boy is mine." Then he's off of me and Magne's grappling with him, pulling down half of the curtain to pin him to the floor, and the pressure in my head is gone, but the pounding is still there.

The door. Alex's voice yelling, "Panya! Are you all right? Su!"

I get the door open and when I see the look on her face – shock, embarrassment, and maybe (just maybe) a bit of envy – and I realize how things must look. Magne and me in our underwear (when did I take my shirt off?) and Evgeny naked (didn't he have clothes on?), the bed clothes strewn about and the curtain on the floor.

Magne's wrestled Evgeny to the post but can't tie him up without help, and he's having trouble just holding him still. In good health, Evgeny's stronger than Magne, despite his much slenderer build. Or he *was*, at least, with *hexen* in him. As a normal vamp, maybe he's not. But if a possessed Evgeny is almost getting away from Magne, then at least his body is recovering.

"Long story," I say, and turn to help Magne with the rope. Once again, we didn't think to bandage Evgeny's arms ahead of time, and I'm not going to stop and do it now.

He snarls and says a lot of stuff in Russian, most of which I don't understand. *Koldun* is one word I do get, though. Sorcerer. They're something like male witches, but always nasty. And it's not an inherited, genetic thing. I don't think. I'm not really sure what they are. Or what they can do.

Alex stares at him. He stares back, and spits on the floor. "*Ved'ma*," he says. *Witch*, in Russian. She doesn't reply, just keeps staring. Then she sways, and I catch her before she falls, and help her to a chair.

Evgeny laughs and I feel the pressure start to build in my head.

"He's strong," says Alex. "I can't keep blocking him much longer."

"Sorry, Su," says Magne, and he walks over to Evgeny and punches him neatly in the face. Evgeny slumps over and the pressure ebbs away.

"Why did you apologize to me? It's not my skull you just broke."

Magne shrugs. "I'll apologize to him when he wakes up. Anyway, it's not broken. I don't think." He bends to examine Evgeny's face, feels his jaw with one hand. Then he makes an abrupt movement and there's a snapping sound. "That'll fix it," he says.

Alex looks ill.

"*Maybe* I'll apologize," Magne says, then scowls. "He *kissed* me."

"You didn't seem to mind," I say.

"He was in my head. I didn't have a choice to mind." He starts to flop onto the couch, but then seems to realize he's almost naked, and picks up his shirt instead.

When we're both dressed again, I make coffee and we sit and drink it, not speaking.

Then Alex blinks, looks at Evgeny, and her stiff posture relaxes. "It's gone," she says. "For now."

"The… whatever was…"

"Riding him? Yeah."

"*I* was almost riding him," says Magne. He sounds annoyed rather than disgusted. Straight as they come, but not homophobic. Good. Homophobia makes me uncomfortable, and it's not fun being uncomfortable around your friends. They tend not to stay friends for long.

I laugh, and it's not even forced. Not entirely. "You and me both," I say.

"At the same time," says Magne, grin widening so that both dimples show.

Then we both laugh and for a few minutes, we can't stop.

"Want to let me in on the joke?" says Evgeny. "And explain why my jaw is in agonizing pain?"

It doesn't sound as funny when we explain it, and both Evgeny and Alex are blushing fiercely by the end. Then I remember my dream and add that to the story.

"Is that what you dreamed?" I ask Alex.

She shakes her head. "It might be the same place, but no. I wonder, though… could that fox, the fox you were in your dream, be your ancestor?"

"You mean I'm *literally* descended from foxes? I can believe a lot of stuff" – like witches and fairies and vampires are real – "but that might be pushing it a bit far."

She shrugs. "I have dreamed about a woman so blonde her hair looks white. And my mother…" She trails off. She's never told me about her family before. Or maybe she has, but I wouldn't remember, would I? "My great grandmother. Great-great-great. I'm not sure how far back. There's a lot weird about my family. Things I never really thought much about, but that sort of make sense now that I know I'm a witch. *Hexen.*"

She gets up and paces back and forth across the width of the room. It's a wide room. Evgeny watches her, like she fascinates him. And I realize he's still naked. It doesn't seem to bother him, but now that I've noticed, I can't stop looking at him.

Evgeny really is beautiful. He's all sleek muscle, but not bulging muscle like Magne, and his olive skin and black hair make his bright blue eyes look unearthly. Both his nipples are pierced with stainless steel rings, and the right side of his torso is decorated in a blackwork tattoo of a raven, one wing wrapping around his chest and belly, and the other around his back. He's got gorgeous high cheekbones, too, and curvy, kissable lips.

Magne flares his nostrils at me and I can see a teasing grin quirk the corner of his mouth. I can tell he wants to say something cheeky, but instead he gets up and takes Evgeny some clothes, and unties him.

"My mother wasn't married," Alex says. "And I never knew my father. Her mother wasn't married, either, or hers. I don't know how many generations. Maybe some of them weren't interested in men, though Mom wasn't a lesbian. She had a few lovers over the years. But my last name, Holz, has been passed down from mother to daughter for who knows how long."

"It means 'forest', right?" I say. "It's lovely."

She nods. "But some great-grandmother or another was so pale blonde her hair looked white. They say she defied all conventions of the day and took up a trade. She was a toymaker. But they also called her a witch. I always assumed it was a fairy tale growing up, an amusing colorful story to tell the other mothers over tea. Now I'm not so sure."

"Rose-Perle," I say and she looks startled.

"That was her name," she says. "Rose-Perle Holz."

"She was the woman in my dream. The younger witch."

We stare at each other, and I'm wondering what it means, that our ancestors are connected somehow.

"Your grandmother, your ancestor, taught mine how to take human shape." If my dream has any basis in reality, which it might very well not.

Evgeny sits beside me on the couch, and Magne opts for the floor. I shift over a little. I know it wasn't Evgeny, pinning me to the bed and forcing himself on me, but it *was* his body, and it makes me jumpy. Ev seems to realize and moves away a little, too. I can't look at him, because I know he'll be hurt. I would be in his place. But I also know he'll understand.

"Who's hungry?" he says suddenly. He gets up again and starts rummaging in the kitchen. Evgeny may be a vampire now, but when he was human he liked to cook, and he was good at it. That's one more pleasure he refuses to give up, even though it means he mostly cooks for me. I'm not going to complain; before I met him I usually ate take away.

"I could eat," says Magne, and we all agree.

"So we sort of know what my dream meant," I say to Alex. "But not yours, yet. What about… Evgeny?"

Alex shakes her head. "He was too strong for me to get much."

"He said 'sorcerer'."

"He did?"

"*Koldun*. It means 'sorcerer'." I glance over at the bookcases, wondering again if I have anything on Russian folklore.

"Well, he could be one. He's not *hexen*. I mean, there aren't supposed to be any male witches, anyway." She flicks a glance at Evgeny, then back to me. "But yeah, a sorcerer maybe. The other witches couldn't really tell me the difference, just that there was one."

I remember where I've heard the word before. "When I broke you out of Charleston's menagerie, the older witch, she said Evgeny's ancestors… the Russian royal family… they were protected by a *koldun*. He was supposed to ensure their safety, and when the revolution started he got the youngest, the boy Alexei, away into hiding. But they didn't say what happened after that."

"They don't know," says Alex. "I asked. And the internet's not much help. There are all kinds of stories about Rasputin and how he's immortal, or he was poisoned and didn't die, or he was shot three times and then drowned, or he vanished into thin air. No two stories are the same."

At the name "Rasputin" Evgeny turns from the hot plate (it makes it harder for him to cook that I don't have a proper stove, but he manages) and looks at me. He's breathing fast again and at first I think he's about to be possessed.

"I remember something my father used to tell me," he says. "As a child it terrified me."

We all look at him, and even Magne seeming serious for once.

"'Dead and buried and may God never let him in Heaven,' my dad would say. His father taught him that. 'Bones and ash, Rasputin is, but a child is left behind.' He insisted I remember it, and teach it to my own kids, but he didn't know why."

"That doesn't sound so frightening," Magne says.

"It wasn't so much the words as the way he said them."

"Anyway, it doesn't say much we don't already know."

"But I thought he was a good guy," I say. "Protecting the witch boy and everything."

"I suppose that depends on which side you favored in the revolution," says Magne. "He'd be the bad guy if you were on the side of the revolutionaries."

"So the child, that refers to Alexei, the prince?" I say.

"Or to Rasputin's own child, perhaps," says Evgeny.

It seems such a simple thing, an innocent thing, leaving a child in the world. But I've seen the photographs of Rasputin, and he was one creepy-looking guy. The idea of a child version of him sends a shiver right to the end of my tail.

Chapter Six

WE THROW IDEAS AROUND as we eat, but mostly we're just pulling shit out of the air. There are lots of "maybes" and "ifs," and not enough facts.

We know that whatever, or whoever, keeps taking over Evgeny's mind is, or has something to do with, sorcerers. *Koldun*. He – and we all agree it's a "he" – is Russian, and is able to recognize Alex as a witch and me as a fox. Probably Magne as a were. We know he has strong abilities to influence our minds, and that he's got a nasty sense of humor and a need to dominate, and controlling people sexually gets him off. Well, not literally, but you know what I mean. Hell, maybe literally, too.

And that's really it. He may or may not be connected to Rasputin, and if he is, we've got a real strong theme of old ancestral connections going on, which could mean Alex's dreams of danger and mine of her great grandmother are somehow connected to this whole mess.

Finally, Evgeny pushes his plate aside. He's hardly eaten anything, but he doesn't usually eat more than a few bites, anyway. Just enough to sample the flavors. I wonder if he's refraining from blood-drinking to avoid making Alex uncomfortable.

"There are at least two things we can do," he says. "To start."

We all look at him. Magne keeps eating, but Alex and I both pause.

Like eating might interfere with hearing, beside being impolite.

"First, we can look through the books." He indicates the shelves holding what used to be his sire's library, and is now mine. Well, ours, but we originally took them to try to find out what I am. "See what information we have on Russian folklore that might help." He looks at me. "German fox folklore, too," he says, a tiny hesitant smile on his lips.

I smile back, and he looks relieved.

"And it might not hurt looking online again," says Magne. "Now that we have a better idea of what to look for." He pops a slice of carrot into his mouth and adds, "A slightly better idea."

"And the second thing?" I ask.

"Find some way to shield our minds."

I immediately think of the stupid-looking science fiction hats Charleston had to protect his technicians from the *hexen* he held captive. But there's not much chance we can get our hands on one of those. Then I think of the *kitsune*'s mask.

"I'll go talk to the fox women tomorrow," I say. If they'll see me.

"I'll try to get something more out of the other witches," says Alex. "Though they seemed to think this was a good learning opportunity."

"One of the other wolves might have some ideas, though most of us tend to avoid other… *others*. But maybe my granddad can help."

Then we look at Evgeny. He looks back at us. He has no contacts here but us. His family is dead, fed to him one by one by Papa Vamp when he was still brand new and didn't yet remember his human life. His friends he left behind in Great Valley when he fled a bad relationship, and he's kept mostly to himself since then. What few people he knows are human.

I've never realized before, but he's as alone as I am. More, because at least I discovered the fox women. They're not exactly social, but they're a connection. I reach across the table and squeeze his hand and he looks grateful. Like he was afraid I'd leave him because of what the…whatever possessed him did.

"I think I'll go talk to Liam," he says. "Before it gets light. He knows more about a lot of things than he lets on."

I leave Magne and Alex in my loft, sorting through books, and head out with Evgeny. He doesn't say anything, but he probably knows I'm going with him because it's too dangerous for him to go alone.

Not that Liam's a threat. He's afraid of Evgeny, with good reason. And not that I could do much if Evgeny's visitor comes back. But at least I could run and get help. And if he gets sick, I can get him home.

Halfway down the stairs, Evgeny stops and turns and pulls me into his arms. He doesn't say anything, he just holds me, buries his face in my hair, and breathes.

I hold him, too, not sure if I should speak. So I don't. And after a moment, I realize I'm perfectly happy just standing there in his arms, feeling his vamp heart beating faintly under my hand where it's resting between his shoulder blades.

He murmurs something into my hair, and I know he doesn't mean me to hear it, because it takes a real effort to say anything I *can't* hear from this close up.

"I know," I say. "I love you, too."

"How did you – " He pulls away enough to look at me.

"All I heard was 'mumble mumble'," I say. "But now I know for sure that's what you said."

He smiles. He gets this look sometimes, the shy boy all bashful. With any other man, I'd say it was put on, calculated to make a girl's heart melt. But with Evgeny, I'm pretty sure it's genuine.

He bumps his forehead against mine, gently. "You are amazing," he says. "I can see why she still loves you."

"Ev," I say. "Alex doesn't – "

"She does, and I think you know she does. It's okay."

"Aren't you jealous?" I say, playfully.

"Fiercely," he says. "But I intend to be such a spectacular boyfriend you won't ever dream of leaving me."

"You're a spectacularly silly boyfriend," I say, and I kiss him, bite his lower lip gently, and feel his heartbeat speed up, just a fraction, under my hand.

Then he kisses me back, and I can feel all that fierce jealousy he's been hiding so well as he presses his mouth against mine and slides his tongue between my teeth. His hands on my hips pull me close so I feel as he gets hard and I feel the flush of warmth under his skin as his circulation speeds up to something closer to human.

I want him. I mean, I pretty much always want Evgeny, like a constant, delicious ache in my crotch, but just then, standing on the stairs, I want him more than ever.

But what if the *koldun* returns while we're fucking? I'd say "making love," but hasty sex in a stairwell doesn't really qualify.

He senses my hesitation, I think, because he backs off. "I hate when you're afraid of me," he says.

"It's not you I'm afraid of."

"I know. It's the… whatever. The sorcerer. You're afraid he'll come back."

"We know he'll come back, it's just a matter of when."

"I suppose we should get to Liam's, anyway, before he locks up."

Reluctantly, I step back. If we dally here too long, we'll miss the opportunity to talk to Liam tonight, and who knows how much time we have to sort things out before the *koldun* is able to take over Evgeny completely. If that's his goal.

Then, just before we leave the building, I grab Ev for one more kiss. I make it long and deep, and we're both gasping and flushed when I pull away.

"Keep that in mind for later," I say. "I intend to pick up where I left off at the soonest convenient opportunity."

Then Evgeny takes my hand and we walk down the street, almost like a normal couple.

Not surprisingly, Liam doesn't seem happy when we walk in to his market. Thanks to us, he's lost a very lucrative client. A client who paid a lot for custom drug cocktails.

I can't believe I used to think Liam was an all right guy, for a vamp. I can't believe I used to think he was sexy.

"How can I help you," he says, his voice clipped, like there are a lot nastier things he'd like to do besides helping us. And I'm sure there are.

"Liam," I say, leaning across the grimy counter. It puts me a lot lower than his eye level, because he's tall, and while I'm not short, I don't exactly tower.

He relaxes a little bit, I think. It's hard to tell with vamps. Most vamps. The symbiont smooths out most of their involuntary reactions, so you have to be looking real close. An excellent sense of smell helps.

I don't like being lower than he is, but it's a calculated ploy. Let him think I'm the weaker one, and he won't feel threatened. Well, not by me. He can't help but feel threatened by Evgeny. Last time Liam tried to pull rank on Evgeny, Ev swatted him down like an irritating bug too insignificant to even bother killing.

The pupils of Liam's eyes dilate and his scent changes. He's nervous about something, and it's not me or Evgeny. While I try to put the tall vamp at ease, Evgeny wanders into the candy aisle and selects a lollipop from an ancient, dusty display. All the merchandise out here is for show. The real goods are kept in back.

"What's new?" I say. I should probably have planned what I was going to ask him before we came here.

"I got a little something in the other day you might be interested in," Liam says, shifting position so he can look down at me and keep an eye on Evgeny at the same time.

Ev has decided to investigate the ice cream cooler. "Maybe you should plug this in," he says, pulling the lollipop out of his mouth. "You know, for the verisimilitude."

"Fuck off," says Liam, then is forced to step back as Evgeny crosses the shop so fast it's difficult to see him move, and stops nose-to-nose with Liam. He's shorter that Liam, and slighter, but there's no question which of them is in charge.

"You sold me out," says Evgeny. "Don't think I've forgotten." He stares into Liam's eyes – they both have blue irises, but Evgeny's are more intense – and Liam doesn't look away, to his credit.

"It was business," Liam says.

"Well, I have some more business for you," I say, before this can turn into a biggest dick contest. "Two weeks' groceries, and if it's tainted, drugged, or otherwise altered, I will not hesitate to take it out on you."

Of course, he assumes it's Evgeny who will do the dirty work. He should pay more attention, because though I may not be naturally inclined to violence, I use it when I have to. And I've had to rather a lot lately.

"And all the information you can find from your sources on Russian sorcerers. Or any sorcerers," says Evgeny.

"Or any Russian *others*," I add. "And if anything turns up on *hexen*, throw that in, too."

"What's in it for me?" Good old, reliable Liam.

"I don't rip your throat out," says Evgeny.

"You know we're good for the cash, at the usual rate," I say. "Unless you'd rather barter for my blood again."

I have no intention of actually giving him any of my blood, but I traded it once, when I was desperate for information. Thing is, I smell really good to vamps. To all *others*, I guess. It's a fox thing. We have super sex powers or something. But for vamps who like to mix fucking and feeding, they think I smell good to eat. It's a damned nuisance, and another reason besides the tail that I haven't been going out much.

But as it turns out, my blood tastes vile. Worse than *hexen*, even. Maybe it's toxic, too. I didn't ask Liam after we'd traded.

"Cash is fine," he says. "And for this, too." He slips a box from under the counter and sets it down.

Just a plain kraft jewelry box, like any small jeweler might use, and a little bigger than my palm.

"What is it?" I ask.

He just looks at me, so I take the lid off. Inside, there's an elegant brass pocketwatch with a simple but beautifully executed knotwork design on the case. I don't have to open it to know that when I do, I'll see visible gearing through the transparent face. Or that if I pry off the back, I'll find some lines of poetry in Latin.

Liam's anxious smell intensifies – it's something to do with this watch that makes him nervous.

"Where'd it come from?"

He shrugs. It's an awkward gesture, smooth from long practice, but not natural to him. Most vamps really have to work at human movement after they're reborn. Liam's old enough that he can fool most people, but he can't fool me.

"It was among the effects of an… acquaintance who recently passed.

"This acquaintance have any connection to Charleston?"

"Charleston was a bit player. The real council – the elders – let him play because he was doing useful work."

He didn't seem like such a bit player to me, when I broke into his high-tech lab to steal back my lover, and ended up fighting him hand-to-hand.

"And this comes from one of these elders?"

"They're secretive. That's all I know. I don't know the circumstances under which the watch came into my acquaintance's possession."

Liam tries to stare me down, but I don't intimidate easily and in the end he's the one who shifts his eyes aside.

"How much?"

"Owe me a favor."

"Fine," I say. "But I reserve the right to refuse any favors I don't like."

"Within reason. I need to get my money's worth."

"If the favor's reasonable, I'll do it," I say.

The pocketwatches, and the verse inside, are another thread of weirdness we encountered while searching Papa Vamp's things, and again in Charleston's lair. We thought Charleston gave them to his closest associates, but it looks like the puzzle goes deeper than that.

"What about for the information?" Liam says.

"I'll pay the usual rate, like I said. If the information is good."

"And the groceries?"

"Same. But I'll have to owe you."

Liam stops trying to pretend he's ignoring that Evgeny's standing too close, and glares at me. He's obviously practiced glaring a lot, because it's almost convincing.

"You know I'm good for it," I say.

He furrows his brow into a frown. *That* looks put on. "Fine, but you cost me a lot of business."

"And you almost got me killed," Evgeny says. "You *did* get me locked up and experimented on. How about I do that for you?" He opens his mouth and lets his fangs extend. From where I'm standing, it looks like he's about to bite Liam's nose off. If vamp fangs weren't so unnerving, I'd be tempted to giggle.

Then Evgeny's expression changes, his face goes slack, and he drops to the floor, thrashing. Not quite like he's have a seizure, but more like something is trying to claw its way out of him, like a werewolf in an old movie tearing off its human skin to reveal the monster. Except instead of trying to let it out, Ev's trying to keep it in.

"What the fuck?" says Liam.

"Help me get him home," I say.

Evgeny croaks something, so I bend over him, thinking all the while about how the *koldun* could suddenly take over and since Evgeny's getting stronger, physically, he could easily overpower me.

"No... time..." he says.

"We have to get you back to the loft," I say. Then to Liam, "Do you have any ropes or chains?"

"What the fuck?" he says again.

"Su..." Evgeny's voice is barely audible. Not only is it quiet, but it's sliding up the register into high-pitched vamp-speak, a difficult-to-hear way of talking to each other that Reborn have. "I can't hold him back."

"It'll be all right," I say. "We'll restrain you and get you home. Liam – "

"I don't want anything to do with this."

"Help me," I say, looking up at him.

He shakes his head and backs away as far as he can in the space behind the counter. "Fuck," he says. "I don't know what the hell you've brought into my shop, but you can get the fuck out."

Evgeny says something, but it's so garbled I can't make out words. It sounds like it hurts him to speak.

"You'll be paid, Liam," I say. "Just get me some chains, or some rope. Help me get him home."

Foam dribbles out of Evgeny's mouth and he stops thrashing as suddenly as he started. His whole body has gone rigid, his eyes open and staring. He says a few words in Russian. At least I think it's Russian. His voice is so distorted it could be English or Swahili for all I can tell. Or any language, really.

He closes his eyes, takes a careful deep breath and says, "Lock me up.

Now. He's about to take over and I can't stop him. There's no time to get me home." Then he clamps his mouth shut so hard I hear his teeth grind together.

I look at Liam. He's still the way only a vamp can be. Barely breathing, so you can see exactly where the idea that vampires are dead came from. He's staring at Evgeny, pupils dilated.

"What the hell is he?"

"In trouble," I say. "Do you have a… a storage room or a meat freezer? Somewhere I can lock him up?"

I don't know if something like compassion penetrates Liam's brain, or if he realizes how much we'll owe him if he helps us, but he finally relents.

"I have a cell in the basement."

I really wish I didn't know that. I wish I didn't *need* to know that.

"Show me."

But then it's gone, whatever trace of compassion might have softened Liam, and he's back to hardass.

"Fuck this. Get out of my store and take that freak with you."

Usually it's fear that makes me angry, being so close to being killed or worse than killed, being helpless, that suddenly pisses me off so much the terror goes away and rage takes its place. Angry Su is Strong Su, because for reasons I've yet to figure out, anger is what brings out the fox powers.

At least the ones the three fox women gave me. Vengeance is especially good – they said, anyway. I've never been that interested in it. But this time the anger comes all on its own.

Not that I'm not afraid. I'm terrified for Evgeny, and yeah, worried abut what the *koldun* might do if it takes over when he's not restrained. But mostly I'm just pissed that Liam is so devoid of anything resembling decency that he won't help someone spasming on the floor of his shop.

So I lose it. I launch myself from a crouch and land on the counter, sprawled over the cash register, one hand gripping Liam's collar. And I growl at him, a growl so fierce it would make a werewolf proud.

I don't know if my face does something weird, but my vision loses a lot of color and sharpens, so I can see normally invisible muscular twitches in Liam's face. My sense of smell increases, too, and I'm surprised to smell fear. Liam's fear.

It's difficult speaking around teeth that are suddenly too big for my mouth, and one canine catches my lip and I taste blood.

"You will help me, you worthless piece of shit," I say, right in his face. "Or I will rip off your cock and shove it down your throat. And then I will feast on your entrails."

Chapter Seven

He stares at me for one slow vamp heartbeat. And another. Then he's the one who looks away first. Again.

"Follow me," he says.

He locks the door of the shop while I drag Evgeny to his feet. I hang on to the anger that propelled me to the countertop and take most of Evgeny's weight. Without the extra boost the anger brings, I couldn't hope to hold him up, no matter that I am stronger than a human, even on a bad day.

I follow Liam in to the back of the shop and wait while he opens what looks like a meat freezer door. Behind it is another door, heavy steel with a keypad. He tries to hide the code with his body as he punches it in, but I slam my hand down on the numbers, so he has to clear it and start again. This time I make sure I can see.

"If you change it, I'll – "

"Rip my cock off. I got it the first time."

He fills his voice with contempt, but I know it's not genuine. Audible feelings in vamp voices are rarely genuine. Normally, they have almost no inflection at all, like robots or telephone help lines. And anyway, I can smell his fear.

I've scared him enough that it oozes from his pores. That means I *really* scared him, and it takes a lot to freak out a vamp. I wonder what my face looked like, back there when I lost my temper.

"Hurry," says Evgeny, his voiced strained almost to breaking.

Down some stairs, and I don't know how I keep Ev from falling headlong and taking me with him.

There's a hallways of doors, several of them open, and inside are people. Most vamp. A few human. I get the impression of squalor, illness, need. I don't look too closely.

At the end of the hall, there's a cell. Classic metal prison bars and everything.

"I'm sorry, Evgeny," I say.

He looks up with an effort, sees the bars. I can feel in the tension of his muscles how hard it is for him to keep going, to drag one foot forward and then the next. By the time we stop in front of the cell, he's shaking so violently I can't hold him still. It's not withdrawal making him shake, I don't think. Not this time.

Liam opens the door.

Evgeny's panting, harsh, terrified breaths. "Lock me in," he says. "Hurry."

So in we go and I hope Liam doesn't get all vengeful all of a sudden and lock me in, too. But then he wouldn't get paid that way.

"I have to leave you here," I say. "I have to go see the fox women. But I'll be back for you."

"I know."

I help him onto the bunk.

"I'm sorry."

"Go, Su. Please. Be safe."

"We'll figure out how to fix this."

Then I leave him there, locked up again. Last time I saw him in a cell, I was breaking him out, intending to make sure he'd never be locked in one again. But now, here I am, slamming the door shut myself.

I get out of there quickly, before the other presence can take over Evgeny, and I practically run up the stairs.

As I'm about to leave the shop, Liam stops me.

"I'm helping them," he says.

I have no idea what he's talking about, and it must show on my face, because then he says, "The people in the basement. They're sick, junkies, destitute. I keep them safe, and in exchange, they trade me… groceries."

It takes me a while to process what he's told me. I'm not really thinking about anything other than the fact that I've just locked the man I love in a cage and left him to be taken over by a sorcerer. Then it sinks in.

"You keep those people down there and use them like cattle?" Maybe they're down there of their own free will, but it's way too close to what Charleston was doing for my liking.

His nostrils flare, just the slightest indication of anger. "Most of them would be dead without me."

"The blood you sold Evgeny – "

"Pure black market medical grade," he says. "The other stuff is special order."

"You're disgusting," I say, and turn back to the door.

"Fine way to talk to someone who's helping you."

He's right. He's still disgusting, but he's right. "I appreciate it," I say. "I really do. I also know you expect to be well paid."

"Naturally."

"You will be." Then I push open the door. "Just don't get too close to the cell if you can help it. Or talk to him. He's…possessed or something. By a *koldun*. A sorcerer."

"Sorcery isn't real, Su."

"Fine, think of this as a really powerful witch."

"What if he gets hungry?"

"Toss him some bloodbags. But cut them open or something. He'll be like a newborn sometimes. Just don't let him into your head."

"I have a special hat for witches."

I almost laugh. "Charleston gave you one?"

"Yeah."

"Good. Use it. And keep your…people away from the cell. I don't want anyone hurt."

Then I push out into the street and walk away as fast as I can. I won't cry. I won't.

But I do, a little.

I head for the bus stop and sit on a bench even though it'll be at least an hour before the buses start running. It's not even light yet, not even a hint of dawn in the sky. I should go home, sleep for an hour or two, eat something.

But I won't be able to sleep. Not after what I just did. I know it was necessary, I know I had no choice, but I still feel like I completely betrayed Evgeny. I not only locked him in a cage, but I left him with *Liam*. And why the fuck does Liam have a cell in the basement of his shop, anyway? No, never mind. I don't want to know why.

The light from the nearest streetlamp is flickering and uncertain, but I slide the pocketwatch out of my coat pocket and look at it anyway. It's identical to the one Papa Vamp had, and the one Charleston had. The ones I got from two of Charleston's…well, they were too high up to be minions…associates, let's say, are the same too, but a little smaller.

Was that because they were women, and women are supposed to have smaller watches, or was it a rank thing?

Five pocketwatches, each with a different line of poetry in them. It must add up to something, but what? It's not likely to have anything to do with our current predicament, I don't think, but it seems it also has a lot less to do with Charleston than I had originally supposed.

The tip of my pocket knife works nicely to pry the back off, and just like the others, this one's got poetry. Latin's not one of my best languages, it seems, because I recognize "vengeance" and the rest doesn't mean much. I'll have to get Evgeny to translate.

Evgeny. I snap the back onto the watch again and shove it in my pocket. That distracted me for all of, what, five seconds?

I thought – I hoped – that as Evgeny recovered, as his body got used to being drug- and *hexen*-free, that he'd be able to keep the *koldun* (if that's really what it was) at bay. Defeat him and drive him away for good, even.

But as Evgeny's body gets stronger, the *koldun* seems to get stronger, too. The withdrawal-caused weakness may have let the sorcerer in, but now that he's been in once, he keeps coming back.

There's no point in thinking in circles, but there's also nothing I can *do*. Not until I can get the bus to the formal gardens – the place I used to work, where I met Alex, where I was raped and beaten and left for dead. The place where the only three people who might be able to help me with my fox nature live.

The sound of a motor approaching cuts through the stillness. The bus already? The sky has taken on a pink tinge, but the city is still asleep. The motor gets closer and I realize it's not big enough to be a bus. A car, then. I think about hiding in an alley, in case it's a cop. But why shouldn't I be out? Maybe I have a super-early work shift.

It's not a cop. It's a battered, but well-cared-for Subaru wagon in forest green, and it pulls to the curb next to the bus stop. The window rolls down with an electric whine.

"Su! I thought you might want a ride." It's Alex.

I get in and she hands me a travel mug – I recognize it as one of Magne's. It's steaming and smells of bitter, dark coffee.

"Magne made you coffee. He's a bit worried that you and Evgeny didn't come back. And I thought since the garden won't be open anyway, we might as well go now, while there still won't be too many people around to see us break in."

Of course. It's December and the garden is closed for the season.

"Where's Evgeny?"

I realize suddenly that I haven't said a word to her since she arrived.

"I had to leave him with Liam," I say. "The *koldun* – "

She puts a hand on my knee, squeezes it, then withdraws to put the car in gear. "Is he going to be all right?"

I notice she doesn't ask, "Is he all right?" which would be kind of a stupid question, but, "Is he going to be."

"I don't know," I say. "But I had to…lock him in a cell." I look at her and I wonder if my face looks as stricken as I feel. I sip the coffee and try to be strong. I need to be Strong Su.

"Shit," she says. "I'm sorry." She fishes in her pocket and pulls out her cellphone. She hands it to me and says, "Maybe you could let Magne know."

"I had to leave him with fucking Liam."

"Is Liam that bad? He seemed all right to me."

"He did to me, too, when I first met him, but he'll do whatever will profit him the most." I stare out the window, but nothing in the landscape stays in my mind. I might as well be watching a blank television screen.

"But right now, his best interest is served by helping Evgeny, right?"

"Yeah. I hope so."

"It'll be all right," she says.

I nod and sip some more coffee. It's strong and sweet, just the way I like it. I wonder if Alex put the sugar in, or if Magne did. Then I remember I'm holding Alex's phone, so I call Magne and let him know where Evgeny is. I don't say much, just give him the facts, and I hang up.

Then it occurs to me that I have friends, and it's a startling thought. And how pathetic is that? To be surprised to find out you have friends? But until I met Evgeny, I didn't get close to anyone. Not that whole year from the point I lost my memories till Ev stumbled into that bar, newly re-born and lost. Even though Magne lived downstairs the whole time, I only talked to him in passing. And almost slept with him once. But then I almost slept with Liam once, too.

"Alex," I say. "That memory I have of you... of us – "

"It's okay, you don't have to say anything."

"I do. It's a good memory. A *really* good memory." I glance at her and she's staring ahead at the road, but there's a flush to her cheeks. I wonder if she's remembering it.

"Even with what happened after, it's a fantastic memory. But – "

"You're with Evgeny. I know. I'm happy that you're happy."

"I don't want things to be awkward with us." I look out the window again, and I'm starting to see the scenery, to actually *notice* it, that is. It's familiar. Not in an I-see-this-place-every-day kind of way, but in a déja vu sort of way.

Sometimes the déja vu gets so strong it lets real memories back in. It's how I started to remember the fox women – I saw a miniature Japanese *torii* gate and an Inari fox figure in the window of an Asian variety store and it gradually pulled up a memory of an actual gate and a full-size fox statue, which lead me to the Japanese garden at Chesterly Formal Gardens.

This time, though, the sensation fades and no other memories surface.

"I don't want to lose you again," I say. "I mean – "

"Yeah," she says, voice hushed. "I know. I know we can't be together. But you're too important. If friendship is all I can have, I'll take it."

We drive in silence for a moment and then she says, "Shit. I made that sound like friendship is somehow a lesser thing."

I chuckle, and it feels good. Like something had eased. "I know what you meant," I say.

"Can you tell Evgeny I'm not a threat? That I'm not going to try to steal you away from him?"

"I don't know," I say. "He said jealousy would drive him to be the best boyfriend ever. I'm not sure I want to give that up."

She smiles, and a lot of the tension goes out of her face. "If he's not the best boyfriend ever, anyway, then he doesn't deserve you."

"I'll tell him you said that."

"Please do." Then she grins at me and I think that maybe things will be all right. Between Alex and me, at least.

There's on-street parking right in front of the gates. During the active season – late March to early November – it's either a loading zone or ridiculously expensive meters with blue handicapped parking signs. But it's off-season now, so parking is free.

But we pull up down the block instead, and sit looking at the gates, trying to figure out what to do next. We need to get inside, obviously, but I'd rather avoid getting arrested.

"There's a caretaker who does rounds once a day," says Alex. "Or at least there was a year ago. And a security guard who's stationed in the main building. I think he walks around three or four times a day."

"What about alarms or cameras?"

She shrugs. "I was a gardener, I didn't pay that much attention. I think the buildings all have cameras on the entrances."

"I think I remember alarms on the main building."

"Right. Probably all of them have alarms, then. Even the sheds, though they'd be disarmed during the day. Too many people in and out who could set them off by accident."

"But not this time of year. And what about the fences?"

She considers, tapping a finger on the steering wheel. "There will be a few gardeners in part time, to make sure the plants are overwintering. So at least the main greenhouse will be active. That might be enough to keep all the alarms off during working hours."

"Let's see if anyone comes in to work, then. If they do, then we just have to find somewhere out of sight of cameras to climb the fence."

"And if no one comes in?"

"We'll just have to hope there aren't any alarms on the fences anyway."

So we wait and watch, and I try to think of something to say to the fox women. They're like the fairies in old folk tales: you can't just start asking questions and expect answers. You have to come at it the right way, and wait for them to permit you to ask.

"Listen, Alex," I say. "The fox women… they use sexual attraction like a tool. A weapon. Last time I was here, they took turns trying to seduce me." Granted, they hadn't tried that hard, and I'd been so distracted by Evgeny they teased me about him. "If I'd… if I hadn't already started falling for Evgeny, I'd probably have let them."

"Would that be bad?"

"I don't know, really. I suspect they'd have thought less of me if I wasn't able to resist them.'

"Is that one of the powers you have?"

I wonder if she's thinking that's how I attracted her, or how I got Evgeny.

"Sort of," I say. I don't really like admitting it, but it's part of who I am now. "Apparently vamps and weres, probably most *others*, find they like the smell of me. It makes them want to sleep with me, and for vamps it also makes them want to feed on me."

"That explains a few things," she says.

"I didn't have this… power… curse… whatever before the fox women found me. What they did to save me also gave me some of their abilities."

"I didn't mean you made me fall in love with you. I meant it's really hard not to think about getting you naked." She says it with a grin, so I know she's joking, but only partly.

"Oh," I say. Lame, but I can't think of anything more intelligent.

"Anyway, I thought your fox thing was genetic – like in your dream your ancestor was a fox somehow."

"I think the dream was just a… like a fairytale. Metaphorical. It's not possible for humans and foxes to, you know, make babies. Plus there's the very disturbing bestiality theme."

"But she learned how to take human form," Alex says. "And anyway, not too long ago I wouldn't have believed witches were possible, let alone vampires or werewolves, or beautiful women with fox tails."

Right then, my tail decides to remind me of its presence by getting pins and needles from being sat on so long.

"Good points, all," I say. "But I don't really know which abilities came from my genetics and which came from the fox women. Hell, I still don't even know what my abilities are or how to turn them on and off."

"I'd think turning them on would be more important," she says. "Especially since you really need to know how to block the *koldun* from your mind."

"No offence, but I wouldn't object to learning how to block *hexen*, too."

She frowns, guilt flickering across her face. "I'm really sorry about that."

"It's not just you," I say. "If Ev's *hexen* nature, or whatever you'd call it, is going to develop, I'd like to be able to shut him out if I need to." Not that I think he'll start trying to get into my head, but you never know when it might happen by accident. And I don't like my lovers having power over me.

Then I say, to lighten the tension, "Anyway, I'd really like to turn off the sexual attraction thing. You try walking down the street at night when vamps think you must taste extra-nice."

She smiles.

"And maybe I could learn how to tone down my own sex drive a little, too."

"Well. If Evgeny's ever not enough for you, you know where to find me." Her voice is teasing. I suspect there's some sincerity, too. Even better reason to turn off the sex appeal.

"Yeah, Magne says that, too," I say lightly.

Finally, another car pulls up near the gate and a lanky older man gets out.

"My old boss," Alex says. "Dean. Decent guy. Brilliant with plants."

I don't remember him, but all that means is that I didn't see him during the one day I remember of my old life.

"If I liked men, I'd probably have a crush on him," Alex says.

I smile. I appreciate how she's trying to turn the weirdness between us to humor, but I'm not sure it's working. Not yet. Not quite.

The gardener goes to the gate and unlocks the smaller portal set into it and steps through, then locks it behind him. It would be too much to hope he'd leave it unlocked, I guess.

"The security guard must already have disabled the alarms," Alex says. "If there are any."

"Okay," I say. "I guess we follow the fence around to the right, and climb it somewhere close to where it borders on the Japanese garden."

Fortunately, Chesterly Gardens is at the very edge of the suburbs, and it's surrounded on three sides by national park land. The groundskeepers are allowed to trim back the trees and undergrowth just outside the fence, to keep it from encroaching, but otherwise there's just forest and meadow. Several areas of the garden make good use of the park as a backdrop, with wrought iron barred fences that show off the forest beyond.

We follow the fence into the trees, after first having a good look around to make sure no one's watching. It's still early enough that car traffic is sporadic – and this isn't such a busy area this time of year, anyway.

Soon, the iron bars give way to stonework. The fence becomes an eight-foot wall.

"The herb garden should be just on the other side," says Alex.

I don't remember the herb garden, but I can smell it now, faint because most of the plants are dormant.

"I spent a whole summer trimming a tiny box hedge laid out like a Celtic knot, with tufts of lavender growing between. It was lovely, but a huge pain in the ass."

"And you probably loved every second."

"Well, not *every* second."

After what seems like miles, the stone wall gets shorter, its height made up with bamboo screening. Every ten paces or so, the stone drops a foot and the bamboo gets longer until it's eventually all bamboo. Backed by more wrought iron.

"That should be the koi pond, now," says Alex. She gestures at the ground, which is damp. "This side of it becomes marsh, and then solid ground." Ahead of us, the damp becomes mud.

"Maybe we can go around the wet part and see if there's a place to climb over beyond the koi pond."

"Or we could go back to the stone wall," says Alex.

I think about that for a moment, then shake my head. "Then we'd have to go all the way around the pond, in the open. I'd rather aim for the maple grove and head up the hill from there."

"Through the pines? Is that where the fox women are?"

"I don't know where they actually live," I say. "But last time I found them on the top of the hill, near the shrine."

There's a little Shinto shrine here, which seems an appropriate place to find Asian fox women. The shrine is guarded by three sets of Japanese Inari fox sculptures.

The mud proves harder to skirt around than I thought, and requires fighting through heavy undergrowth which in the end seems more trouble than slogging through wet dirt.

When we do get around it, it's to find the bamboo fence now backed by smooth, expertly-fitted planks of cedar, with not a chink or a foothold in sight. Most inconveniently, there are also no large trees with overhanging branches growing next to the fence, either.

I guess I should have listened to Alex and gone back to the stone wall.

But she says, "Look at this." She's running her hand along a section of fence. At first, I don't see what she's seeing and she has to point right at it: a hinge, perfectly painted to match the fence.

There's a hidden gate, just where we need to get in. It seems far too convenient, but my vague suspicions are quashed when we find the equally cleverly-hidden keyhole. It's a sophisticated, strong lock. I'm a pickpocket, not a pick-lock, and though I can open simple locks, I've left my hair in a long braid down my back today instead of putting it up, so I don't even have bobby pins. If bobby pins would work on a lock like that.

"Damn," I say. "I guess we keep going. Or go back."

"No, I got this," says Alex. She takes a knife out of her pocket and cuts into the wood experimentally. "It's just a matter of deciding whether to cut out the lock or the hinges. I think the lock will be less noticeable."

I stare at her and it takes her a moment to notice. She laughs when she does.

"I'm good with plants, remember?" she says. "Cedar is a plant, and even better, it's a softwood. Emphasis on 'soft.' If they'd used oak, we'd be in trouble."

Chapter Eight

EVEN THOUGH THE WOOD is soft, it's thick, and the lock is deeply-set, so it takes a long time for Alex to cut and chisel and pry the wood away enough to wriggle the mechanism out. It turns out it probably would have been faster to go back to where the fence was climbable.

But this way we're less likely to be seen, and we also have a handy escape route.

When the lock is out, it leaves a huge hole in the gate, big enough to stick an arm through, easily. Alex leans down and peers in.

"Not much to see," she says. She keeps her voice low, just in case anyone's nearby. She steps aside to let me look.

On the other side of the fence is a grove of lace-leaf maples. Their reddish branches are bare, and form intricate, twisted shapes in the air. The deep green moss, browning in spots from the cold, forms a backdrop that makes the red twigs startlingly bright.

To the left, the maples give way to willows with drooping golden branches. Just beyond them, but out of sight, is the koi pond. I can smell the water – icy and clean with a hint of fish. It makes me hungry – one reason I don't keep an aquarium even though I love the bright colors of tropical fish. I might be tempted to eat them. I wonder if the fish here stay in the pond all winter. It's not cold enough yet to have frozen solid, but by

January it might be.

I turn my head, put my other eye to the hole, and look to the right. There, the maples continue. Somewhere ahead, they'll be mostly replaced by pines which clad the hillside up to the Shinto shrine on top.

There's no one around.

"Ready?" I say.

"I'm about to meet three fox women," says Alex. "If they're anything like you, I'm not sure I *can* be ready." She grins.

"They're way more dangerous than I am." I say it as a joke, but as soon as it's out, I realize it's true.

Alex pushes open the gate and steps through. I follow and she closes it again. There's a broad scuff mark in the dirt and leaf litter where the gate scraped the ground, but it's unlikely anyone will come here. There's no path to the gate, and except for the gaping hole where Alex cut the lock out, it's almost invisible in the fence. And even the hole is less obvious from this side.

"Which way?"

"Up," I say, and take the lead. The trees are the ornamental kind, and not more than ten feet tall at the most. Many of them are much smaller, pruned and twisted like oversize bonsai. We have to take a winding route, ducking under the branches we can duck under, and going around those we can't.

I consider aiming for the pathway to make the going quicker and easier, but we don't know the guard's or the caretaker's schedule. If I was alone, I'd chance it, because I'd hear anyone long before they heard me, and I'd be able to get out of sight before they got close, but I don't know yet how well Alex does in the woods, or how quick her reactions are.

As we near the top of the hill – I know we're almost there because it gets a lot steeper for the last bit – I catch sight of her face. She looks at peace.

"You really love it here, don't you?" I say, softly.

She blinks, startled. "Not so much here, specifically, but around plants, trees, gardens. Yeah. I feel like I belong." She smiles and brushes a tree branch with her palm. "It does seem odd to be in the Japanese garden without hearing the deer scare, though."

Odd that I didn't notice the absence of the singular, regular deep bamboo-on-wet-stone "thunk." But I suppose there would be no point in keeping a water feature running with no one to enjoy it.

"We miss it, also," says a voice. Female, on the high-pitched end of pleasant. It takes me a moment to realize she's speaking a Chinese dialect, because I understand her perfectly.

Alex stops and looks at me uncertainly, but follows when I step out of the trees.

She's shorter than I remember, the *huli jing*, but then I spent most of my time with them – the part I remember – sitting down and sipping tea.

"Hello," I say. It seems too informal, but I don't really know what the proper etiquette for greeting a fox woman is.

They seem to me – the *huli jing*, the *kitsune*, and the *kumiho* – to be somehow more than vamps or weres or witches. Closer to deities, more… supernatural, somehow. It's silly, because none of the *others* I've met are really supernatural. Exactly.

But she doesn't seem to mind my casualness. "Little sister," she says and holds out her hands to me. I take them and instantly feel the flush of warmth under my skin. She giggles. "We must teach you to be master of your senses," she says.

"That would be useful," I say.

She regards me solemnly, looking me up and down, as if searching for signs of change since she saw me last. So I look back at her. She's dressed simply in a deep red cotton quilted coat and pants. Her feet are bare, but covered in red fur, and fox ears poke out between strands of her long black hair. Her almond-shaped eyes are amber, like mine, pupils slitted like a cat's against the bright sun.

Then she seems satisfied with what she sees and drops my hands to look at Alex.

"You've brought company," she says.

"My friend Alex," I say.

The *huli jing* sniffs the air. "Witch woman," she says. "Have you come to save her from us?"

"I thought you were her friends," Alex says. She's blushing fiercely, so I know the *huli jing* must be turning on the charm.

"Sisters," the fox woman says. "Not the same thing." I find that interesting, because last time I visited, they called me "daughter." I wonder if they've changed or if I have.

She walks in a circle around Alex, then touches her hair lightly. "Red hair,' she says. "So lovely." The she turns abruptly back to me. "You've stopped cutting yours, I hope."

I pull the braid over my shoulder. Two weeks ago, I could just sit on it; now the end of the braid reaches mid-thigh when it hangs down my back. Longer if I unbraid it. "I haven't cut it since before I saw you last."

She smiles and her long fox teeth become visible.

"Come have tea. The others were just having a shooting match near the pond."

"Won't they be seen?" asks Alex.

Instead of answering, the *huli jing* looks at me.

"A fox is unseen when she wishes to be," I say. It's what they'd told me. "I wish I had the hang of that trick, too."

"Are you sure you don't?" The fox woman leads us to the gazebo that looks out over the garden. Nearby is the Shinto shrine, flanked by a pair of white fox statues.

In the middle of the gazebo table is a bronze pot filled with glowing coals, over which an iron kettle steams. Under the table is another pot of coals, to warm the feet of anyone sitting there, I suppose.

I pause to look at the view. The top of the hill is steep enough that it's possible to look over the tops of the trees and see the garden spread out below. At the foot of the hill is a green lawn and beyond that, the koi pond. There's a tea house there, and a wooden deck, where Alex and I –

I glance back at her and she's looking that way, too. I wonder if she's remembering making love there, and how the hard wood planks might have been the softest bed, for all we noticed.

Deliberately, I think of Evgeny. Not as I last saw him, sick and scared and locked in Liam's basement. I think of him stepping out of the shower, skin gleaming with moisture, nipple piercings catching the lamplight, raven tattoo emphasizing the lines of his muscles.

I think of the way he'd look up suddenly, see me watching, and smile shyly. How his cock would get half-hard just from me looking at him.

"Still besotted with your vampire boy?" says the *kitsune*, the Japanese fox woman.

While I was daydreaming, she and the Korean *kumiho* arrived from below. They're carrying bows. The *kitsune*'s is a traditional asymmetric Japanese longbow, and she's wearing traditional garb, too, but all in dark reds. The fox women like red.

The *kumiho* is dressed more simply, and her bow is shorter and curvier. She always seemed the most practical of the three.

"Who won?" I ask. They each hold up a duck.

"Join us?" says the *kumiho*.

So we all sit and sip tea and look at each other. I try to think of what to say.

"You look tired," the *kitsune* says. "And I think it's not just because your lover keeps you awake pleasuring you."

I look into my tea cup and try to control the flush of heat. I must manage to at least keep from blushing visibly, because the *huli jing* says, "See, controlling your reactions is not so difficult."

"I am tired," I say. "There's a *koldun*, a – "

"Sorcerer," say all three fox women together. The word hisses between their teeth, a fierce sound.

"You know of him?" I ask. I try to make it sound like a statement, because they haven't invited questions, and one constant in folklore – so often repeated it almost certainly has some truth to it – is that fairies, spirits, demons, whatever you want to call them, don't like being asked questions. It's a bad idea to expect answers unless you've made a proper bargain, or unless they invite you to ask.

"We know the type," says the *kitsune*. "*Koldun* in Russia, *madoushi* in Japan. Many places have names for such as they."

The *kumiho*, who is sitting on my left, pats my hand. "Usually men who want what little power women have."

The *huli jing*, across from me, adds, "As if men didn't have enough power already, they have to steal ours."

All of them look at Alex, who shifts just a little closer to me.

"You, little witch," says the *kitsune*. "Did you bring him?'

"No," says Alex, confused. "I – "

"They lurk around *hexen*, around witches," says the *huli jing*. "They call themselves protectors, but really they drain the witch's power like leeches drain blood."

"Bloated parasites," says the *kumiho*. "They don't even know what to do with the power once they've got it." She turns her head and spits.

I dare to ask a question. "Are they always evil? Hasn't there ever been a good one? One that really wanted to protect?"

Three pairs of bright fox eyes look at me.

"It's not impossible," says the *kitsune*. Of the three fox women, she's the one I'd be most inclined to trust. When I first came to visit them (well, not *first*, but I don't remember when they saved me much, because I was unconscious for most of it), she encouraged me to choose joy in my life.

The *kumiho*, who advocated vengeance as the quickest way to awakening my fox nature, says, "They may begin by protecting, but they always end up using. They always corrupt."

I think of Evgeny. Most non-vamps say vamps always end up nasty, too, but Evgeny's always been sweet. And I've met one or two other bloodsuckers who weren't all bad. I'm inclined to believe people can rise above whatever they're said to be, if they really want to.

The *huli jing*, she who said I should balance kindness and violence, says, "I have never met an honorable sorcerer, though I have heard they exist."

"What does this one want?" the *kitsune* asks.

"Who is he?" says the *huli jing*.

"What has he tried to do to you?" asks the *kumiho*.

So I explain. I don't include every detail. Some things are too personal. But I tell them everything that seems possibly relevant.

Then, when I run out of details, and they look at me like they're expecting more, I say, "I was hoping you could teach me how to… to shield my mind from him."

They exchange glances, then they all look at Alex, then back at me.

"This is a thing you should simply be able to do," says the *kitsune*.

"As your witch friend does," says the *huli jing*.

"He was too strong for me," says Alex.

"You have untapped strengths," says the *kumiho*. "I can feel them in you, ready to burst."

The *kitsune* nods. "Oh yes. Like spring under the soil, you are. Soon you will be alive with it."

"You will be very strong," says the *huli jing*. "Your sisters should be instructing you more."

"I'll let them know," says Alex.

"We'd rather you didn't," says the *kitsune*.

"We'd rather they didn't know we were here," says the *huli jing*.

"We'll take your memory if must be," says the *kumiho*.

"I don't think you need to do that," I say.

"No," says Alex. "They keep secrets from me, so I'm not too broken up keeping this one from them. But – " She glances at me. "Is…" She doesn't finish, remembering what I said about questions.

But the three fox woman smile.

"Pretty *and* smart," says the *kitsune*. "You want to know why we wish to remain secret."

Alex nods.

"Witches like foxes for familiars," I say.

The fox women smile wide, which with their long canine teeth is not exactly comforting. Foxes have the longest canines, proportionally, of any in the canid family.

"So they do," says the *kitsune*.

I look at Alex. "In my dream, my ancestor became your ancestor's familiar. It's how she learned to look human."

And then the fox women insist I tell them that story, too, and they ask my genealogy and I tell them what little I know. My names are Korean, Chinese, and German. I look mostly Chinese, so I figure I'm half Euro, half mostly-Chinese with a bit of Korean. Aside from the German Fuchs, which means "fox," I don't know any family surnames.

I don't remember anything else. Maybe I knew more before.

"You really must break this memory block," says the *kumiho*.

"I don't know how," I say. "As far as I know, it happened when you saved me. When you tried to take the memory of…"

The *kitsune* puts her hand on mine, over the *kumiho*'s which is still there. The *huli jing* adds hers, too.

"We know," they say together.

"But we returned the memory we took," says the *kitsune*.

"If that was the case, it should have repaired you," says the *huli jing*.

"If it did not, you may never remember," says the *kumiho*.

I carefully don't look at Alex when I say, "It might be better not to remember. I'm not the same person now. Maybe it's better I just be who I have become."

"You *are* different," says Alex. There's a realization in her voice. Not a wondering sort of thing, but not entirely negative. "You're not the gentle woman I fell in love with. You're not Panya."

Then I do look at her. Her gaze is steady, her face serious. Then she smiles, just a little. "But I like this you. Su. The Su-you." Her smile widens. "This you I can be friends with."

I let out a breath I didn't realize I was holding. And I'm big on breath control. My kung fu teacher – little though I remember of him – must have emphasized it, because I almost never hold my breath, or do anything out of the ordinary with my breathing, without doing it deliberately and consciously.

But I didn't realize how much the thought of disappointing Alex bothered me. I'm not sure how much time I could spend with her if she stayed in love with me.

"Interesting," says the *kumiho*, looking from one to the other of us.

"Never mind," says the *kitsune*.

"There isn't much we can tell you," says the *huli jing*. "We were born as we are, or made to be as we are fully and all at once."

"Or else so long ago we have forgotten the process," says the *kitsune*. "But from us you should have the ability to block any influence on your mind no matter how strong."

"You should be able to turn your sexual appeal, and your own desire, on and off as you will," says the *kumiho*.

"And you should be able to see and sense what others cannot, and remove yourself from their sight and senses as you choose."

"At some point, you will simply be able to do these things," says the *kitsune*.

"Or maybe you will not," says the *kumiho*.

The *huli jing* adds, thoughtfully, "If we had made you as we intended to that night, you would be what we are."

"But the… the *fuchs* I already have in my DNA… that changed things."

"Indeed," says the *kitsune*. "And we don't know precisely how."

"It would have been disastrous if your heritage was not fox," says the *kumiho*.

"*Other* and *other* of different types do not often mix well," says they *huli jing*. "Nor do *kin* and *kin*. That is why many of those that are made become unable to bear young, and those that are born cannot be made."

I can see Alex thinking. She gets a faraway look and her eyes dart back and forth like she's watching her thoughts on an invisible movie screen.

"But Evgeny…" she says, and she looks at me. I know what she's thinking.

"Evgeny," I say, "is a vampire. He was made a vampire. But his lineage, his genetic heritage, is Russian witch."

"No matter," says the *kitsune*. "Witches are female, and he is not."

"He's descended from the royal family," I say. "The Romanovs. They had male witches. Super rare, but now and then, they had them." I look at Alex.

"That family died out," says the *kumiho*, with a little too much relish. "Slaughtered during the Russian revolution."

"No, I say. "The youngest son, Alexei, he lived. The witches told me was protected by a *koldun* and escaped."

They snarl, all three of them, when I say *koldun*. Then they look at each other.

"Does this Evgeny have witch abilities? Not even every royal male did. It was still rare, even in that family." The Korean fox woman looks fierce.

"We've never been sure if it was being force-fed witch blood or if it was his own abilities manifesting," I say.

The *kumiho* abruptly spits again. "*Hexen* blood," she says. "That's one way a *koldun* is made."

"Someone was trying to turn your Evgeny into a far more dangerous creature than a vampire," the *huli jing* says.

"If he's being taken over by something, then someone is still trying, though in a different way," says the *kitsune*.

"You better hope his witch powers develop soon," says the *huli jing*.

"Or else feed him more witch blood," says the *kumiho*, leering at Alex.

Alex looks calmly back. "What will that do?"

The *kumiho* grins her fox grin. "Boost his ability to shut the other out. At least temporarily. It would give you more time, at least."

Alex looks at me, eyebrows raised.

"No," I say.

She shrugs. "I'm game."

"You don't even know him."

She shrugs again. "One, I want to kick this *koldun*'s ass. And two, you love him and that's good enough for me."

The fox women tilt their heads at once, listening to something. I listen, too, and it takes me a moment to hear it.

"Guard coming," I say, and the fox women give me approving looks.

"Good luck, little sister," says one.

"Work on your abilities," says another.

"I love your tail," says the third.

Then they get up and disappear into the woods. Alex and I head the other way, back into the pines and down the hill. I stop her before we get back to the gate. There's someone there, ahead. Then I hear hammering. Someone's discovered our break-in and is nailing the gate shut.

Chapter Nine

I LOOK AT ALEX and she looks at me.

"If it's Dean, I could go talk to him," she says, voice low. She doesn't whisper, she just speaks quietly, and I'm impressed – she's good at being quiet.

"And say what?"

"I was trying to impress my girlfriend? He'd buy that."

"Maybe," I say. "But you'd be stuck paying for that gate."

"I feel guilty about that, anyway."

I stare in the direction of the hammering. "No," I say. "It's not that big a setback. We can climb over somewhere else. Or wait till he's gone and pry the boards off."

"Okay," she says. "But we'll have to circle around through the woods, as far away from the gate as we can, once we're out. In case they've called the cops."

Behind us, there's the sound of a stick hitting bushes. "I know you're around here somewhere," says a belligerent male voice.

Alex's eyes widen, but I listen, then shake my head. "He's moving away from us."

"But they know we're here."

"They know someone's here."

We wait a bit longer, then work our way down the other side of the hill, aiming farther back into the gardens than where we came in through the gate. Alex isn't as quiet as I am. But she's much better at moving through the woods than most people.

We reach the fence before I hear a sound that makes me nervous: the distant wail of sirens. Two cruisers at least. Spending a year as a pickpocket has made me leery of cops. I've never been caught – I'm very good at my job – but cops make me nervous, anyway. And they have guns. We *others* may heal a lot faster than humans, but shoot one of us in the head and we'll still be dead. Well, I'm not sure about vamps, but a bullet to the brain would at least put it out of commission for a long time while the symbiont repairs the damage. *Splatter* the brain with a gunshot, and I'm pretty sure even a vamp is done for.

Anyway, I don't like guns, and police sirens mean guns. And they mean the garden owners are serious about trespassers. But at least they have to leave the black-and-whites at the gate and come into the gardens on foot. I have the advantage there.

The fence here is wrought iron again, tall, without crossbars except at the top and bottom, and with spikes on each upright.

"Lovely," I say. I'm pretty sure I could get over with minimal injury, but I don't think Alex could manage it. Being a witch gives a person extra mind powers, not extra physical ability.

Alex grabs a bar and tugs at it. "It's pretty rusty," she says. "Maybe we can get a couple of bars to come free."

"Stand back," I say, so she does.

I pause a moment to breathe and calm my thoughts, then I turn and spin and kick, my foot landing square on one of the uprights with a loud "bang." It creaks and I feel it give a little under my boot, but it holds. When I stand back, I can see I bent it a little, but it didn't pop free as I'd hoped.

"Jesus," says Alex, and I don't know if she's referring to the noise or the bent iron bar.

"Damn. I guess that was a really bad idea."

"It was worth a try."

"Let me give you a boost over."

She looks at the fence, considers the height. "What about you?"

"I think I can jump it. Maybe. High enough to get a good hold on the top crossbar and pull myself up, at least."

She looks doubtful.

"Worst case, I run back to the fox women for help."

She eyes the height of the fence again, then nods and steps up close to it, her hands resting on the bars. "Okay."

I lace my fingers together and bend over so she can step into my hands. We count together to three, then I heave her upwards.

I'm strong and she's not too heavy, and I think it surprises her that I boost her so high, so she's not quite ready for it. But she scrambles to brace herself on the horizontal, gets her foot on it, and pushes herself over the spikes and clear. She lands hard on the other side, but stands up and turns.

"Your turn," she says. There's a brightness in her eyes, at the adrenaline rush, maybe. It makes her more beautiful, but I've had to fight for my life too many times. I don't want to be chased through the woods by cops.

And speaking of cops, I can hear them approaching. There are several of them, fanned out and searching. Then I hear a sound than quickens my breath. Barking.

I must have some odd look on my face, because Alex reaches through to fence to touch my shoulder.

"Su? What can you hear?"

Because of course she can't hear it.

"They brought dogs," I say.

"Shit."

"Head into the woods," I tell her. "I smelled a creek near where the ground was muddy, but father into the trees." I point in the general direction. "Running water won't fool dogs completely, but it should confuse them for a while. Slow them down. If you get to the car ahead of me, circle the block and park in a different spot to break the trail.. And watch out for cops. Don't look suspicious. Come out of the woods on a hiking trail, if you can find one.

"But you're coming too?"

"I'll be right behind you. But we might get separated, and I can hide from them more easily."

Or I could if they hadn't brought dogs.

She squeezes my shoulder again. "I'll wait in the car." Then she's off into the woods at a fast walk.

I wait until she's no longer visible, then I look at the fence. Can I get over it?

The barking is closer. Two dogs. They must have taken them to the gate to pick up the scent. But there's one good thing: they're barking, not baying. Cop dogs. Probably German shepherds. Still bad, but herding dogs are less of a threat to a canny fox than hunting dogs. Trail-scenting dogs.

Either I read up on dogs before, or else I have some kind of inherited fox knowledge.

I take several long steps back from the fence – the trees grow close against it here, but they're big, so there's room between them. Still no useful branches, though. Then I run at the fence, leap, grab, and haul myself over. My coat catches on a spike and tears, and I land badly, my ankle turning.

"Fuck." But I say it quietly, under my breath. When I stand and try to walk, pain shoots up my leg. Great. I'm supposed to be more than human and I've sprained my ankle jumping a fence.

I ignore it as best I can and head deeper into the trees, angling just a little towards the front of the gardens so I won't be too far from the car when I emerge from the woods. But far enough that I'll give the gate a wide berth.

I can't move as quickly as I'd like, limping along, holding on to trees for support where I can. I must be giving the dogs quite a trail, though if they picked up my scent, their handlers will have to take them all the way around, because I left them on the other side of the fence. And the gardener just finished boarding up the nearest gate.

I have time. Unless they already have dogs on this side of the fence.

Excited barking erupts from the two cop dogs. They've found my trail. Shouting from the cops. That would be them discovering that the trail goes over the fence.

Then more shouting, closer. There *are* cops on this side. They crash through the trees to where their colleagues wait, penned in the garden. I try to walk faster. And then comes a sound that makes panic flood my limbs, makes me stumble to a halt: the deep "wow wow wow" bay of a hound.

I force myself to breathe, force my limbs to keep moving, but an irrational terror is choking me. Even in my dream, when I was a fox fleeing hunters, I don't recall this much panic.

I stumble, keep going, agony in my ankle sending stabs up my leg. The hound gives voice again and I start to run. My vision goes grey… no, not quite back and white, but colors are muted.

She bays again and somehow I know she's a she, and pregnant, and excited by the smell of me. I wonder if she's a fox hound, bred for generations to chase my kind.

Her voice is full of joy. Chasing me is her passion and her destiny. The panic floods my nose with scents, fills my eyes with impossible detail while leaching out color.

She bays and I leap ahead through the trees, am suddenly entangled in my clothing, claw free and run flat out. My ankle doesn't hurt so much, now that I have three other legs to take the pressure off. When I splash into running water, a little sense comes back and I turn and follow the stream, keeping in the deepest part.

Minutes later, just as I come on Alex's scent, I hear the hound's confusion. I hear men exclaiming as they find my empty clothes. Then the hound finds water and her voice shows her consternation. It won't slow her for long. She knows to search up and down the bank for where I must eventually come out.

I follow Alex's trail. She can't run under branches as I can, so it's easy to run full speed after her. Each time the hound behind me gives voice, my guts clench briefly in fear, but otherwise I have begun to enjoy the chase.

A tree ahead has a branch half broken free, hanging low, and I run up it, out along another branch and into another tree. There, I have to leap down, and I re-discover my injured leg.

When I hear the hound call out that she's found my trail again, I push aside all thoughts of toying with her, and I just run, black paws flashing below me, red tail streaking out behind.

She's closer, that dog, so I push faster and run right out into the road. I hear tires squeal. I forgot about cars. How could I forget about cars?

A voice curses me, the car roars away. Then I hear, "Su?"

It's Alex. I run towards her voice. She's standing next to her green station wagon, holding the door open.

The hound is closer, so I leap for the door and Alex closes it behind be, then gets in the other door and drives.

"I really hope that's you, Su," she says, eyeing me from the corner of her vision.

I loll my tongue out at her and turn to look out the window, where a tri-colored hound emerges from the trees to stand in the road, looking almost sad to be left behind. I feel sorry for her, though she'd have torn me apart if she caught me.

Then I look at Alex again. She's trying not to, but she keeps glancing over at me.

That's right. I'm not supposed to be this shape. I'm not supposed to be all fox. I should be mostly human.

It's really hard to concentrate, to keep human thought patterns foremost. I want to curl up in a ball on the seat and sleep while I have the chance. Or crawl into Alex's lap.

She smells like magic. Or at least something like I imagine magic must smell. To my fox nature, it smells like safety, but also something less pleasant. Subjugation? But the safe part is almost overwhelming. I can see why witches like foxes as familiars. We must be very easy to tempt into servitude. And if I don't keep pulling human thoughts out of my memory, I might happily do whatever Alex tells me to. I might let her use me, use my… power? Magic? Fox abilities.

And *that's* deeply unsettling, at least to the human part of me.

So I do what I can to focus on human problems, human concerns. I stand on the seat and look out the window, watch the houses and streets pass and try to remember if we came this way on our way to the gardens. When we pass out of the suburbs and through downtown, I hunch down a bit so I can just see over the door. The city makes my fox-self nervous.

Then we're out of downtown and into the industrial district, and I'm glad when I recognize my building, when I can even pick out the windows of my loft. It's a small thing, maybe, but it would be so easy to lose myself in being a fox.

I'm pretty sure I wouldn't even miss being human.

We go inside. The front door doesn't always shut properly, so we can just walk right in. I keep meaning to see if I can fix that, but I always forget until I'm coming home and tired. The loft door is locked – Magne must have gone back to his own place – and of course my keys were...

I panic. Did I take my keys with me? Are they still in my coat? What about my wallet? At least my ID had an old address on it. Did I even take my wallet with me?

No. I calm myself down by thinking slowly and carefully about what was in my pockets when I left. I almost never carry my wallet. Just two keys – one for the building in case the door actually *does* shut properly, and one for the loft – and a little emergency cash. Just in case I get nicked picking pockets, I started taking only the bare minimum with me when I leave home. The keys are a fairly standard type, so they're unlikely to lead any cops back here.

And hopefully none of the neighbors near the garden took note of Alex's car.

I am going to miss those boots, though.

Alex doesn't hesitate at the door, but takes a key out of her pocket and unlocks it. She glances at me, a little sheepish-looking, and says, "Magne gave me the key. He said it's a spare for emergencies."

Of course. I'd given Magne the key a week ago, when Evgeny first started showing symptoms of withdrawal. Just in case we needed help.

Inside, I sit in the middle of the floor and look around. Now what? I have no idea how to get myself back into human shape, and while being a fox is fun – tempting, really – I can't fuck my boyfriend like this. Even the thought is gross.

Not that that's the only thing I want to do as a human. Conversation is nice, too, And food. As a fox I'd be happy eating mice and grasshoppers. I miss curry already.

Alex sits on the couch and looks at me. She's got that thinking expression, eyes flicking side to side, focus distant.

"My great-great grandmother... however many greats. She taught your ancestor how to be human. Maybe I can help you change back somehow."

I get up, walk over, and sit at her feet. Trust Alex to have realized that I'm not staying in fox shape because I want to. She laughs. "Not this instant." But she bends down and puts a hand on each side of my head, concentrates. I feel pressure behind my eyes, and it builds until my eyes water. Then it stops suddenly.

Alex shakes her head. "I just don't know what I'm doing, and I don't want to hurt you."

I nuzzle her hand with my nose, hop up on the couch, and curl myself into a neat circle. Just before I fall asleep, she says, "Tomorrow we'll go see one of the other witches. She doesn't know I found out where she lives."

Then I sleep, but fitfully until a thought that's been trying to surface comes clear suddenly: the pocketwatch I got from Liam was in my coat, and it had more lines of poetry, more pieces of the puzzle maybe. If not for this puzzle, then for another puzzle.

Then the thought fades and so does consciousness.

I'm running under the trees again, four-footed, and another fox runs beside me. The witch has sent us on an errand, to fetch some particular feathers for a spell.

We make a game of it, to see which of us can catch the bird first. It is a small bird, brown, but with a glorious voice. A small flock of them prefer a particular tree I know of, this time of year, this time of day, so I go there and wait. The other fox knows another tree.

While I wait for my birds, a human man wanders along a deer trail, whistling. He's young, a boy from a nearby town, perhaps, off to seek his fortune.

I crouch in the undergrowth – here, we are near a meadow and there is more sunlight than close to the witch's house, where the trees are tall and shade out all but the most hardy plants. Witch plants.

Here the shade is green and dappled – even my color-deficient eyes can see that. It makes me sleepy.

The young man sits beneath my bird tree and takes a loaf of bread from his pack. As he begins to eat, the birds arrive, one by one. They watch him. They are curious, unafraid. People do not often come here. The man smiles in delight and offers a crumb on his hand. A bird lands on his finger, pecks the treat, and sings for him when it is done. He laughs, but no sound comes from his throat, and the bird flies back into the tree.

I feel saliva pooling in my mouth. Both bird and bread look delicious, but I mustn't eat the bird. That is for the witch to pluck. Maybe she will let me eat it later.

Then I have an idea. I retreat farther into the brush, then I stand up on two legs, and put on the seeming of a human woman. I take leaves and make them seem a simple green dress. Then I step out of the wood and into the young man's view.

He smiles, but doesn't speak. When he offers me bread and a place to sit with gestures, I know he can't speak. I smile and sit and eat some of his bread.

He whistles and a bird lands on his knee. He gives it a crumb. Another lands, and another, until the birds, every last one, sit somewhere on his person, and none are left in the tree.

He gives me bread to tempt the birds, too, but they are wary of me. They know what I am. But I keep trying, because it makes him smile. He has a nice smile, warm and honest.

The witch rarely smiles. My fox companion says she used to smile a lot when she was younger. She smiled so much that sometimes even the older witch smiled, too. But now she smiles hardly at all, and the old witch seldom visits.

I wonder if she would be happier if her house and her garden were in the sun instead of deep in the gloom of the Hexenwald.

The young man gently shoos the birds away and they perch back in the tree. I hold up my handful of crumbs for them, but my arm is getting tired. The other fox will surely have returned to the witch by now. How long have I sat here?

My arm wobbles, and the young man places his hand beneath mine, steadying me. His touch is warm, his hand gentle but strong, and a feeling goes through me I have not experienced before.

It is akin to the winter heat I had earlier in the year, when the male fox and I romped in the woods and attempted to make kits. We were not successful, but it was fun.

But this is not quite the same. It is softer, less urgent, but stronger for all that. I look into his eyes – blue-grey – and feel heat in the flesh of my cheeks. My skin tingles and I want to be closer to him.

Then a bird lands on my out-stretched hand, pecks at the bread. It pauses to sing and I smile, and the young man smiles. Then it pecks again.

I wait until it has eaten all the crumbs before I snap my hand shut around it, stuff it in my mouth (alive, as the witch would prefer), and run.

I am the first back to the witch's house, and she praises me when I arrive. I pretend it is enough to make up for the shock in the young man's pretty eyes.

Chapter Ten

I WAKE AT TWILIGHT and see Alex has fallen asleep in the chair, a book open on her lap. There are other books around her on the floor and the coffee table. A cup of tea, half-full, sits so close to the edge of the table, I want to push it back towards the middle. I reach out, and my arm is a human arm, not a fox paw.

Sometime during sleep I changed back. I've got goose bumps all over, and I'm naked – the cold is probably what woke me.

I start to adjust the position of the tea cup, then instead I pick it up and sip the cold tea. Maybe thirst woke me, too, or the throbbing in my ankle.

When the cup is empty, I limp into the washroom, use the toilet, and wrap myself in my robe. I should do something useful, like look through some of those books.

I should go see how Evgeny is doing, locked in Liam's basement.

But I'm so tired, every muscle aching from fleeing the hound. My ankle hurts. Not as much as when I twisted it, but enough that just standing is painful.

So instead of doing any of the things I should do, I pull the curtains off the bed – they're still where they fell when Magne pulled them down tackling Evgeny – and get in bed.

I curl up as small as I can and think about sleep. I'm so weary, but now that I'm lying down, I can't sleep. I imagine practicing kung fu in my head – sometimes it helps me stop thinking – but I keep getting tripped up because I can't remember if I have a tail or not.

Finally I free an arm from the covers and reach around to feel my own ass. No tail.

Just a few days ago, I'd have given a whole lot to be rid of that silly red brush. Now I miss it. I feel oddly incomplete without it. Completely human.

And just a couple months ago I'd have given almost anything to feel merely human. To not be *other*. Now I can't stand the thought.

I curl up tight again. Once, when I couldn't sleep, when Evgeny was stolen from me, I'd been able to sort of… I don't know what to call it. To consciously dream myself into his mind. I consider doing that now, assuming I even can – I figured at the time it was *his* witch ability that made it possible. But if the *koldun* is there, who knows what could happen?

I shiver.

Other times, alone in bed, when Ev stayed at his own place, I would think of him, how he touched me, and pleasure myself until I felt sleepy. But Alex is across the room and I can't do that. Even if I could be quiet, which I rarely am.

If it was daytime, I would lie in the sun until its warmth soothed and relaxed me. But twilight is fox time. I should be up and about.

I start to get up again, but the ache in my muscles stops me. Then I *do* get up, but not to get dressed and walk to Liam's market. Instead, I go back to the bathroom, run a hot bath, hot as I can stand it.

There's a bottle of purple jasmine-scented bubble bath on the shelf – a gift from Evgeny that I usually save for when he's over. My tub is huge and we both fit comfortably.

He teases me about having a boyfriend who smells like flowers, but I know he doesn't mind.

I squirt some under the running water and the scent almost makes me cry. Here I am, taking a bath when Ev is in a cage, at Liam's mercy.

When I climb into the water, it feels so good that I decide not to feel bad about Evgeny for a little while. A few minutes, maybe an hour. Then I can worry again. For now, I will let a soak in the tub restore me.

So I lie back, half floating, and close my eyes. The jasmine scent fills my nostrils and I can almost imagine Evgeny is there. He would be behind me, so I could lie back against his chest, and he would put his arms around me, kiss my neck, nibble my earlobes. His hands would cup my breasts, just like this, and his fingers would tease my nipples until I arch my back and dig my fingers into the muscles of his thighs.

When I realize I'm copying those remembered touches with my own hands, I think, *I should stop.* Alex is in the next room. Maybe asleep, maybe not.

But I don't stop. I sink farther into the hot water, until bubbles tickle my nose, and let my hands caress my skin, my breasts. I slide one hand between my legs and the heat there is greater than that of the bath water, the moisture more slick.

I move my hips to the stroke of my fingers, thrust up until my body opens and push my fingers inside myself. I want to moan but my mouth is under water, so I blow air out my nose instead, frothing the bubble bath on the surface of the water.

Then I slide my other hand down to join the first, find my center with my finger and tease gently, then rub, faster until the orgasm builds and I feel I have to scream. But I bite it back, let the waves of pleasure flow through me until I can be still and calm again.

Then I just float in the hot water, able at last to think of nothing in particular. Able, finally, to sleep.

The next time I wake I'm sure I'm drowning. Lukewarm water floods over my head and I thrash to stay afloat. Soap stings my eyes and my paws scrabble on slick porcelain.

When Alex gets the door open and sees me, I'm clinging to the side of the tub, holding my head up, but not quite able to get enough purchase to get out.

She grabs me quickly, lifts me out and sets me on the floor. Then she starts to laugh.

"Oh, Su," she gasps. "I'm sorry, but you just look so ridiculous. All wet and skinny and forlorn. If only you could see yourself."

I turn my back to her and put my nose in the air.

When she finally stops laughing, she pulls the drain on the tub and gets a towel to dry me off like a lapdog.

"Unless you figured out how to turn taps with your paws, I'm guessing you were human again for a bit."

I touch her cheek with my nose.

"But you… Did you fall asleep in the tub?"

I nod. It's not a natural gesture for a fox, but I assume she'll see it as a human movement.

"We'll go see a witch or two in the morning," she says. "Obviously you *can* change back. We just have to figure out how to make it voluntary. And how to make it stick."

I follow her back out into the main room. I guess I won't be going to see Evgeny like this. I whine softly and Alex looks at me.

She sits down and says, "You want to go check on Evgeny, don't you? That might not be a good idea, with you like this. But what if we asked Magne to go?"

I nod.

She gets up again, finds her coat and rummages. She pulls out her cellphone, and then another object, shiny and brass. She sets in on the coffee table. The pocketwatch from Liam. I stare at it.

"It fell out of your pocket when you got out of the car," she says. "I was so distracted I forgot to mention it."

That's one thing that's gone right, then. If we ever manage to fix Evgeny, he can look at the inscription and see how it fits with the others.

Alex presses a few buttons on her phone, holds it to hear ear, and waits. "Magne," she says. "It's Alex. Su's – Yeah. We got home a few hours ago. No." She looks at me.

I shrug, or try to. I think she understands the gesture.

"She's a fox. Yes, I mean literally. She… Well, I thought maybe you could go to Liam's and check on Evgeny."

Then she has to explain, as best she can without having all the details. Because I didn't tell him much when I called earlier. I only told him that Evgeny was staying at Liam's because the sun was coming up. I can hear

Magne cursing.

Alex's eyebrows go up. "Okay," she says, and pushes a button to end the call. "He says he's on his way, and he'll bring food when he comes back. And he hopes you're still a fox because he wants to see what you look like."

I'm curious about that, too. All I can see of myself is black paws, black legs, red flanks, and white-tipped red tail. I suppose I must be an ordinary-looking red fox.

I wonder if there's one human detail left about my fox shape, the way I have a fox tail sometimes in my human shape. An ear maybe, or a naked patch of skin between my shoulder blades.

I hope not.

I fret, waiting for Magne to come back. I pace back and forth across the loft while Alex tries to ignore me and flips determinedly through Papa Vamp's folklore books.

I try not to think about why it might be taking so long, because really it probably isn't taking that long at all. Finally, Alex gives up trying to do research and watches me pace.

"You're going to drive us both nuts," she says, so I sit down and watch the door.

I completely understand, now, why dogs wait for their masters by the door. There's nothing else to do but watch for the first signs of their return.

I'm not sure when the wanting Magne to come back so he can tell me how Evgeny is turns into needing to see Evgeny myself *right now*. But it does and it's so intense I actually start scratching at the door like a dog.

"What, do you need to pee or something?" Alex says. "Can't you use the toilet somehow?"

I glare at her, but I have no way of knowing whether or not she can read my expressions in this shape. I scratch at the door again.

Finally she gives in and opens the door and I run to the stairwell and scratch on that door. I whine to convey the urgency. I can't explain, even to myself, why I suddenly have to get out, to get to Liam's, to make sure Evgeny and Magne are all right. I just know I do.

And yeah, I know it could be a trap. The *koldun* could somehow be reaching out to me through whatever connection I have to Evgeny, and drawing me in. But what would it want me for? I disgust it.

"Just let me get my coat," says Alex.

It might not want me, but it could want Alex. The fox women said that *koldun*s somehow drain witches, steal their abilities while seeming to protect them.

I have no way to tell Alex this. And anyway, I saw the look in her eyes when we were trapped in the gardens. Even scared, she loved it. A *koldun* is probably more danger than some cops and their dogs, but I get the feeling that she figures she's part of the story now. Part of the gang.

I have friends. It's still a weird thought, but I'm getting used to it. I like it. It makes me feel stronger, almost like I can be Angry Su, Strong Su, whenever I need to be. If only it let me change out of this fox shape when I need to.

Alex steps out of the loft and shuts and locks the door.

"I suspect you have more in mind than a quick trip to the nearest fire hydrant," she says, as she pockets the key and steps forward to open the stairwell door.

Maybe she can sense something of my thoughts. She's a witch after all. And maybe if I'm thinking loud enough, I can *let* her hear me.

So I try. *Magne*, I think at her. *Sunrise.* Because it's got to be almost dawn now. I've got that itchy feeling I get at twilight, both ends of the day. A tingling in my feet that says it's the best time for action, if any action needs doing.

She doesn't answer, so I can't be sure she's understood, but she hurries down the stairs after me, opens the door at the bottom and then the one out of the building.

"We can drive," she says, but I'm already off and running. It's not far to Liam's. Too far to carry Evgeny when he's about to be overtaken by a sorcerer, but not too far to run in a few short minutes. It would take just as long in a car, what with the getting in and starting and parking and all.

Alex curses under her breath, but follows. I don't wait, but she can run pretty fast for a human. Well, mostly human. So she's not too far behind me.

Liam's market is locked, the sign turned to "closed." I look up at the sky, and the black has a distinctly pale hue. The sun is rising.

I scratch at the glass and metal as Alex tugs on the handle in frustration.

"I suppose we could find something to break the glass." She looks around; it's a dodgy neighborhood, and there are lots of stray chunks of concrete and broken bricks.

But as she's bending to pick one up, I catch movement back in the darkness of the shop, a flash of dim light, as of a door opening farther inside. A blobby grey shadow. Magne?

But no. The height is close, but not the bulk. This is a thin shadow. It wavers, almost, as if the person who forms it can't quite walk in a straight line. Like a drunk.

I want to bark, to yip, to warn Alex, but all that comes out is a whine.

She straightens, moves towards the door a step, then stops. Maybe she can hear my thoughts, or maybe it's my body language – rigid, staring.

The shadow makes me nervous.

Alex steps back again, to the side, and watches the door with me, waiting.

"Can you tell who it is?" she asks.

No.

"Oh, wow," she says. "I caught that thought loud and clear."

So she's sort of been able to hear me. Perhaps that single word was simple enough to carry clearly.

Not Magne, I think.

"No," she says, her voice going quieter, as if she feels the sudden need to be inconspicuous. I feel the same.

"Not Magne," she says. "Liam?"

The shadow weaves closer, resolves into a more solidly human – or vampire – shape. A tall, thin person with short sticking-up hair. The face is still shadowy, but yes, it could be Liam. I think as much at Alex.

We wait and watch. The person takes a step to the side, almost falling, then catches himself awkwardly on a shelf. There's the muffled sound of several things falling to the floor – some of Liam's grocery display, maybe.

The person stands swaying for a moment, then continues towards the door. Now that he's closer, he looks zombie-like in his movements, stiff, struggling.

Finally, he reaches the door and the early dawn light falls on his face. Liam. What the hell is he doing?

He closes his eyes, clenches his teeth against the burn he must feel from even that wan light. His hand fumbles for the lock, clumsy. Like he's fighting himself.

The same thought must occur to Alex, because she curses under her breath.

"Is the *koldun* riding him how?" she asks, but it's not so much a question as an expression of worry. *What is this thing we're facing and how can we hope to defeat it?* her words seem to say.

Liam unlocks the door in spite of himself, and begins to push it open.

Then Alex moves, rushes forward to try to hold it closed. I help her, but my weight as a fox is insignificant. In my human shape, I might have some hope of keeping Liam inside, though soon the full light of morning will flood the windows – though they have blinds, they're not closed.

Liam's an old vamp, and strong, and Alex has only human strength. I try to force myself back to human shape, so I can help her.

Though I will never consider Liam a friend, and he's done enough nasty things I can't say I'd be too sorry to see him leave this life, he's a thinking creature, and I don't believe any sentient being deserves to suffer the way Liam will if he walks out into the sun.

He won't immediately burst into flame and disappear in a puff of ash, like in the movies. Instead, the sun will first burn him like anyone getting a sunburn, only at an accelerated rate. Then his skin will crisp and char and burn away, and each layer of flesh will follow as it's exposed, until the only thing left is a few scraps of bone, too small to identify as anything.

It's a torturous way to die.

But he's old and strong, and we only slow him a little. He shoves, and Alex staggers back from the door. I lose my footing and tumble a few feet.

Liam looks at us. His skin is flushed, not burning yet, but in a moment the sun will clear the buildings across the street.

There is pain in his eyes. I expect the *koldun* to speak, but when he opens his mouth, it's Liam talking. The *koldun* may be controlling him, but it's making him fully aware of his own death.

"Thanks for trying," he says.

"Oh God," says Alex.

We have to kill him, I think at her. *Or else he'll suffer.*

"I can't," she whispers.

No, she is a nurturer of life, tough though she may seem. I think killing, even if she could bring herself to do it, would destroy her. Or at least fuck up her brain good.

"Please," says Liam. Then, "I don't mind dying."

I look at Alex. *Turn away*, I think at her.

A tear runs down her face, but she nods, turns her back.

With a great effort, fighting the sorcerer, I suppose, Liam drops to his knees.

Fox teeth are not built for tearing the throats out of creatures bigger than they are, but I manage it somehow. It's messy, and it takes too long, but it's less painful for Liam than burning alive. As the life fades from his eyes, I think I see something like peace there.

Or I could be imagining it.

Chapter Eleven

I TASTE BLOOD and charcoal.

Liam's body seems to shrivel, then bloat, the processes of decay suddenly accelerated by his death, instead of slowed as they would be if he was still alive. Then the sun finds a gap between buildings and strikes him. For a moment he almost seems to glow, then his flesh crisps and curls and burns to nothing.

What's left is scattered by a light breeze that smells like roast pork left a bit too long in the oven.

My stomach rumbles and I want to vomit, but either foxes don't puke, or else they have stronger constitutions.

"Wow," says Alex. Her eyes are big, haunted maybe, and she stares at where Liam was a moment ago. "The sun does that?"

Yeah.

We both look towards the door of the shop. I'm suddenly reluctant to enter, afraid of what I might find. But the urgency that drove me here is still there. Something is still wrong.

So we step cautiously through the door and into the market, step over spilled packages of cereal and granola, and make our way to the inner door.

I notice that Alex leaves the outside door unlocked, and I'm glad. We might need to make a hasty exit.

In the back room, there isn't really anything out of place – there isn't much to *be* out of place – but I spot smeared greasy handprints on the glass door of the cooler, like maybe Liam leaned on it in passing. Or tried to find purchase to slow himself down.

I stop in front of the door disguised as a meat freezer and Alex looks at me questioningly, then opens it. Inside, a red light glows next to the keypad. Carefully, precisely, I think the numbers at her and she punches them in, and all the time I hope that Liam – or the sorcerer – didn't change the code.

We wait and I force myself to keep breathing, to not hold my breath, until finally a green light blinks on and the electronic lock clicks and Alex pushes the door open.

I slip in front of her to lead the way, but pause at the top of the stairs to listen. Breathing. I can't count how many, but a few at least of Liam's… residents are down there. One breathes more strongly, but also more erratically – that might be Magne, but if so, he's not in his usual state of calm.

I can smell blood and fear, but I could smell those things last time I came down here. They're stronger now, though, which is probably not a good sign.

Then I hear voices. No words, just odd sing-song, wordless sounds, groans. A yell. *That's* Magne.

I want to take off at a run, to help him, but I force myself to descend slowly, cautiously, one step at a time.

Alex follows, placing her feet with care and moving as quietly as a *hexen* can. She breathes slowly and deliberately, and I can tell from the odd catch that she's carefully drawing in and releasing each breath to keep herself from panting.

From the bottom of the stairs I can see all the way down the hall. All the doors are open now, and several of them have bodies in them.

The first one we reach is dead, limbs crooked at awkward angles, throat punctured by two neat holes, needle-small. This vamp was eaten by one of his neighbors. The corpse is bloated, which for a vamp means a few hours dead at the most.

The next body is not dead, but dying. She's emaciated and has the vacant eyes of a drug addict, and she's sucking feebly at a wound on her own wrist. Is it possible for a vampire to drain itself to death? I'm not sure the question even makes sense.

I step over her legs and keep going. Three more bodies, all dead, all fed on by another vamp. Then two vamps, limbs entwined, fucking and feeding on each other. They're silent, except for their accelerated breathing. Their mouths are fastened on each other's necks, hips thrusting together. They move more and more slowly and by the time we step past, they've lapsed into stillness, their breathing barely audible.

I can see the bars of Evgeny's cell, but I can't see him in it. I really, really hope he's not the one who did this.

Then we reach the last room and I hear feeble movement within. I round the door and there is Magne, huddled in a corner, arms over his head, three vamps clustered around him. One has fastened its fangs into his shoulder and he's weakly trying to pull away. Another seems to be trying to bury its head in his crotch, but his curled-up posture thwarts its intentions. The third stands near him, watching, pale member in hand, slowly jerking off.

The standing vamp turns to look but doesn't look down, so he sees Alex and not me. I hear her breath catch, and she stops.

He grins, turns father so she can see him stroke himself, flicks out his tongue at her. He doesn't appear to have any wounds, and he seems strong, so I'm guessing he's the one who did in the others. Except for the ones who did in themselves.

For a long moment, I freeze, uncertain what to do, then the thought kicks in that my friend is here, hurt, *being* hurt even in front of my eyes.

Then it's almost like I'm a passenger in my own body, observing my actions from an objective point of view. Except it's not like that at all, because it's not a stranger controlling my body, it's me. No, it's more like I only have to think what I need to do and my body does it. Or not think, even, because it's like kung fu, where actions happen faster than thought.

So let's just say I can't explain it. But my fox body moves faster than any mortal creature can, my teeth are sharper than they ought to be, and the two vampires on Magne are dead almost before I realize it.

Too bad I couldn't do this when I needed to kill poor Liam.

Then Magne stands up and snaps the neck of the third vamp while it's still jerking off for Alex.

I leap at Magne, burrow into his arms, so glad he's all right. He laughs and almost falls over, because he's weak and killing that vamp probably cost him what energy he had left.

"Boy, am I glad to see you two," he says. And then he does fall over, clutching his head.

"No fucking way," he growls.

The koldun, I think at Alex.

She nods, crouches by Magne, and puts her hands on his head. Then she sways and takes her hands away.

"I can't block both Magne and myself at the same time," she says.

And I realize I don't feel any pressure in my head at all. Either the sorcerer doesn't recognize me, or my fox shape comes with mind-protecting abilities. Or those powers I should simply naturally have, according to the fox women, have finally started to work.

Hat, I think at Alex, and try to picture Charleston's protective headgear, with its wires and electrodes, like a prop from a cheesy SF movie.

"Oh," she says, and hurries from the room. I hear her retreat down the hall, then come back at a run, the hat in her hands. She must have spotted it as we made our way past. Obviously, I'm going to have to work on my observational skills.

She places it on Magne's head and he immediately sits up and sighs in relief.

"Thanks," he says. Then he looks at me and grins. "Aren't you just adorable?" Then he frowns and adds, "But completely impossible according to my understanding of the universe."

"I'm starting to think Su is not anything like normal, even for an *other*," says Alex.

Evgeny, I think, loudly and pointedly.

"She wants to know how Evgeny is," Alex says.

"She wants – How can you – Never mind," says Magne. "You can explain later. Ev's fine, more or less. Still locked up. The... sorcerer or whatever seems to have left him alone while it sicced this lot on me." He waves his hand around to indicate the dead vamps.

"It might not leave him alone now," Alex says. "Now that all its playthings are dead and the rest of us are untouchable."

"What about Liam?"

Alex looks away, then back, and shakes her head. She doesn't seem quite able to actually say what happened, but Magne must get the idea. He probably knows it's morning and that Liam left up the stairs.

"Poor bastard," he says. "That can't be a nice way to die."

Alex doesn't say that I put Liam out of his misery first, but maybe it's not important.

"Let's go check on Ev, then," Magne says.

I can hear Evgeny's breathing, have heard it all along, I think, but didn't realize it was his. It's light and regular and quiet and slow, just as a healthy, resting vamp's should be. Just as Evgeny's hasn't been for some time.

I don't feel the tension, the fear that brought me running here, but I can't quite feel at ease, either.

The three of us leave the room and walk slowly to the cell. It's still locked, still secure. Several empty bloodbags lie on the floor just outside it. It's dim and shadowy within, but my fox night vision picks out Evgeny's shape on the cot.

That's why I couldn't see him before, because he's stretched out peacefully on the bed, blanket pulled up over him, asleep.

Alex steps up close to the bars and frowns in concentration. "It's gone, for now," she says.

"Does that mean I can take this ridiculous hat off?" asks Magne.

"I wouldn't advise it," says Alex. "We don't know when it might come back."

Then Evgeny stirs on the bunk, opens his eyes, and smiles.

"Su," he says. "You're a fox." He twists around to look at the others. "Am I still dreaming?" He focuses on Magne. "I must be."

"No, you're awake," says Magne.

Evgeny blinks at him. "Why are you wearing that?"

"Apparently, it keeps witches and sorcerers out of my head." Magne turns to Alex. "No offense."

"I wonder if Charleston designed it to look stupid on purpose." She grins.

And for a moment, everything is perfect. Except I'm still a fox.

Evgeny swings his feet over the edge of the cot and sits up. "I actually don't feel crappy," he says.

"Maybe it's over," says Magne. "Maybe the sorcerer dude got bored and decided to find somebody else to toy with."

"Maybe," says Evgeny. "But I'd rather not take any chances."

I step close to the bars and Evgeny touches my fur. He smiles. "You look lovely," he says. "Though I'm rather fond of your other shape."

"She seems to be stuck," says Alex. "We planned to pay a visit to an elder witch today, to see if she can help."

"What about the fox women?" Magne asks.

"They seemed to think she should automatically know everything. Though they did admit they didn't remember how they learned anything, so they could be wrong."

"Helpful."

"You should go see this witch, then," says Evgeny.

"What about you?" Magne leans on the bars and pokes a finger in the lock. "I wonder where Liam keeps the keys."

"I hope they weren't in his pocket," says Alex.

Magne frowns and Evgeny looks from one to the other, then realizes what they mean. Something like mild regret flickers across his features and is gone. He never did like Liam.

"I should stay locked up for now," says Evgeny. "You could bring me some books, though, if you want me to be useful."

"I'll stay with you, then," says Magne. "After I get those books and some food for both of us."

So I stay with Evgeny while Magne and Alex fetch and carry – and Magne drags the vamp bodies into the farthest-away room and shuts them in. I press close to the bars and Evgeny strokes my fur like I'm a cat, and it's a little bit comforting.

I miss his touch on my bare skin, though, and I miss the constant ache of attraction. In fox shape, I have no thoughts of wanting sex, and no interest in Ev beyond friendship, companionship.

I suppose it would be seriously creepy if I *did* want to fuck him in this shape. Yeah, definitely gross. But that's a really good reason to get out of fox form, because the absence of desire is like having a basic part of my emotional makeup shut down.

I must whine, because Ev's hand stops and he says, "What's wrong?"

I shake my fox head, then I think *I miss you* at him.

He blinks in surprise, then his sweet smile spreads across his lips, reaching all the way to his eyes.

"I *heard* you," he says. "In my head." He stares at me wonderingly for a moment, then says. "But I'm right here. How can you miss me?"

So I think I a picture at him, us naked, limbs draped across each other.

"Oh," he says. "That." Then he gets that little thinking furrow between his eyebrows.

"Yeah, that's gone, isn't it?" he says. "I don't like that very much."

Then Alex and Magne return, arms full of books and bloodbags and takeaway food. Alex and I eat, too, and then it's time to go see a witch about a fox.

A girl stuck in fox shape.

We take Alex's car and drive a route I don't ever remember taking before.

At some point, without me noticing when, it's become much easier to focus on human things, less alluring to just succumb to fox thoughts and fox instincts.

Maybe it happened when I somehow knew Magne and Evgeny were in trouble. Or maybe it was just a gradual return to my proper mind, the way a newborn vampire gradually remembers their past and becomes a thinking creature again, instead of a beast of instinct.

Whatever caused it, it's welcome. One less thing I need to worry about, because hell, I've got quite enough things to give me giant ulcers for the rest of my life.

I wonder if there are any *other* shrinks out there. Our lives are so messed up – or mine has been, anyway – that you'd think there'd be a demand. Some were or fairy or something could make a nice practice out of it. But then, where would you go to school for something like that? And where would you advertise?

We pass through a suburb, then another. Each is full of houses nearly identical in color and shape, but each suburb has its own look to distinguish it somewhat from the others.

One is mostly grey houses, ranch style, with big yards and garages hidden around the side. Another is huge faux-tile-roofed beige monstrosities, so close together there's barely room for a path from front to back yard on each side, and each has a double-car garage stuck on the front like an advertisement for the occupant's affluence. Or like the house belongs to the car, and the people are just the hired help.

Eventually, we reach a neighborhood that's sprawling, stretched out, with fenced and treed yards in a variety of odd shapes. The houses are similar to one another – split-level, mostly, with 70s yellow glass windows next to the front doors, but they're different colors, with different types of siding. A lot of them have mature flower gardens, and few have garages, though carports are common.

It's not an especially pretty neighborhood, but it's more comfortable than most of the others we passed through.

Alex slows to read addresses. "I only came by once," she says. "And I didn't stop."

There are several cars parked out on the road in front of one house, which also has a driveway full.

"That's it," says Alex. "Looks like she's got company."

I look at her, wondering if we should try again later.

Alex circles the block, then parks a few doors down. She taps her hand uncertainly on the steering wheel, moves to get out, but then settles back in her seat.

"It looks like company's leaving," she says.

We watch and I see someone I recognize, a not-quite-middle-aged curly-haired witch I met when I broke them all out of Charleston's prison. She was the one who first called Evgeny an abomination.

Then I see a tall, slender black woman I also recognize from Charleston's. I notice her because aside from Charleston himself, she's the only *other* I've seen who's a person of color. Then I look closer at the rest, and realize I've seen them all before. They were all there that day, held captive. Even the little witch-child is there, leaving hand-in-hand with a plump elderly lady

– the only one I don't remember from the escape.

"What the hell?" says Alex. "I guess I didn't get invited to the party." She doesn't sound miffed, or sad to be left out, just a bit confused. Suspicious, even.

Hexen, I think.

"Yeah, every last one of them."

I'm not sure if she means all of them are *hexen*, or that all the *hexen* she knows of are here.

We wait until they all drive away. I don't know about Alex, but something about it all makes me uneasy.

"Maybe you should wait for me here," says Alex.

But if something weird's going on, I want to know about it. Right away.

No, I think at her. *We're stronger together*. I'm not really sure what I mean, even. Strength in numbers, maybe. But when I put the thought into words – even mental words – it seems to mean more, somehow.

Alex nods sharply. "Okay. Let's go." She gets out of the car and holds the door for me, and we cross the street and walk to the witch's house side by side.

I think, from the stiffness in Alex's movements, that she's putting on a show of more bravado than she feels. It makes me proud of her, of her strength, and for a brief moment I imagine what it might be like if I chose her instead of Evgeny.

But then I think of her face after I killed those vamps in Liam's basement and I know that even if I *had* chosen to be with her that it wouldn't have worked. I'm too different from the woman I used to be.

I'm glad she's here as my friend, though. I'm a bit of a loner – though that might be my fox nature – but I'm starting to find that friends are a very nice thing to have.

On the front step, Alex hesitates, then takes a deep breath and rings the bell.

It echoes inside the house, a peculiar deep "bong" like a grandfather clock.

Then nothing. I've begun to wonder if maybe the witch who lives here left with the others. But then there are footsteps down the carpeted stairs inside, muffled by what sounds like a deep-pile 70s shag.

The door opens and I recognize this witch, too. She's the older woman who spoke for the others in Charleston's lair. Their leader, I suppose.

She sees Alex and blinks rapidly, surprise widening her eyes, and something that might be dismay. She recovers quickly and smiles a grandmotherly smile.

"Alexandra, how nice to see you," she says. "What brings you here?"

"I wanted to ask for your help," Alex says. "For my friend."

"Which friend, my dear?" Then the witch notices me sitting next to Alex's feet. "Oh, I see," she says. "You've brought your familiar."

Chapter Twelve

THE WITCH – I don't know her name – stands back to let us in the door. I have the sudden urge to flee, but I push it aside. I can't help but stick close to Alex's legs, coming dangerously close to tripping her.

"She's not my familiar," says Alex. She eyes a boot tray with several pairs of shoes neatly lined up on it, looks at the witch's slippered feet, and toes off her sneakers. "She's my friend, Su, the one…"

"Yes, I know," says the witch. "The *fuchs* girl who freed us from captivity."

She bends over, hands on knees, and speaks to me slowly and loudly, the way some people talk to children. "We're quite grateful." Then she ignores me.

"She's a perfect familiar for you," she says, taking Alex by the arm and leading her up the stairs and onto the main floor. Ahead I glimpse a kitchen, to the left it opens up into a living room full of plush furniture.

There's a fireplace at the far end, functional, but more for the show of open flame than for actual heat. Where most old ladies might have ceramic cats on the mantel, and decorative fireplace tools, the witch has a collection of cauldrons – some of them looking quite functional and well-used – and an upright iron rack holding several heavy pokers.

I can smell smoldering wood, and I wonder if the gathering of witches involved fire.

"Tea?" asks the witch, and Alex mutters something non-committal. The witch nods and goes into the kitchen, leaving us standing. "Make yourself at home, Alexandra," she says.

Alex steps uncertainly into the middle of the living room, and I follow, keeping as close as I can without getting stepped on. You'd never know I was the same fox who'd just dispatched several vampires with only her teeth. But last time I met a witch other than Alex, I was rescuing them. I was in a position of strength, though they were actually considerably more powerful than I – especially in a group as they had been. Here, I'm weak and vulnerable, or at least that's how I feel. My fox nature might be able to keep the witch out of my head, but who knows what else she might try?

I think of that urge to crawl into Alex's lap that I felt after escaping the cops' dogs, the desire to do whatever she told me to.

"There now, it'll be a minute to boil," says the witch, bustling back into the room. I'm pretty sure the grandmother act is put on, but I can't imagine why. To put us at ease, maybe, but unless she's working against us, then why not just be herself? Why pretend?

"Please, sit," she says, and Alex sinks automatically into the nearest chair. I wonder if the witch controlled her just then, but when I look at Alex's face, peer closely into her eyes, she looks herself. Just uncertain, as if she's trying to work something through in her mind.

"She's stuck in fox shape," says Alex, finally. "That's why we came to ask your help."

"Ah, well," says the witch. "That's part of binding your familiar, isn't it? It's your responsibility to teach her to take human shape, your gift to her for her service. And part of being a witch is learning how to do that for yourself."

"That doesn't seem very efficient," blurts Alex. Her eyes are flicking side to side; she's thinking. And I think just filling the air with whatever pops into her head to buy herself time.

"Perhaps not, but it's tradition," says the witch. She goes into the kitchen again and there's the sound of water, dishes clattering, a refrigerator opening, and she returns with a tray. Tea pot, cups and saucers, milk and sugar.

"She's not a fox. Not really," says Alex. "And I don't want to *bind* her. She's my friend."

"She is a fox," says the witch, pouring tea with precise movements. "Though not an everyday fox, of course." She hands a cup to Alex, who inhales the fragrance, but sets it aside without drinking.

"But not *all* fox," says Alex. "She's human, too. Mostly human."

The witch sips, sets her cup in front of her on the coffee table, and regards Alex sternly.

"Whatever else she may have in her ancestry, however many humans, she is most definitely *not* human anymore. She is *fuchs*, fox, with a fox's magic." The witch frowns as she regards me. "Her human… remnants have been tampered with, so even they are entirely *other*."

She must be talking about whatever the fox women did to me, the parts of themselves they conferred upon me in order to save my life.

"She might look like a China doll, sometimes, but my dear, what she *is* is a German *hexenfuchs*, with some Asian fox magic thrown in."

She lifts her tea and sips again, entirely unaffected by the disbelieving way Alex is staring at her.

Then Alex shakes her head. "You said a witch binds her familiar by teaching it how to be human. Are you saying all familiars can take human shape once they're bound?'

"Goodness, no," says the witch. "A very few gifted familiars can display the *seeming* of human shape, but touch destroys the illusion, since they are not actually in a different form. The *hexenfuchs* is a rare and much-sought-after beast, because she can put on an actual human form. Though of course she remains a beast in mind and in all other ways."

The witch contemplates Alex for a moment, then she says, "You have the potential to be a very strong witch. I feel it in you. And a strong witch needs a strong familiar. It is only destiny, fate, that has brought you two together. All you have to do is reach out and take it. Take her."

The witch's eye glitter and I notice, abruptly, that they are colorless grey, flat like old ice. My fox vision lacks many of the colors of my human sight, so I had assumed they were just an ordinary blue. I shiver and crouch closer to Alex's leg.

"You see," says the witch. "She already seeks your protection. All you need do is give it to her. She will soon enough come to enjoy her life. Her fox nature will predominate in time, and she will be more content than she could ever be as a human woman. Eventually, she will even be grateful you took her away from that abomination she is so taken with."

I remember my dream, where I was in the forest, hunting birds for a witch. Or my ancestor was. I defied the witch, just a little, to enjoy the company of a handsome young man who could charm the birds down from the trees.

Maybe it was only to use him to catch a bird, but I remember the way my skin tingled when his hand touched mine, and I think not.

I think this witch knows nothing about love. Maybe it's a disease of witches. I hope Alex never suffers from it.

Alex picks up on the mention of Evgeny. "Why do you call him an abomination?" she asks. "I mean I get that it's bad that he was made a vampire, so he could never develop his witch heritage, which is bad because witches are so rare. But what if he *could* become a witch and still be a vam... a Reborn."

The witch looks like she wants to spit, but she doesn't. She smooths the disgust from her expression with a long sip of tea.

"That is not possible," she says. "It would make him something – No, it's not possible."

But I think she's wrong. I think it *is* possible. Hell, I think it's happening.

Alex considers. She picks up her tea, stares into it, sets it down again. "What's a *koldun*?" she asks.

The witch sits very still, but I see her eyes flick to focus on the fireplace, then away. She's forcing herself still. Something about the word makes her uneasy, but is it because the sorcerer is a threat to her and the other witches? Or is it possible they've decided to help the *koldun* attack Evgeny, because *Evgeny* is the threat to them? Because he's becoming something that shouldn't exist? But how could he endanger them just by *being*?

"A Russian sorcerer," says the witch. "Didn't we go over this once already?" Her voice is sharp, chastising a student for asking a stupid question.

"Is he evil?" asks Alex. I want to tell her to be cautious, to warn her that her mentor – if that's even the right word – is hiding something from her. But I don't dare try to think it at her. Not with the other witch so close.

I pretend to groom my tail like a cat so I can get a better look at the fireplace. There are objects clustered on the hearth, maybe decorative or maybe recently used. An iron cauldron, burnt black on the bottom; a dark-colored dish of pale liquid, milk I think, from the smell, though I'd have to sit up to see inside; some pieces of paper; a pencil; a candle stub.

Objects almost too stereotypically witchy to be believable. But behind the cauldron, almost out of sight, a set of Russian nesting dolls. Or I assume a set, because I can only see the biggest, outermost one. It's not a plump peasant woman in a headscarf, though. It's a man with a long beard, and a long black outfit. Like a priest, or a monk. Rasputin was a monk. Does that mean something?

I still don't think it's likely witches are behind whatever's taking over Evgeny. Or do I? It seems too preposterous, but there is something going on that this witch doesn't want us to know about.

"That depends on your definition of evil," says the witch after a pause so long I almost forgot what Alex had asked. "To the average human, he might seem so. To a witch, the *koldun* is a protector."

I look back at the witch. I can't always smell a lie, literally, but something in her words just seems off. She's relaxed now, though, confident that Alex is just looking for information in general and not suspecting something about the other witches.

"I was told that a *koldun* protects while stealing a witch's magic, because he has none of his own."

"Told by whom?" The witch looks concerned, but not like she's hiding something.

Alex just shrugs.

"I'd like to meet this anonymous source," says the witch, looking at me, then away. "It sounds like they have some odd misconceptions."

Alex shrugs again.

"Now, take my advice, dear, and bind this fox to you before she gets too many ideas beyond her station."

"If I teach her how to change back to human shape…" Alex looks at me, worry in her dark eyes.

"You will bind her to you, yes," says the witch. "That's one way to do it." She stands up, ready for us to leave, but not wanting to look like she's booting us out, I guess.

Alex nods. I wonder if she's considering it. If I really could somehow bring out her strengths as a witch, maybe she'd do it. I know I sometimes think I would give a lot – or give up a lot – to gain my full fox abilities. Maybe becoming a witch is a process of losing your humanity. But I haven't given in to any of the tempting shortcuts I've been offered, not yet, and I have to trust that Alex won't either.

I think of the pale-haired witch in my dream and how my fox ancestor thought she'd be happier if her house was in the sun. I wonder if this witch ever goes out in the sun.

And then I wonder why she had company so early in the morning. Or had they stayed from the night before? I make myself not look back at the fireplace, but I still wonder what they were doing here.

Then Alex asks, right out, looking up at the elderly witch. "Why were all the other *hexen* here?"

"Pardon me?" says the witch, pausing in the middle of collecting Alex's untouched cup of tea.

"The other witches, they were all leaving when I got here. Why was I left out?" She lets a whine creep in at the end, just a touch. I hope it's an act.

The witch smiles, so suddenly it's almost a grimace. "Jealousy, Alexandra? It was just a meeting for more experienced *hexen*. You'll be included when you've come into your powers fully."

I think of the witch child. She must be only eight or nine years old. Has she come fully into her witch powers?

"Oh," says Alex. "I see." She stands up. "I suppose I should go see what I can do with this fox, then."

This time, the witch's smile seems genuine. "Good girl. She'll be eager to please you anyway. It's in her nature. It shouldn't take much to make her yours."

Alex nods, heads for the stairs, and pauses to jam her feet into her shoes without untying them.

"Come back when she's bound. It's traditional to begin passing on more knowledge then." The witch hugs Alex and beams at her.

Sure, I think, once the student has proven she's no longer constrained by human decency by binding another sentient being to her will.

I think that must be what a *hexenfuchs* is. A "witch fox" because witches like them for familiars, but also because they're something more than ordinary foxes, the way *others* are something more than human.

Hexenfuchs. I'm not sure I like how it's connected to witches, but at least I have something to call myself now.

Alex doesn't say anything until we're well away from the witch's house, passing by a treeless beige housing complex. Maybe she's paranoid about being overheard, like I was not long ago, or maybe she was just thinking.

"There's definitely something not right," she says. "She wasn't telling me something. Maybe a lot of somethings."

She pulls the car off the road, into the drive-through lane of a coffee place, the kind that serves cheap, acidic beverages that must contain some addictive ingredient because so many people drink it even though it's terrible.

She orders a large with lots of milk and stares absently ahead while we wait.

I hide on the floor when we pull up to the window. It's probably not a big deal if I'm seen – how many people in this dull neighborhood have even seen a real fox before? But I'm still uneasy and don't want to draw attention to myself.

As we pull back onto the main road, Alex says, "If it means turning out like her, I don't think I want to be a witch."

They can't all be like that, I think, but my mind isn't clear, so I don't know if she hears. I think I might be slipping back into the fox's mindset, a little. I force my thoughts back to our problems.

I'd like to tell her how about how Evgeny hasn't become like most vampires, how he hasn't let the extra power turn him into an obnoxious prick or an evil monster. But maybe to her he still is an evil monster. He's killed. Vamps, mostly. But then so has Magne. So have I. Maybe we *can't* fight our natures.

We're quiet the rest of the way back, thinking, I guess. There's a lot to think about and so far all we've found is more questions.

"Your place or Liam's?" Alex asks when we get out of the car. The sun is high now, and it's making me sleepy. Even in human shape, patches of sun make me want to stretch out in them and nap. In fox shape, it's almost too much to resist.

I do want to check on Evgeny, but he's probably sleeping, and I should let him have some peace while he can. So I go to the door of my building, wait for Alex to open it, then lead the way in.

The loft feels empty without Evgeny, and I realize that even though we're not living together, he spends so much time here it's as if he belongs.

We both sit on the couch and stare into space for a while. When I feel the lure of my fox nature creep in, tempting me to give up on human life – because after all, it would be so much easier to just be an animal and let Alex look after me – I sit up.

Teach me how to take human shape, I think at her, forming each word precisely in my head to be sure I'm clear.

She looks at me, startled out of whatever she'd been thinking.

"First of all," she says, "I don't know how. And secondly, if I do that, you'll be bound to me as my familiar."

Good. For a little while back at the witch's house, I though maybe Alex *would* decide to bind me. I feel ashamed that I thought so, but I'm so used to trusting nobody but myself, it's hard to let go of suspicion.

Trusting Evgeny again, once all this is over, is going to be really difficult.

Unbind me after? I think.

"I don't know how to do that, either," she says. "I'm not sure it's even possible."

You don't know what's possible. I don't mean it to sound harsh, but maybe it comes out that way because she frowns.

But then she says, "The other *hexen* haven't really been very informative, have they?'

Even less than the fox women, I think.

She gets up. "Can I make tea?" she asks. "I was so nervous I couldn't drink the witch's tea, and that coffee I got on the way home isn't kicking in."

I wonder if maybe Alex doesn't know the elder *hexen*'s name, either. Or if she just doesn't use it for some reason of her own.

As she fills the kettle and plugs it in, she says, "I have an idea how maybe you can change back, but I don't want to tell you directly." She leans against the counter, looking at me. "I won't teach you, but maybe I can help you teach yourself."

When she has a cup of tea for herself, and one for me – maybe in case I'm successful at changing back – she sits cross-legged on the floor. I sit in front of her.

"When you changed back last night, and had a bath, were you dreaming?"

I nod. I start to form words in my head to tell her about it, but it's too difficult to relate that way, so instead I think pictures at her. Running as a fox, seeing the young man.

Oh. She wants me to remember whatever might have made me change back in my sleep. That would most likely be the part where the fox – me – in the dream took human shape so she could meet the man.

I get up, pace across the room, trying to recall every detail. I ducked behind some bushes and assumed a human likeness, made the seeming of a dress out of leaves.

But in the dream, or the ancestral memory, or whatever it was, I was a fox, an actual fox, only seeming to appear as human. Or was I? The witch had seemed to think *hexenfuchs* could actually take human shape.

Either way, I'm not a fox that can take human form, but a human that can take fox form. Aren't I? Does that work the same way? But it's all we have.

"Wait." Alex gets up. "Just in case, I'm going to leave. In case the... the binding starts to happen. I'll go wait with Magne and Evgeny."

She gets her coat and goes to the door. "Good luck," she says, and then she leaves.

And I lay on the floor and close my eyes and remember every detail of that dream. I can picture every vein on every leaf, every insect, every chirp of every bird.

And I know what it felt like to be a fox putting on the shape of a girl. And then I know how. Or rather, I don't know how, but I simply can.

When I open my eyes, I'm no longer small and furry. I'm naked and human and full of desire. And I have a fox's tail.

I know how to make it go away, but I let it stay. I like it.

Chapter Thirteen

Of course, it would be too easy, too *helpful*, if that was that. Oh hey, now I can turn into a fox whenever I want, and change back in a snap. Look, I have a tail! And now I don't!

No. Instead I lie there for five minutes, exhausted. And then suddenly I'm a fox again. And I don't mean I changed back on purpose, either.

Damn, I think. So I go through the process of remembering the dream again, of bringing to mind every detail. And it takes even longer, and I'm even more tired after, but I'm human again.

I relax, and bam! Fox again.

Fuck.

But the third time, taking human shape isn't quite as hard. Instead, it leaves every muscle and joint aching. And then I'm afraid to relax. I must lie there for an hour at least, naked on the hardwood floor, rigid and afraid to move.

And then I realize I'm lying on my tail and it's going numb, so I sit up. That's when I realize just how strangely humans are put together. I mean, we're basically quadrupeds who figured out how to balance on our hind legs. It's weird. And after running on four legs for… how long? It *feels* weird. Really bizarre.

I get to my feet and walking across the floor feels like a tightrope balancing act, like I might topple over at any second.

And putting on clothes. Hell, that's just downright peculiar. And kind of binding. But it's winter and I live in a big drafty apartment and I've already been naked too long.

When I look in the mirror, my lips are blue-tinged, so I find a sweater and wool socks.

And then I have to look in the mirror again. It takes me a while to spot what looks off. My face is still the same, rounded and sort of bronzy. Same insanely long hair so straight you could use it for a plumb line. Same amber eyes.

No, not the same. Same color, same shape, but my irises are bigger. So big there's hardly any white. And my pupils – a stray shaft of light catches them and they contract – my pupils are slitted like a cat's. Like a fox's.

I guess I'm going to be wearing sunglasses a lot. Unless I can make them go back to human, the way I can make my tail disappear.

For now. I let them stay. I'm too damn tired to expend the effort. For now, I'm happy just to stay in human shape.

The thought of walking to Liam's – now that he's dead, whose place is it? – makes me want to curl up in a ball on the bed. But my sex drive has returned with my human shape and I want to be near Evgeny.

So I find shoes – footwear is even odder than clothes right now – my coat. Not my favorite coat, that one that got left behind in the woods when my dog-induced panic made me turn into a fox in the first place.

Then I head down the stairs, clutching the rail like an old lady. I'm glad it's still daylight, because if a vamp decided to attack, I'm not sure I could hold it off. Then again, since I freed all those *others* from Charleston, I haven't had nearly the problem with vamps as I used to.

Even bloodsuckers can be grateful, I guess.

When I get to the market, I bang on the door, wondering if anyone can even hear me. Finally, it occurs to me to *think* at them, *Hey, it's Su, let me in!*

I hear back, faintly, something that might be a reply, if it's not my imagination, but in a minute or two, Magne opens the door.

He grins. "Glad to see you're yourself again."

I smile back. "I feel about a hundred years old," I say.

"Changing for the first time will do that to you," he says. I think he says it just to say *something*, because werewolf changing is a totally different thing.

They don't really turn into wolves. Instead, the connections and articulations between their bones and muscles and all gradually alters, sometimes over many, many years, until they can be reconfigured into a human shape or a more-or-less wolf shape. Magne once compared it to one of those transformer robot toys.

I always imagined their tails are sort of nestled inside their asses like those extendable marshmallow roasting sticks.

We go downstairs and Magne has dragged a couple of cots out into the space in front of Evgeny's cell. There's more takeaway food – I smell curry – and a pot of tea has materialized from somewhere. I can't picture Liam as a tea-drinker, but I didn't know him, not really.

"Hey," says Alex. "You're you again."

Evgeny says nothing, but he smiles, and when I go up to him, he puts his face up against the bars so I can kiss him. His fingers wrap around mine and I let go of some of the tension.

"We've been researching," he says when I step back. There are books scattered around, places marked, some of them propped open.

"What have you found out?" I say.

"Nothing that makes sense."

I sit next to Alex on one of the cots and lean against the cell bars. Evgeny drags his own cot closer so he can sit right on the other side.

Alex picks up one of the books and flips it open. "According to the little we found, *kolduns* shouldn't be so powerful. They steal a witch's abilities, but only gradually, and their own use of those abilities is weaker, more subtle."

"Seems like they were usually physically powerful, too, or else had charismatic personalities, so they could be protective in other ways. And they use the stolen power efficiently. But one could never have taken over another being the way whatever-it-is took over Ev," says Magne, picking up a container of curry and passing it to me.

I'm ravenous, so I don't talk, just eat. And listen.

"So either it's not a *koldun* we're dealing with," says Alex, "or else these books are all wrong."

I look from one to the other of them, and they all seem to be waiting for a reply, so I say, "What if the *koldun* stole power from a lot of witches?"

"Maybe," says Alex.

"But witches have always been so rare, it doesn't seem likely."

"There are, what, a dozen *hexen* here in Riverbend?" I point out.

"And how many years did Charleston and the vamp council spend collecting them?" says Magne.

"And they didn't all come from here," says Alex. "Me and Mathilde are the only ones from here." So she does know the old witch's name. "I thought the rest had gone home, but either they stayed for some reason, or she called them back."

"Which is suspicious," says Evgeny. "*Hexen*, according to everything we've been able to find and that Alex has told, tend to scatter, to stay far apart for protection."

"They – we – only get together in pairs or sometimes threes to pass on knowledge to new witches when they've... once they've found a... familiar."

A thought occurs to me. "I didn't see a familiar at the witch – at Mathilde's house."

"She has several," says Alex. "I've only seen one, but she has a couple of cats and some birds, I think. Maybe more."

"No fox?'

"No. Foxes are preferred, but not that common. I guess *hexenfuchs* are even rarer than witches."

I try to remember if the other fox in my dream, the male fox, could take human form, or if he was an ordinary fox.

"So…" I try to assemble the scraps of information into something that makes sense. "What, then? It's not a *koldun* after all? Or it's an unusual one? And the witches are up to something."

Alex nods. I look at Magne and he shrugs. Evgeny quirks an eyebrow.

"Are the witches up to something entirely unrelated?"

"Probably," says Magne. "Why would they want to control Evgeny?"

"Or make poor, greedy Liam walk out into the sun?" says Ev.

"Because they can?" says Alex, at the same time as I say, "Because they think Ev's an abomination?"

"So now what?" says Magne.

I turn to Alex. "Did you see what was next to Mathilde's fireplace?"

"The cauldron? Tacky, isn't it? She said once she finds it amusing to collect things that witches are supposed to have, according to popular lore. She says it draws attention away from the real stuff."

"Like the Russian dolls?" I guess she didn't notice, because I have to describe what I saw.

"Creepy," says Magne.

"I guess I'll have to go see her again," says Alex. "But I won't take you with me. If she sees I haven't bound you, she might decide to try to make you *her* familiar."

"When will you go?" I pick up the curry again and pass choice bits to Evgeny through the bars. It feels good to be my proper shape again, though I have to admit being a fox *is* fun.

"Tonight. I might as well go right away. And maybe I'll catch another gathering of *hexen* and find out what they're all up to."

"You'll be careful?"

"Of course."

Magne leaves soon after Alex. He's got a job he can't neglect too often, though his boss is lenient – another were, apparently. Before he goes he asks me about six times if I'll be okay and makes sure I know where all of Liam's phones are in case I need to call.

And he brings down a whole box of bloodbags so I won't have to go upstairs if Evgeny gets hungry.

"You don't have to stay," Ev says, once everyone's gone. "I can't get out, so I'll be fine here."

"Do you want me to go?" I try to keep a straight face, but I'm not good at that, and I end up laughing.

"You just can't do pouty," says Evgeny.

"No," I say.

"It's because you know I'm crazy about you."

"Oh, are you?" I say, feigning doubt. I'm not very good at that, either.

A pathologically honest nature doesn't lend itself to that kind of teasing.

Evgeny wedges his hand through the bars to catch a strand of my hair – I didn't tie it back properly before I left the loft, and bits keep slipping free of the hasty braid. He tugs gently and pulls my head closer until he can bump his nose against mine. If we wedge our chins into the gap between bars, we can just kiss, but it's not comfortable.

"You know I am," he says.

For a while we just sit close together, content with a bit of peace. But we won't get real peace until we get to the end of this mystery.

"You seem a lot better," I say finally.

"I think my body has recovered, anyway," he says. "No more withdrawal."

"So did the weakness from all the drugs and *hexen*… is that what let the *koldun*, or whatever it actually is, into your head?"

"I suppose," he says. He's twirling a strand of my hair around and around his finger. It's so long he ends up looking like he's got a ball of wool stuck on his hand. He lets go and it slowly unwinds, and just before it slips free he catches it and starts winding again. "And now that it's got in once, I can't seem to keep it out."

I'm fascinated by the way he's playing with my hair, absently, but also concentrating on it as if it's important.

"Like a hacker who gets past some big corporate security system, then leaves a crack somewhere so he can always get back in, even when they patch the original weakness."

He looks up, mild surprise in his look. "I wouldn't have expected you to use a computer metaphor," he says. "But it could be something like that."

I don't even own a computer, but must have been familiar with them, before. I've used both Magne's and Evgeny's to look for stuff online, and I didn't need to ask how. Maybe I was even good with them once. Mostly they don't interest me at all, now.

"In fact," says Evgeny, voice growing thoughtful – and unlike most vamps, the emotions in his voice are real. Somehow, his symbiont didn't change a lot of things in him that the vamp symbiont usually alters. "I think it's a really good analogy."

"So find the back door," I say, "and we can find a way to… uh… update your security… um… firewall?" Okay, maybe I wasn't so good with computers.

Ev laughs and it's nice to hear him relaxed and happy. "Something like that."

"Why do you think he… it… whatever, only comes at night? Is it because you're less vulnerable when you're asleep?"

"Maybe. Have I ever woken up already taken over?"

I have to think about that. "I'm not sure. I don't think so." Though the time he tried to get me and Magne both to have sex, he might have been awake before it took him over, or he might not have. *I* was asleep.

"It could be that, then. Or maybe he's awake at night."

"Could he be a vamp, too?"

"I doubt it. Unless maybe he was drinking *hexen* and gaining witch mind powers that way."

"But vamps who can metabolize witch blood are even rarer than witches."

"Right. And so are vamps who have captive vamps who can metabolize *hexen*."

Because Charleston, who fed on Evgeny after force-feeding him witch-blood, had gained some pretty impressive mind-fuck powers.

"We only know of one of each, and Charleston's dead."

"And I'm the one who's being possessed. Besides which, I haven't been drinking witch blood since we escaped."

I slump against the bars. I can feel Evgeny's faint body heat on the other side and it's comforting.

"So really," he says. "We still know nothing."

I sigh. "Yeah."

"Have you tried turning back into a fox?" he says, I think just to change the subject.

"Hell, no," I say. "I just figured out how to be human again, and that took me three tries and all my energy."

"I notice you still have a tail," he says, a smile tugging at the corner of his mouth. "It's cute."

I stick my tongue out at him and his smile grows.

"I can make it disappear," I say. "I'm just too lazy."

"And I like your eyes." His voice gets softer, a little shy.

I look into *his* eyes. "Yeah?" I say. "You don't think they're weird?"

He shakes his head. "I always liked your eyes, but now they're more... I don't know. More *you*."

And that makes me smile, so for a while we sit there grinning like idiots. Dumb, lovesick children.

Then I look at the books scattered around, and the neat freak in me makes me pick them up and arrange them on one of the cots.

"Did you go through them all?'

"Pretty much. I did come across one odd thing, though, in one of the Russian ones. One of the books *in* Russian, I mean."

I sit up.

"My Russian's not that great, really. I learned as a kid, but I speak it better than I read it."

"So what did you find?"

"Just one story that mentioned that there's another kind of *koldun*, something different from what's in the fairy tales. But it didn't actually say what was different about it."

"That's helpful."

"Well, it implied that it was an older tradition. That is was the real thing. The real *koldun* where the rest are just stories."

"So maybe *that's* what we're dealing with?"

He shrugs. "I guess there's no way to know."

So we sit and feel useless and wait for Alex to come back and report whatever she finds out when she confronts the witches. I wonder what she plans to say to them.

"Will you show me?" Evgeny says.

"Show you what?"

"Changing into a fox?"

"You saw me as a fox."

"But not changing. Or would that be too personal?"

I can't help but smile at his concern. He's seen me have screaming orgasms, and there's not much more personal you can get than that.

"I think you've seen it," I say. "When I was fighting Charleston."

"I didn't really see," he says. "It happened so fast."

"Well, I can try," I say. "But what if I get stuck again?"

"I don't think you will."

I don't really think so, either. What I'm more afraid of is not being able to take *fox* shape again. That it was just a fluke. And now that I've done it once, I don't want to give it up. It felt like something that's a part of me, the way my tail feels perfectly normal now. Perfectly *right*.

But if I do fail, I'd rather be with Evgeny than alone. We've each shared parts of ourselves we haven't shared with anyone else. The good and the bad.

So I take off my clothes and fold them into a pile on the cot.

Evgeny pretends to leer at me. "I love looking at you naked," he says. "I can't wait until this is over and I can make love to you again."

His skin is dark enough I almost can't tell he's blushing, but he is. He hardly ever talks about fucking, but almost always about making love. And it's how he touches me, too, as if it's more important to be close, and intimate, and loving, than to just get off. Though it always comes to that, too, eventually.

Evgeny's rarely in a hurry in bed.

I think about touching myself for him, since he can't touch me. It would be awfully sexy to lie back on the cot and pleasure myself while he did the same on the other side of the bars. It's that thought, as much as the cool air on my skin, that makes my nipples stand up.

I know he can smell my arousal, and I can smell his.

"Evgeny," I say. My voice comes out low and husky.

"I know," he says. "I know."

"It's a bad time, isn't it?"

He nods, and he's got a little crease between his eyebrows, like his thinking-wrinkle, but this one's from regret.

"If he came back into my mind now, or in the middle of… I couldn't stand it."

I reach out, touch his fingers where they're wrapped so tight on the cell bars his skin is stretched white across the bone.

"Okay," I say. Then I close my eyes and think about being a fox. It doesn't work. Nothing happens until I hear a sharp cry from Evgeny, wordless and vamp-high-pitched, and open my eyes to see him collapse against the bars.

When he looks up at me, the leer is real, and he speaks with the *koldun's* voice. "*Lisa.*"

And then I am a fox, and leaping for his face, and snarling.

Chapter Fourteen

MY TEETH SNAP shut just short of Evgeny's nose and my face bangs painfully against the bars. Which is probably a good thing, as much as it hurts, because if the bars were spaced any wider I'd have my head stuck through them.

I'd also have bitten off a good chunk of my boyfriend's face.

I drop to the ground in front of the cell, teeth bared. I can *feel* the *koldun* inside him, looking out through his eyes. Except it's not a him, it's a *they*.

Multiple presences, focused through one stronger personality, and overlaid by a sort of shadow of something male and nasty. The mind-influencing powers of several… a dozen, maybe.

"*Hexen*," I say, and startle even myself with my own human voice coming out of my fox throat. Which shouldn't even be possible. Hell, I shouldn't be possible yet here I am, so maybe I should shut up about what can and can't be.

The directing presence realizes I've seen them.

"*Fuchs*," I hear her say. It's Mathilde, the older witch, her German accent somehow more pronounced than it was in person. "So," she says. "Now you are a problem, just as your Irish friend was."

My Irish friend? Liam? Had Liam somehow figured out what was going on while he was watching Evgeny for me, and that's why they made him walk into the sun?

You killed Liam, I say. Liam. *He never would have given you away if you paid him to keep quiet.*

"Bah," she says. "He was only a Reborn." She says it like someone might talk about an irritating bug. "Easier to kill him."

Nice, I think at her. *You're as bad as they are. Do you give up your humanity to gain your powers?*

"I am *hexen*. Not human." I can almost hear her spit.

Good for you, I say. *Now get out of Evgeny.*

"He is an abomination."

So you've said.

"He is a threat to all *hexen*."

No. I snarl. *He wasn't a threat till you made him one. Now you've made him mad.*

"Well, then, lucky he's so far buried in his own mind he can't do anything about it, isn't it?"

Ah, but you forgot about me. You hurt someone I care about, and you have to deal with me.

"And you are nothing but a *hexenfuchs*. An animal too big for its britches. If Alexandra won't take you, I will."

And then I feel something more behind her voice, her presence, something besides the other *hexen* lending their powers. She's distracted, just a little, by something else. I can't tell what, but it makes her focus waver.

That's all I need. But I resist the urge to attack immediately. There might be more I can find out.

What about koldun? I ask.

"A fairytale to make every witch a good girl when a strong, powerful man tells her to be, to make her obedient. A strong male protector to make everything all right."

Koldun are not real?

"How would a powerless human steal strength from a witch? No, all that's needed is obedience, that's how a *hexen*'s power is taken. By making her do as she's told."

Why make us think one possessed Evgeny?

"To keep you looking elsewhere while we took his mind." But there's a ripple of something from the other witches, a dissent I can just barely feel through Mathilde. She's not telling me everything.

Now I know.

"Now it's too late. He is ours."

All I need is to keep him locked up and you can't harm him or me.

"You will slip up. It is only a matter of time."

But now we know who is responsible. Now we can stop you.

"Unfortunate that you know, but you cannot stop us." Her attention wavers again.

Then I realize. Alex. Whatever Alex is doing is distracting Mathilde.

"You should not have tried to turn one of our own against us," Mathilde says. "She is what she is, and she will stand with us."

She'll be what and who she wants to be. I growl.

Then I feel something from Alex. Just for an instant, she reaches through the connection from witches to Mathilde, to Evgeny, to me. There are no words, but I know what I have to do.

I don't know how to do it, so I just assume I can. I do what the fox women say, and I just act.

It's almost like flinging myself, my small furry body, at Evgeny's face, except what I'm really doing is flinging my mind into his.

His blue eyes widen, startled, and for a moment it's not him, then it is him again, returned to his own head.

"Su," I hear him say, but then I pass through him into Mathilde's mind and then I sort of… I don't know… explode.

I don't think I hurt her or the other witches, except for maybe a nasty headache, but I burst apart their connection and I drive them from Evgeny's mind.

And as I pull back into myself, I smooth shut the cracks they made in his defenses.

When I come to, I'm me again. Human. I'm naked on the floor in front of Evgeny's cell, and Magne's shaking me urgently.

"Su!" he says. "Come on. Fuck, wake up!" He gathers me up and sits on the floor with me in his lap. "Fuck."

I push weakly against his chest. "I'm okay," I say. My voice sounds like I haven't used it pretty much ever.

He holds me away so he can see me, then hugs me so tight I swear I feel my ribs rubs together. He's strong, Magne.

"I'm fine," I say. My voice is more normal. "How's Ev?"

I hear movement, blankets, a cot creaking.

"I seem to have another one of those really incredibly terrible headaches," he says. "But I'm alive, and witch-free."

I wriggle free of Magne so I can put some clothes on. He doesn't even ogle as I get dressed. He must really have been concerned.

"You were both out cold when I came in," he said. "Good thing I forgot to lock the door on the way out, since apparently you couldn't hear me ring the bell."

"There's a bell?" I say, feeling a little stupid for how I had banged on the door and then announced myself by *thinking* at Alex.

"I thought you were…" He trails off.

"Dead?" finishes Evgeny for him.

"Yeah."

"Well," I say, punching his arms playfully, "We're not only alive, but well."

"Quite well," says Evgeny.

"And if you have any idea where Liam's keys are, it should be safe to unlock Ev now."

"Are you sure?" says Magne, eyeing me dubiously, perhaps wondering if the *koldun* is controlling both of us now.

So I give him the rundown on what happened, as well as I understand it.

"Shit," he says. "A whole pack of witches."

"Yeah," I say. "And Alex went to them for answers."

"I hope she doesn't switch sides," says Magne. "I was starting to like her."

"She won't," I say.

"I agree," says Evgeny, and when I look at him with eyebrows raised he says, "Those of us who love you are very loyal." Then he looks away, acting nonchalant.

Magne laughs. "He's right, there. You do inspire a certain... dedication in your friends."

I ignore him. Both of them. "Why didn't we find any stories about witches banding together to take over other people? You'd think it's something they'd want to use against their enemies."

Magne shrugs. "Witches have always been rare. Maybe there were just never that many to band together."

"Somehow they knew it could be done," I say. "Even before now. When I rescued them from Charleston, they were able to take over his minions by working together."

"They were weak-minded anyway, those minions," says Evgeny.

"The problem is," says Magne, "We don't have a lot of facts about *hexen*. They've been rare and secretive for so long."

"And suddenly they're everywhere," I say.

"Funny how that happens," says Magne.

"I wonder if there's something more to it, though," I say. "Anyway, help me look for a key to this cell."

"Try Liam's office," says Magne, and points. There's another hall, running to the left of the cell, and at the end, there's a door. I assumed, from the "exit" sign over it, that it leads out to a stairwell up to the alley behind the market. Turns out it does, it just opens into an office first.

I find a set of keys in the desk. Under the desk, there's a sort of wooden hatch in the floor. I'll bet there's a safe under there, but I don't say anything to Magne. He might suspect I'm a thief, but I'm not sure I want him to know for certain. For some reason, I want him to think well of me. I didn't used to care. But he didn't used to be my friend.

When I unlock the cell, the first thing Evgeny does as soon as he's clear of it is kiss me. And kiss me. And kiss me. Finally Magne clears his throat and says, "I'll be back at my apartment if you need me."

Then I suppose he leaves. I stopped paying attention to anything but Evgeny a while ago.

Somehow, I can *feel* that it's him, and *only* him. I can tell there are no witches, no koldun trying to get in. He's *my* Evgeny again.

And he's kissing me like nothing else matters besides pressing our lips together in just exactly the most perfect way. When he kisses me, when he touches me, he puts all his concentration into it, like our being together is the central most thing in the universe. It makes a girl feel special, let me tell you.

It's been a few days since he had the luxury of bathing properly – a good soak in the tub would leave him vulnerable, and he hasn't exactly felt up to a shower – so he's a bit ripe. But I don't care. It helps, maybe, that my fox nature isn't bothered by the same kinds of stink that my human nature doesn't like. Or maybe I'm just so wound up from lack of sex that I can ignore it.

Thing is, Evgeny doesn't like to smell. He's very particular about hygiene, which isn't something all that common among guys in my experience, and it's very nice, usually.

So he pulls away. "I need a shower," he says.

I pull him back to me. "Shower later." I sit on one of the cots and pull him down after me. Maybe it's one of my fox powers awakening, or maybe he just feels the need for intimacy as much as I do, but he doesn't pull away again.

He wrinkles his nose when I pull his shirt over his head, so I say, "I don't care what you smell like as long as you're touching me." Then I duck my head and tug gently on one of his nipple piercings with my teeth.

When I look back up into his face, his eyes are so bright they seem to glow. He looks like he's going to say something, but instead he touches my cheek, just brushing the skin with his fingertips.

A smile tugs at the corner of his mouth as he traces the line of my nose, the curve of my lips. I kiss his fingers.

His smile grows, sweet and a little wicked. He slides his hand into my hair, pulls my head close, and kisses me, hard, his tongue slipping between my teeth to slide against mine. I feel like I can't get close enough. Then he pulls away long enough to peel my shirt off and unhook my bra. He presses his skin to mine.

I can feel his heart beat faster, and every stroke of my hand on his skin brings more heat to his flesh as his circulation picks up.

We're twisted awkwardly sideways on the cot, so I half-stand, just enough to push him back on the mattress. Then I kneel over him, one leg on each side of him, and let my hair fall like a curtain around us.

He reaches up to run his hands over my belly, my ribs, cups a breast in each hand and brushes his thumbs across my nipples. They're already erect, wanting his touch and I'd gasp if I wasn't busy kissing his neck.

Then I sit up, flip my hair back and look at him. My own heartbeat quickens and my keen fox nose can already smell the scents of our desire mingling in the air. It makes me want him more. I wonder if he can smell us, too.

"Su," he says, and that's all. It's all he needs to say. When he says my name, it holds the world.

"Evgeny," I say back.

He slides a finger under the waistband of my jeans, pops the button and works down the zipper. I wiggle backwards to get his pants down, and while I'm down there, I slide my mouth over him as soon as he's free.

I missed the taste of him.

I suck until his breathing goes harsh and his back arches, and he pulls me away to lie on top of him.

"You first," he says, then rolls me over, works his way down my body with his mouth, leaving kisses and cool trails of saliva down my breasts, my belly.

He tugs my jeans off, then pauses the bury his face in my crotch and inhale my scent. He always does that. He moans, softly, turns his head to kiss my thigh, then nudges my legs apart.

His mouth feels like fire on me and his clever tongue reaches every swollen fold until I'm ready to scream.

I muster enough presence of mind, just barely, to say, "Wait."

"What's wrong?" he says, and looks up at me, eyes full of concern. The lower half of his face is wet with my fluids and I just about come thinking about how it got that way.

"I want you inside me," I say. "Now."

"I don't have – "

"In my jeans pocket." Yes, I keep a condom in my pocket. I like sex, and you just never know. I may be more resistant to a lot of things than humans, and my vamp boyfriend may be sterile, but neither of us is stupid.

We're not immortal and we can get sick. So even though neither of us cheats, we're careful.

It seems to take forever for Evgeny to get the condom unwrapped and rolled on, and the whole time I'm aching with desire.

Finally, he crawls on top of me and I wrap my legs around him. He holds back, teasing, rubbing himself on me. Then he kisses me and I feel his tongue probe into my mouth, and he twists his hips and he's inside me, filling me up, filling me with lust.

I can taste myself in his mouth and it's exciting, maddening.

He moves slowly against me, sliding in and out, but I want more. I pull him against me with my legs, hard, harder, faster. I don't think I've ever come this way, just from fucking, but I want him inside me when I orgasm.

Then I hear a door open, footsteps on the stairs, and Evgeny stops, holds still, inside me, and I can tell he's on the edge of climax.

I listen to the footsteps, inhale the air. "Magne," I say.

"Sorry."

"You're going to have to wait a minute."

"I – "

I fling up a hand to cut him off, not caring if he can even see it from where he stands on the stairs.

"Su," says Evgeny, softly in my ear.

I open my eyes and he's looking towards the stairs, towards Magne.

"Look at me," I whisper, and he does. Then I tighten all my nether muscles, pull him close with my legs, and watch his eyes widen.

"Su, we can't – "

I cut him off with a kiss, release and tighten my muscles, again and again until he can't resist any longer.

He buries his face in my hair. "Oh god," he moans, quietly.

I don't care if Magne's watching, I don't care what's so important, I slide a hand down my own belly to my crotch, find my center with the tip of my finger and let Evgeny's thrusting into me do the rest.

I make one concession when I come. I don't yell my pleasure out loud the way I'd like to, but instead I clench my teeth and pant into Evgeny's collarbone.

He buries his face against the mattress to muffle his moans.

Then we lie still for a moment, catching our breath.

"Okay, Magne. What was so vital you had to interrupt us?"

I'm annoyed, and I get rude when I'm irritated, though I know it would have to be a big deal for him to walk in here, knowing we'd be making love.

"It's Alex," he says.

That gets my attention, I wriggle out from under Evgeny, and we both sit on the cot, groping for clothing and putting it on.

"What about her," I ask, spotting my bra on the floor.

Magne has stayed put on the stairs, and I can see now that he's facing sideways, staring at the wall. I can't tell for sure, but the slope of the ceiling might even have blocked us from view. I can also see the bulge in his trousers that shows he was not unaffected by the wet sounds of us.

I feel guilty, but only a little.

"She's back," he says.

"Why do you sound worried?"

He looks up at that, and there's nothing to see, because we're both dressed and tying our shoes.

"She's..."

"Is she all right?'

He shakes his head. "She's not hurt, but ... she's shaken up. Bad."

I get up and Evgeny's right behind me. I think, briefly, of Liam's safe and what might be in it, but there will be time for that later. Rent's due, but Alex is more important.

Chapter Fifteen

ALEX IS NOT JUST shaken up, she's shaking. She sits on my couch with her hands clenched together in her lap and a muscle bulges in her jaw from trying to hold herself still.

There's a half cup of tea on the coffee table in front of her, and wet patches on the thighs of her jeans show that the other half of the cup was probably spilled rather than sipped.

She turns to smile when we walk in, but it comes off as a grimace.

"Hey," she says, and her voice is surprisingly steady.

"What happened?" I say. "Are you all right?" I sit next to her and put my arm around her. Then I realize that I probably stink like sex and maybe that's not such a welcome thing.

But she relaxes marginally and leans against me a little.

"I will be," she says.

"What happened?" says Evgeny. He sits on the other side of me, close, so I can feel the faint heat of his skin. If it were some other guy, I'd think he was being possessive around his girlfriend's ex. From Ev, I think he's just showing support. The thought is confirmed when he gets right back up again and starts making tea. He even digs out the bottle of cheap Scotch and pours a good amount in each cup.

Alex takes a deep breath, and lets it out slow, and when she inhales and exhales again, her breathing is steady. She's calm enough to unclench her hands.

"I went to Mathilde's, like I planned. It was just getting dark. I waited in the car, to see if the others would show up again, and sure enough they did. So I went to the door, pretending like I was just there because I wanted her to teach me, to let me take part in what the rest of the group were doing."

She pauses when Evgeny hands her a steaming mug, takes it and sips. He hands me one, too, and I gulp the hot drink, feeling heat and booze both burn their way down my throat.

Then Alex sets the cup next to the half-full one still on the table.

"She asked if I'd made you my familiar, and I told her you ran away into the woods, still in fox shape. I'm not sure she believed me, but she decided I could help them with whatever they were doing."

As Alex speaks, she must be using her witch abilities, because I start to *see* what she's describing. Maybe she's just trying to make things clearer in her own head, but she's started projecting it to me. I wonder if Evgeny can see her thoughts, too.

By the time she starts talking about being invited inside and greeting the other *hexen*, I'm almost fully inside her memory, experiencing it with her.

She went into the living room, where there were ten or eleven other witches, all women of course. They sipped their tea and regarded her silently until she said, "Hi. I guess I'm allowed to join you this time."

"Has Mathilde told you what work we're doing?" says one witch. I recognize her from Charleston's. She's even paler than Alex, with curly brown hair. She was the one most disgusted by Evgeny, who practically spat the word "abomination" when I had mentioned him.

"Not yet," said Alex. "But I gather it has something to do with joining all our powers together."

"Indeed," said Mathilde, appearing with a mug of tea and handing it to Alex. "Drink this to help you focus."

I can taste the tea in Alex's memory – it was bitter, minty, a little mouldy, even. *Valerian, maybe?* That last thought is Alex's. I don't know much about herbs, but I know valerian's supposed to help people sleep, so maybe it's good for helping extraneous thoughts slip away.

Alex joined the others, sitting around the room, sipping, and saying nothing. Then Mathilde began a low chant, full of the names of different goddesses – mostly Norse and Germanic, which makes sense, I guess, if most *hexen* have German ancestry.

It reminds me a lot of neo-pagan worship, though I'm not sure how I know that. Maybe I was a Wiccan before. I certainly haven't followed any religious practice since I lost my memory.

Soon, all the witches were swaying slightly to the sound of Mathilde's vice, and one by one they joined in the chant, but each on a different beat, like singing a round. Alex joined, too, but merged her voice with the witch next to her – maybe to keep herself apart a bit, or maybe just because she was unsure of the words.

Then, abruptly, they all stopped at once and were quiet again. Mathilde collected the tea mugs – Alex's was still half full – then went to the fireplace and lit a fire. When it was going nicely, she tossed a handful of plant matter into the flames and the room filled with the scent of the forest.

Through Alex's memory, I inhale deeply. It's a lovely smell. Pine and fir and damp soil. It makes me ache to run as a fox.

Then I feel Evgeny against my back, a solid presence. His chin rests on my shoulder and his breath tickles my ear. The desire to change shape fades and I lean back against him.

The witches moved to sit on the floor around the hearth, as close to the fire as the size of the group would allow. Mathilde stayed in the middle, and Alex sat a little apart, observing.

Then Mathilde held up an object in her hands, rounded, painted wood. The Russian doll.

"From an old enemy comes the power to focus a new enemy to our will," she said.

"The old enemy allows us to defeat the new," said the other witches.

Mathilde opened the doll, set the top half to one side, and removed what was inside. It was not another doll, as one would expect – doll inside doll until the last was too small to hold anything. Instead, she lifted out a jar, old, bubble-filled glass with drab grey dust and shards of yellow-white inside.

A jar of someone's ashes.

I feel Evgeny's breath sudden on my neck, and I know he's sharing Alex's memory, too. Maybe through me, or maybe directly from her.

"Rasputin," he says, so quiet I'm probably the only one who hears.

"Thanks to our enemy," said Mathilde, and placed the jar in front of the fire, where the glass caught and refracted the firelight, almost making the ashes inside seem to writhe and dance.

She turned to look at Alex. "It is our focus," she said. "You and the others will focus your mental abilities on me, just as you did when we escaped the vampire's lair."

Alex nodded.

"And I will focus through the old *koldun's* ashes, to reach out to the new enemy and bend him to our will.

Alex opened her mouth to ask something, but Mathilde held up her hand. "You may ask all the questions you like when the work is done. For now, follow the others and see how we can become more than lonely women working our spells in the woods."

Then Mathilde stood up and held her hands out towards the jar and began to hum softly. The other witches held their hands towards her, looked up at her from their seats on the floor.

Even only in Alex's memory I can feel the power they built up, mental energy streaming from each witch, stronger from some, weaker from others, I feel a surge of pride to find that Alex is stronger than any of the others. Mathilde noticed, too, and paused to turn and nod approvingly, before focusing again on the jar. She pulled out the stopper.

And it seemed like all the energy in the room streamed out of Mathilde, through the jar, and vanished. Except it didn't vanish, exactly. Instead, it caught hold in its target, leashed him to it, and forced his consciousness into hiding. And then the witches controlled Evgeny. The witches and whatever was in the jar.

And they, including Alex and me sharing her memory, looked out through Evgeny's eyes, between the bars of the cell. They … we … saw me naked and my shape seemed to waver like heat distortion and instead of me, instead of *human* me, there's fox me, leaping and snapping.

I watch my own transformation with shock. It is nothing remotely like the parts of Magne changing shape that I've seen. Nothing like a vamp's jaw unhinging and becoming a new configuration. It looks completely magical, and completely impossible.

One moment there's me, a slight Asian woman, a little too tall and a little too pale to look properly Chinese, long black hair falling around her. Then the air does something so the eye can't quite focus and there's a fox, rusty red with black legs and a bright white tip on her tail, long teeth snapping together so close the air of them moving feels like a breeze.

I feel Evgeny's arms tighten around me, then relax.

Then, of course, in the memory I forced them out. But it was Alex pulling herself out of the meld of witches, refusing to take part in subjugating Evgeny or fighting me that distracted Mathilde, that let me gain enough presence of mind to just *act* and shove them away, burn out their connection, and seal their path back in.

Then Alex stumbled away from the witches, all of them clutching their heads from the nasty headache I'd left them with. She looked at the jar of ashes, but Mathilde had snatched it up, jammed the stopper back in, and shoved it back into its wooden case. She held it tightly to her chest.

"Damn," Alex muttered, and then she ran from the house, got in her car, and drove. She was confused and got lost several times on the way home. I felt vaguely ashamed that I'd been busy fucking my lover while she'd been trying to get back to us.

She shakes her head now, and says, "You couldn't have known," and I blink and the memory is over.

"How did you do that?" I ask.

"Do what?"

"Pull us into your memory," says Evgeny.

"I wasn't in anyone's memory," says Magne.

"I guess…" Alex hesitates. "I must have been broadcasting my thoughts while I was trying to keep the memory clear. You and me, Su, are sort of connected, so you could pick them up, I guess."

"*Hexenfuchs*," I say.

She shrugs. "And Evgeny …" She stares at him. "If the witch blood is out of your system, then you either saw through Su, somehow, or else…"

"Or else?" Ev's voice is calm and low, even though there's something weird in the way Alex is looking at him. Fear, maybe, or something …

"Or else you *do* have witch abilities, even though you shouldn't. Your vamp… According to Mathilde, being Reborn should have destroyed any chance of that."

"According to Mathilde," says Evgeny. "How reliable a source is she?"

Alex shakes her head and picks up one of the mugs of tea, sips. "I don't know. There's a lot she didn't tell me, that she said I'm not ready for yet. But I wonder how much of that was just that she didn't know if she could trust me yet. Or that she didn't know herself."

Later, Evgeny and I curl up in bed together, the curtains back up and blocking out the sun, creating a comfortable den.

Magne offered Alex his couch to sleep on, because she was exhausted and I guess he thought Ev and I would want to be alone. We had a long shower together, but didn't make love. We just enjoyed being together without having to worry about anything taking over his mind.

Now I'm keenly aware of his naked skin against mine, but it's enough – for the moment – to have him next to me.

"Did you feel it," he says, his voice like a caress in the dark. "When we watched you change in Alex's memory?"

"She's afraid of me," I say.

"And of me," he says. "And she's jealous. She still loves you."

"Does it worry you?" I'm not even sure if I'm teasing or serious. I'm not sure if I *need* to be serious.

"No," he says. "Not yet. It could be dangerous, jealousy and fear. But I think if she were going to side with the other witches against us, she'd have done it then."

"They are her…" I can't quite finish the sentence. "Her kind" smacks too much of racism. Or speciesism. Or whatever.

"Her people," says Evgeny. Better. Not perfect, but better than what I almost said. "She risks losing their help if she ever needs it."

"And if she's going to be as powerful a witch as Mathilde thinks, then she's probably going to need it."

"Or at least think she needs it."

I roll over, bury my nose in Evgeny's neck, and he shifts to put his arms around me and tuck the quilt over my shoulder.

"Do you think those ashes were really Rasputin?" I say.

"It seems pretty unlikely, doesn't it?"

"Maybe that's what your dad – that saying he taught you. Maybe it referred to that. Maybe it's not an actual child he left behind, but a doll. A doll of his ashes."

"Maybe. But whatever or whomever those ashes are, the witches believe they allow them to focus their intent on another. And sometimes belief is enough."

"They called you their new enemy."

"And they called… whomever the ashes belonged to *koldun*."

"But Mathilde told me a *koldun* is only someone – a man – who makes a witch believe he is her protector so she'll do what she's told, that he doesn't really have power."

"And how much is Mathilde *not* telling?"

"That's true. She wouldn't exactly confide in me."

He's quiet for a while, and I lie and listen to his faint, slow heartbeat and his almost inaudible breathing.

Then he stirs, puts his other arm around me, and pulls me close. He kisses the top of my head. "Thank you," he says.

"What for?"

He pulls back a bit, as if to look at my face, but it's so dark in our nest even I can barely see the faint glint of his eyes.

"For kicking those witches out of my head," he says. "And for not giving up on me, or staking me when I was a total ass."

"It's not *you* who was an ass," I said. "It was the …" That makes me pause. "The *koldun*," I say. "Which was really the witches. But which seemed to be a single, definitely *male* person."

"That *is* weird," Evgeny says.

"So maybe those ashes had some effect after all. Like they gave the witches the semblance of another person to hide behind." I don't say, *Maybe they held another consciousness that the witches used, or that used them.*

"Perhaps the ashes even affected how the witches acted," he says.

I think of being pinned to the bed, the *koldun* – or the witches –

controlling Evgeny, dominating me, flaunting his – their – sexual control over me. And Magne, even. Was that the result of … of Rasputin, or whomever those ashes used to be?

"Creepy," I say.

"Yeah."

"We need to get that bottle from Mathilde."

"How?"

"I don't know. I guess we just go take it?"

"Just like that?"

"Hey," I say, poking him in the chest. "I broke into a high security research facility and got you out. I think I can steal a bottle of dirt from a witch."

He chuckles and catches my hand before I can poke him again. "I am forever grateful that you rescued me, my magnificent, foxy woman. But I am beginning to suspect a small group of witches could be a much greater danger than a whole city full of vampires."

Then for a while our conversation turns into kissing and caressing. There's no urgency this time, just delight at the feel of Evgeny's skin, his hair, his mouth. We're leisurely, lazy, and I even doze off once or twice during the lulls. I'm pretty sure Evgeny does, too. And it's not for lack of interest, it's just that for once it doesn't feel like we're running out of time and we'd better get our business done quick in case we don't get to be alone for a while.

Also, we're both tired. Sometime around noon I fall asleep for real, Evgeny's breath tickling my neck and his arm solid across my hip.

I'm dreaming about the past again. The far past, when my ancestor was a *hexenfuchs* familiar to Alex's ancestor witch.

I've had a litter of kits, and the witch examines each one in turn, frowning as she holds them up. They're all chubby, fuzzy little things with vague eyes, and each one is no more than a normal fox. Her other familiar, my mate sometimes, is just a fox, too, though he's been around witches his whole life, so he's absorbed a share of magic.

Even normal foxes make good familiars, according to the older witch.

Almost as good as crows.

When she determines my babies are only foxes, not *hexenfuchs*, the witch ignores them. She allows me to keep them, as long as they don't interfere with my duties for her. I make sure that they don't, and when they're grown – every single one reaches adulthood – they venture away to find their own territories.

And I meet the young man again, the one who charmed the birds from the tree with his gentleness and patience. In fact, I have been secretly meeting him all along, in my human seeming. My fox-mate knows this, but he doesn't tell the witch. He only hides in the bushes and watches as we sit quietly together, share bread, communicate in gestures.

Until one day the young man kisses me and I feel a heat under my skin like nothing else I have felt before. My fox ancestor wants to fuck him like her fox self fucked her fox mate, but he holds her off gently. Frustrated, she grows angry, but he only touches her face softly, kisses her, then lays her down on a blanket by the side of a stream. He doesn't fuck her, he makes love to her, slowly touching each part of her with his gentle hands, with his lips and his tongue.

In the middle of the dream, I think of when I first met Evgeny, how shocked he was when I told him vamps always wanted to fuck me and feed on me, how he said, "I don't want to *fuck* you," and how he blushed fiercely when he admitted that what he wanted was to *make love* to me.

The young man in my dream of the past makes love to my ancestress, whose part I play. And I – she – dares touch him back, imitating the way he touches her, stroking his skin, licking him, putting her mouth over his erection until he cries out in his wordless voice.

And then, before he can roll her on her back again, she straddles him, takes him inside her and rides him until they're both satisfied, until his seed fills her, and something new takes root in her womb.

And then the dog fox runs for the witch.

I am punished – my ancestor is punished – caged like a dangerous beast, and forced to watch as the dog fox is butchered and skinned and stuffed as a toy. And that toy fox arrives, an anonymous gift, at the home of my silent human lover, a present for his little sister, who is shy and loves animals.

The witch shows me this, in her mind. She was a kind woman once, I know she was. But now she is cold and hard and she tells me how the child will sicken and die, and so will my love and all his family.

"Be grateful my curse won't extend to the whole village," she says. "Be grateful I don't strip the young from your womb and skin you for a toy to match your first mate."

Then she turns away to stir a pot on the fire, but I see how the firelight catches a tear that slides down her cheek.

She was kind once. Could she not be kind again?

I wake to Evgeny murmuring into my hair, rocking us gently as he holds me. His chest is damp where my cheek rests against it and I realize I've been weeping.

When I look up, there are tears in his eyes, too.

"I dreamed it with you," he says. "I was there."

"The dog fox?"

"The young man with no voice."

"I love you," I tell him, then I straddle him like my ancestor climbed aboard her lover. I slide myself over him until he gets hard and wait impatiently while he fumbles for a condom, then I ride him like my ancestor rode her young man, only when we're finished there's no new life growing. There could never be, even without the latex sheath between us.

Chapter Sixteen

A S SOON AS THE SUN grows dim enough to bear, Evgeny is up making coffee. I take a little more time, stretching and enjoying the bitter rich scent coming from the kitchen. I'm finally forced to get up and put clothes on when Alex and Magne knock on the door.

"Thought we should figure out our next move," Magne says. He's carrying a couple boxes of pizza and a big paper bag. Not my favorite – dairy doesn't agree with me at all – but Magne can't eat milk either, so I hope one of the pizzas will be cheeseless. And at least I won't have to cook.

"This isn't your fight, you know," I say. I choose a slice from a pizza apparently loaded with everything *but* cheese and take a bite. It just happens to be the slice with the most bacon. Entirely by accident, of course.

Magne shrugs. "You're my friends. I can hardly just stand by and watch."

It's interesting, how we've gone from just neighbors to good friends in the space of a few weeks. I guess thwarting a consortium of vampires who prey on *others* really brings people closer.

"I also brought you this." He stuffs a slice of pizza in his mouth and pushes the paper bag over to me with his foot. I open it one-handed, the other hand being occupied with inserting more pizza into my face. I can't remember the last time I ate.

In the bag I find my clothes, the ones I left in the woods. Even my coat and boots are in there. I set down my food long enough to check the pockets of my coat. Then I remember Alex already gave me the pocketwatch. It's there on the table, under one of the pizza boxes. I dig it out and hand it to Evgeny. "The one from Liam," I say.

He pulls a knife from his pocket, flips it open one-handed, and pries off the back of the watch. He frowns at it.

"Something about a child. 'A child shall lead the way in a blaze of glory.' Or something along those lines."

Alex looks confused, so I tell her about how we found pocketwatches on Ev's papa vamp, on Charleston and his second-in-command, and a couple others. How each one has a line or two in Latin engraved inside the back, that seem to add up to a poem or a prophecy.

"A child," she says. "That turns up in Evgeny's father's thing, too."

"We thought it might refer to the witches' doll," Ev says.

"I suppose it could," says Alex. "Dolls in witchcraft are called poppets, which is also a word used for children. But I don't know if that could refer to a wooden doll, a Russian nesting doll. Or if it even translates."

"Well," I say," We thought these watches had to do with Charleston's organization, and they didn't. Apparently they belong to an even older vampire council, a sort of secret society of elder vamps pulling strings behind the scenes."

"But the only one who actually seemed to know anything about them was Liam," says Evgeny.

"And Liam's dead," says Magne.

"And so are all the other vamps we got watches from," I finish.

"It doesn't seem likely the witches are in league with a vampire council," says Alex. "From what they told me, they really don't like vampires, especially after being held captive and periodically forced to donate blood."

She's looking at Evgeny. I don't see any malice or anger in her look, but she's got to be thinking that a lot of the blood donated ended up fed to him, because he's the only vamp who can metabolize *hexen* blood.

Of course, the vamps fed on him in turn, and he was as much a prisoner as the witches were.

Evgeny looks back at her, his eyes blank. Though unlike most vamps he naturally shows all the range of human expression on his face, he can make it go away when he wants, and now he's vamp-still. It's pretty unnerving. Expected in a regular vamp, that stillness, unless you're not used to it, but not from Ev. I resist the urge to jab him with my elbow so he'll twitch or flinch or frown.

"Still," he says. "There's something weird going on with the *hexen*. We assumed they would be on our side, since we – or Su – released them from captivity. But they are certainly not on *my* side."

Alex looks a little embarrassed. A pink flush spreads across her cheeks and she bites her lip. "I gather the others feel they were about to escape, anyway, and Su just happened along at the right time to open to cell doors."

"So they don't feel any obligation." Evgeny relaxes again and a little frown creases his brow. He doesn't like it when someone slights me.

"Right," says Alex. "And as far as I knew until recently, you were – "

"An abomination," Evgeny says. He interrupts smoothly, but there's a bit of spite in his voice. No, not spite. More mild anger born of confusion. Or something.

"Because of what you are," says Alex. "But I thought that they didn't really care, as long as they didn't have to associate with you."

"I disgust them, but if I stay away I can continue to exist."

Alex blushes again, but she doesn't look away. "That's what I thought. But now it seems like Mathilde has decided you're an enemy to witches, that you need to be defeated before you can harm them – us, I guess." She picks a mushroom off her pizza and looks at it, before setting it aside at the edge of the half-empty pizza box.

"I don't think it matters that you don't *intend* us harm. Mathilde seems to think you'll cause it anyway."

"So she decided to do him in first," I say. "Along with anyone who tries to get in the way."

"So it seems."

"Even me. Even though I *helped* them."

"Yeah."

Then I think about the witch in my dream and how my *hexenfuchs* ancestor thought she was kind once, but had become cold and hard. But she might become kind again. And I think about Mathilde saying she was not human when I asked if she lost her humanity when she gained her witch powers.

I tell Alex about last night's dream, leaving out the details of the sexy parts.

"I'm really starting to wish I never learned what I am," she says. "I don't want to become cold and mean like that."

"Even if it's the only way to protect your people?" Evgeny says. His voice is gentle.

"How are the witches my people?" says Alex. "I didn't even know they existed until a few months ago, and they haven't exactly been helpful since then." She looks around at the three of us, eyes shining, but not with tears. "You guys have been more to me in the past few days than the *hexen* have, ever. And Su – " She stops, looks at me, looks away.

Then she looks at Evgeny, chin tilted up and that fierce Celtic goddess look about her. "Would *you* become hard and cruel to protect *your* people? The Reborn?"

He's startled. I can tell by the short sharp explosion of air out his nose, though it doesn't show on his face. It's the idea of other vamps as his people, I think, that takes him aback. He tilts his head to one side and the little line he gets between his eyebrows when he's thinking appears.

"You're right," he says. "I don't consider the Reborn to be my people." A sneer touches his mouth and is gone when he says "Reborn." "Like you, they have never done much for me." He smiles, all teeth. "Many of them did a lot of unpleasant things *to* me. No, my people are here in this room." He puts an arm around me. "But you *are* wrong about one thing," he says, and his smile grows, not pleasantly. "I *am* hard and cruel. I have killed easily and with no remorse, and to protect those I care about, I would do it again."

Alex stares at him.

Then Magne laughs. "Big, bad, scary vampire boy," he says, and the tension in the room dissolves. "You may kill when someone tries to kill you, or threatens someone you love, but we all know there's at least one person who turns you all soft and cuddly."

Everyone looks at me and Evgeny's vamp-cool demeanor vanishes behind the sweet, shy way he always looks at me. His toothy smile softens.

"I guess I can't deny that," he says.

Magne laughs again. "So stop scaring the new girl and let's figure out what to do next."

"If we can destroy that bottle of ashes," I say. "They won't be able to focus on it again." Then I think about the male presence I felt in the witches collective. "Assuming that doesn't just free whatever might be in there."

"If we can convince them all to scatter again, to go back to their own homes," says Alex, "Then they won' be able to gang up on anyone."

"Still," says Magne. "Who are we to decide who should be allowed to have power and who not?"

"Nice thought," I say. "But they attacked Evgeny first."

"True," says Magne.

"Maybe," says Evgeny, "we need to figure out why they think I'm so dangerous."

It's such a simple idea. All along, we've been reacting to a threat. But it's a threat with reason behind it. I, at least, just assumed the witches decided to get rid of Ev because of their notion that he's an abomination. But what if that's not just a prejudice against a particular, rare combination of *other*ness? What if there really is something to it?

What if the *hexen* are afraid of Evgeny for good reason?

Finding out if Evgeny really is some sort of danger to the *hexen* is going to mean talking to Mathilde again, and I don't expect she's going to be too pleased about that.

Evgeny wants to speak to her himself, but both Alex and I insist it's a bad idea, something she's likely to see as a threat, and even Magne agrees.

Of course, Magne also wants to speak to her – partly because he's never met any witches before Alex, and partly just to be there as backup. But I don't think he'd be welcome, either, even if she'd see him as less threatening than Evgeny.

I suggest he talk to his contacts and see if any of them can come at the problem from another direction. What happens, for example, when someone with an existing *other* heritage is infected by a symbiont, be it vamp or were or something else?

And though I don't say it, I also wonder if asking those questions might turn up something that could help me figure out *my* abilities. After all, I'm an *other* who was both born and made. I have *hexenfuchs* genes from my dad's family – presumably, since I got my German last name from him. And I was given fox demon – well, not *demon*, literally, but for lack of a better word – nature by the *kitsune*, the *huli jing*, and the *kumiho*.

So even though everyone seems to think you can't be born an *other* and also become one through infection, it obviously *does* happen. Evgeny and I are both proof. So surely it's happened before now. Surely somebody has heard *something*, no matter how insignificant it might seem.

And Evgeny, I suggest, could look for similar answers in Papa Vamp's library. And then Ev points out that I won't get any more welcome from Mathilde than he would, due to our last meeting, and even Alex will likely get a cool treatment.

"True," I say. "She's not going to be happy to see me. But I'm also Alex's familiar."

Evgeny stares at me. "What?"

I get the same reaction from Alex.

"Well, not really," I say. "But I'm supposed to be. And Alex didn't do anything more wrong than back away from attacking her friends. So Mathilde won't be happy, but I think she'll be at least willing to hear us out when we tell her we're trying to help."

He still doesn't like the idea, but he concedes that I might be right.

We decide to wait for morning to go see her, so we won't seem to be skulking around at night all the time. That leaves me lots of time to help Evgeny fetch back the books we left at Liam's while Alex goes home to shower and change and call in sick to the temp job she's been doing since the escape, to pay the bills while she figures out what to do with her life.

I first thing I do at Liam's is empty the cash register, and the second is to head for the safe. Evgeny watches without comment.

"I have to pay the rent somehow," I say.

"I didn't say anything," he says. "Besides, I plan to clean out his blood supply."

"Be careful of the 'special order' stuff," I say.

"No need to warn me," he says. "If it didn't come from a blood bank, I'm not going to touch it."

When I slide back the panel covering the safe, Ev calls out from where he's packing books into a box. "How do you know the combination?"

"I don't," I say. "But I know the combination to the lock on the basement door, and I know Liam. A little."

I punch in the same code, and sure enough, the LED turns green and the safe opens when I turn the handle.

"Bingo," I say. "Most people don't like to have to remember more than one combination."

Inside the safe there's a bank deposit bag – from a bank that no longer exists, I notice – crammed full of cash. That should keep the rent paid for a while. Under that there's a box with some old-fashioned-looking jewelry in it. A simple gold ring, worn and bent out of a perfect circle from long wear. It's small, like something that would fit a lightly-built woman. And there's a gold filigree pendant with a garnet set in it. Next to that, a silver baby spoon.

"Shit," I say. I reach up above the desk and grab the sepia-toned photograph that's displayed there. The woman in the photograph wears a necklace that might be the same. The infant in her lap is sickly-looking, but smiling.

"What?" Evgeny appears in the doorway.

"Look at this," I say. I hand him the photograph and the box of jewelry.

"Liam's wife?"

"I didn't know he had one. Or a kid."

"Lots of *others* have lives before they become what they become."

"I wonder how long ago that was."

"I wonder if Liam's maker fed him his own family." Evgeny stares at the photograph.

When Ev was newborn, his maker, his papa vamp, fed him his own family – his mother, his father – before he began to remember his human life. While he was all vamp and instinct, those two people were just food. But once he recovered his human memories, he'd carry the knowledge that he'd devoured his own loved ones forever. That's the kind of parent Papa Vamp was.

While vamps are like people – some are decent and some are dicks – a large proportion of them seem to turn out cruel. Not evil, exactly. Just mean because there's no one to stop them, no one to govern them. And there's often no one to show them that it doesn't have to be that way. That not everything is kill-or-be-killed, be a dick to someone else before they can be a dick to you.

"Are you all right?" I ask. I'm still sitting on the floor, but I lean over and put my hand on his leg.

"Yeah," he says. "I'm fine." He puts the photograph down on the desk, then picks it up again. "I wonder, should we bury these?"

"The photo and stuff?" I say. "Like to honor the dead?"

He shrugs. "I'm not convinced we get an afterlife, but it seems the decent thing to do."

I wonder if by "we" he means vamps or people in general. "Sure," I say. "We can add something of Liam's, too."

Ev nods and takes the mementoes to add to the box of books.

I check the safe for any other valuables and there's an envelope in there, full of papers. Some of the documents look old, and one has a design on it that reminds me of the knotwork on the pocketwatches. It seems to be blank otherwise, but it intrigues me, so I stuff the whole envelope in my pocket.

I shut the safe and slide the wood panel back over it, not to hide what I've done, but just because it's tidier. Then I join Evgeny upstairs, filling another box with bloodbags. We do a quick once-over of the place to see if there's anything else worth taking – I consider taking some food, but it's all so dusty from sitting there untouched for who knows how long that I don't even trust the canned goods to be edible. Hell, they could be so old they still used lead to seal them. They're definitely past their sell-by date.

Ev grabs a handful of lollipops and then we leave. I feel a twinge of sadness as the door shuts behind us – even if Liam was of dubious character, he was one of the first *others* to help me. Sure, I had to pay him for information, but he *did* refrain from having me for lunch, and there was even a brief time when we almost became lovers.

I can't say I'll miss him, exactly, but… Yeah, okay, I will miss him a little bit.

Alex won't be back until after sun-up, so Ev and I have bacon and eggs and peppermint tea – and blood for him – then get a bit of sleep. I'm expecting to dream; I *want* to dream. I want to know what happened to my ancestor.

But I guess I do know. She had her child, and it was too big and killed her. But was she born human, that too-big child? Or was she born a fox? And I want to know if the witch, Rose-Perle, remained cold and cruel, or if she found the sun again and remembered being kind, remembered when she was a happy child who loved animals. But I don't dream at all, or not that I recall.

I wake to warmth and I don't want to leave the bed, where Evgeny snores quietly. But it's time to get on with things. Alex will be here soon, and if Ev's going to research while I'm gone, he'll need me to bring him books to look at in bed first.

And maybe a lamp, because his dark-vision isn't that great.

When Alex arrives, bearing two giant take-out cups of coffee – there's a distinct chocolate smell coming from them as well – I'm as ready to go as I can be.

I've dressed non-threateningly in loose trousers – I vanish my tail, though I've really come to like having it – and a more girly-looking top than I usually wear. And I've put on canvas sneakers instead of my usual boots. My hair is braided and coiled up on my head out of the way.

Alex has also chosen non-threatening-looking clothes in colors besides her usual beige and khaki. Instead she's wearing deep green and blue that makes her hair stand out like her head's on fire.

She laughs when I answer the door, and spreads her arms. "I guess we both had the same idea," she says. "Look soft and non-scary."

I laugh, too. "Let's go and get this over with," I say.

Just as I'm closing the door, I hear Evgeny stir. "Be careful, my heart," he says.

"You, too," I say.

"Yes," he says, "These books might be dangerous. I might get a papercut."

I smile as I close the door. He's never called me "my heart" before. I think I might like it.

Chapter Seventeen

It's strange, watching the same scenery, the same soulless subdivisions and housing projects pass by out the window, but from a human perspective, instead of that of a fox. I mean, it was still me then, and you wouldn't think just being a different shape would make such a difference, but it does.

I guess it kind of shows that who we are has as much to do with our physical selves as it does with some undefinable core of being, whatever you might call it. Yes, I'm still Su, but the way I think in human shape is different from the way I think in fox shape. It has to be; I couldn't function as a fox if I thought like a human.

And maybe that's why it would be so easy to become a fox and never change back. Like Mathilde had told Alex, I wouldn't care after a while. I wouldn't even know *to* care.

But there was still something constant, something essentially me. Though fox and human brains are different, they must be similar enough to retain some of the wiring, because I could *think*, not quite as a human, but as more than just a fox, and I kept my memories. In fox shape, those human memories are harder to access, but in human shape, the fox memories are perfectly clear, if a bit foreign-seeming.

Yes, I remember, my brain seems to be telling me, but those memories *feel* different.

So sitting in the passenger seat of Alex's car, watching the scenery as we pass through it, is familiar but strange, all at once. Like that intense more-than-déja-vu I sometimes get (though not so much, lately) that triggers an old memory coming back to me, from before.

And I notice different things. Then, I noticed shapes, configuration, repetition, the number of trees and places to hide. Now I notice the differences in materials, the way each neighborhood seems to have a predominant type of car – all SUVs in one area, all small efficient cars in another. And I notice the people. Not just how many and where, like the fox did, but what they're doing, how they dress, if they seem friendly with their neighbors.

And I wonder if any of them know what things go bump in the night. Are they aware of vampires and werewolves? Probably not, but maybe some of them notice the oddness in some folks that can't quite be explained by the fact that a lot of people are just weird.

I wonder what those people we pass by would do if they knew vampires exist. Would it matter at all that few vamps grab people off the street to eat? Would they care that werewolves prefer the taste of four-legged prey? Would they envy the mental powers of witches? And what would they think of a woman who can turn into a fox, who has a fox's tail when she doesn't consciously decide not to?

What do I think of myself?

Because, honestly, I haven't taken the time to mull it over much. I've spent over a year not knowing what the hell I was, and I'd worked out quite nicely how much that sucked. Now I do know, and I'm not sure what to think. But like I said, I haven't really had the *time* to think. So I promise myself that once this is over, I'm going to devote as many long bubble baths alone as it takes to suss out how I feel about myself.

And then I wonder what Alex thinks of me. She's afraid of me. Or she was when she saw me change shape through the witches' connection to Evgeny. Is she still in love with me, like Ev thinks? Or is she more comfortable being friends now, like she said?

I have to push those thoughts aside as we pull into Mathilde's neighborhood. This time, Alex parks in the driveway next to a battered but cared-for Toyota sedan with cheerful bumper stickers.

"Ready?" says Alex as she turns the key in the ignition and the car goes quiet.

"As I can be," I say.

I let Alex take the lead. This is her world we're going into, and it affects her future, how this all comes out. If it goes well, if we can somehow become allies with Mathilde, then Alex doesn't have to lose the community she's so recently found. If it goes badly … well, then she can hang out with us misfits who don't have a community of their own. Though I guess Magne doesn't fit that classification – he has us *and* his own pack, plus a lot of non-were friends, too.

It takes a long time for Mathilde to answer the door, and when she does, she's wearing a big fluffy bathrobe and slippers and she blinks at us like the light is too bright.

She doesn't say anything, she just looks from one to the other of us and waits.

"I'm sorry if we woke you," says Alex. "But we need to talk. Can we please come in?" She holds herself confidently, but her body language conveys contrition, like a dog that knows it's done something bad, and wants to please, but that would do the same again. No, not quite like that, not so abject, nor so like a servant to her master. More like a young person who's just gone against the wishes of a parent for the first time, but knows what they did was right, but who wants to repair relations. I can't tell if that's genuinely how Alex feels, or if she's constructing her attitude to put Mathilde at ease.

"I wasn't asleep," says the witch. "I was trying to escape this delightful headache your familiar has given me." She looks at us each again, then turns and walks up the stairs, leaving the door open, so we follow.

"She's not – " Alex starts to say, but I touch her hand and she stops. Let Mathilde believe that I'm bound, if it will make this discussion easier.

But once we're inside, Mathilde turns and says, "She's not your familiar. No, I see that. And yet, knowing you could bind her, she still stays with you. Either she's very stupid, or a very good friend." Mathilde's voice is hard to read. She sounds annoyed, but I can't tell if it's disdain or grudging respect that makes it rough. Odd that they sound so alike.

The curtains are drawn in the living room, leaving a dim, but not dark, room. It seems more pleasant this way. I glance at the hearth while Mathilde's attention is on moving a damp cloth from the arm of the sofa to a dish on the table, but the Russian doll is gone. I wonder where she's hidden it. I wonder if taking it from her would do any good.

We sit, me and Alex together on a smaller couch, and Mathilde alone on the big sofa where a pile of blankets and a pillow show she was resting. There's a bottle of Tylenol on the table.

"Sorry about the headache," I say.

She looks at me, then back at Alex, and says nothing.

Okay. This should be fun. I'm tense and uncomfortable, but I decide that Mathilde doesn't need to know that, so I make myself relax into my seat. I don't quite sprawl, Magne-style, but I know if she looks at me I'll look perfectly at ease. Really I feel like I've walked into the lair of the enemy, even if this enemy is a lot more grandmotherly than my last one.

"Why are you here?" Mathilde finally says.

"We think…" Alex hesitates and twines her fingers together in her lap. She's trying to decide how to explain, I think. "We're wondering why you – why the *hexen* – see Evgeny as an enemy, and if maybe there's something that's a danger to all of us, to him too."

"We?" says Mathilde.

"Me and Su." Alex glances at me. "And Evgeny. And Magne." She tilts her chin up, a little defiance in her look, but not too much.

"I am curious as to why you have chosen a fox, a Reborn, and a cur over your own people." Though her intent, especially calling Magne a cur (and I don't even know how she knows who Magne is, though I guess she must have figured it out from her attacks on Evgeny), is to make us feel bad, her voice is calm and seemingly without malice.

Alex scratches her nose and lets a little smile touch her lips, like she's remembering something pleasant. "They're my friends," she says.

"Are they?" says Mathilde. "Haven't they simply used you to help them? Let you spend time with them so you could help them figure out what was attacking them?"

Mathilde has a point. Leaving aside the fact that Alex and I were once lovers, we *have* used her, though not meanly. We did ask her to help read Evgeny, and to ask the witches for information. But we did it – or at least

I did it – as one asks a friend for help.

She'd have *my* help if she needed it.

I can't tell if Alex has those same thoughts or not. She just looks levelly at Mathilde and says, "They haven't used me any more than you have, and they've helped me just as much." She shrugs. "Besides, I haven't really been that useful."

Mathilde's nostrils flare, but she doesn't argue.

"So we were thinking, " Alex continues, before Mathilde can turn the conversation away to some other topic. "If Evgeny's so dangerous, can't you tell us *why* or *how*? If it's something that endangers all of us, then let us help fight it."

"The best thing you can do, to save all your friends, is to behead that Reborn and lay his body in the sun to burn, then scatter his ashes."

"Why?"

"Because what he will become can destroy all of us – *hexen*, Reborn, were-beast. Because others will seek to control him who will *not* destroy him, but use him to bring about the subjugation of all *others* and the reduction of humanity to the role of beasts of burden and prey."

Alex looks taken aback. I *feel* taken aback, but I force myself to stay calm and relaxed.

I venture a thought towards Alex, hoping the other witch can't also read me. Alex's eyelids twitch, but she doesn't look at me.

"Assuming Evgeny's death is not an option," she says, "What then?"

Mathilde looks like she's swallowed a lemon. "Destroying the abomination" – her glance flicks to me, then away – "would be safest for everyone. As a true witch you should not shrink from the death of one to save many, especially not when some of those many are your own kind." Her emphasis is on *own*.

Alex starts to speak but Mathilde abruptly holds up one hand.

"But since he is your friend and you refuse to let this happen, and since your power combined with that of your fam – of your fox friend seems to be enough to thwart your fellow *hexen* so we cannot force the issue, then you will have to find out who else seeks to use him and stop *them*. Your strength may not be equal to *that* task."

Then Mathilde grimaces and reaches for the pain medication. I wish I could undo the headache for a moment, until I remember how she treated Evgeny. Then I have to resist the urge to make her pain worse.

"Who else is trying to use Evgeny?" asks Alex. "And why? What's so dangerous about him?"

Mathilde swallows her tablet and sets the bottle down again. She closes her eyes a moment, rubs her temples. Then she says, "We don't know exactly what happens when a *hexen* is made Reborn. No, that's not true. Either she dies, or she fights off the symbiont and remains a witch, or the Reborn's disease overwhelms her witch nature and she is simply a vampire. A witch no more." She seems to consider. "It almost never happens that a witch is infected in the first place, and the one instance I know of resulted in death. The other two possibilities are only hypothetical, and are assumed to be what happens if she has come fully into her powers and can resist it, or if her powers have not yet manifested when the rebirth occurs."

"So if a witch is reborn after she's developed *hexen* powers, she might recover but not as a vampire, but more likely she dies? If it happens before then she never develops her powers."

"Presumably," says Mathilde. "Aside from your friend, who is already an anomaly simply by being male, I know of only the one *hexen* who was reborn. Or rather *not* reborn, because as I said, she didn't recover from the ritual death, but simply stayed dead."

The way a vamp is made is they're drained until they die – or *almost* die, I'm not certain on that point – then the parent vamp transfuses them with his or her own blood, and the vamp symbiont uses the body's weakness to overwhelm and take it over and then the person revives once the symbiont has healed them. It's why they call themselves Reborn, and why a new vamp is called "newborn."

So I guess if witch gets drained, and the symbiont can't overwhelm her body's defenses, even weakened as she is, but she's *too* weak to recover without the symbiont, so she dies for good.

Which means that if the draining and transfusion happen before her witch power manifests, the symbiont doesn't have to overcome it. Instead it establishes itself before her witch nature ever wakes, and defeats it on its own home turf so it *can't* awaken.

I prod Alex with another thought.

"But what if a witch's powers could awaken, even after being reborn?" she says.

"It's a truism, that *others* which are born cannot be made, and those that are made cannot be born," says Mathilde. "It isn't supposed to be possible that one can be both born and made."

"It isn't supposed to be possible for a man to be a witch, either," says Alex.

"And what about weres?" I ask.

Mathilde says, ignoring me, "Only one bloodline has ever been known to produce male witches, and even then they were exceedingly rare. Even breeding the boys with other *hexen* families didn't increase the frequency. Essentially, we don't know how they might be different from other *hexen*."

Then she does look at me, and her disdain is evident on her face. But I think I also see respect there. Perhaps she might acknowledge that I am more than a particularly gifted animal, given the opportunity.

"And werewolves are made, not born," she says. Her contempt is moderated with caution, like she suspects I had good reason for asking.

"Magne told me it might be possible for a were to be born a were, if their mother is one."

"Ah," she says, understanding dawning on her face. "Those would still be made, only they are infected within the womb, through sharing the blood of their mother."

I nod. So it's still a symbiont-in-the-blood thing, not a genetic thing.

I decide not to mention that I'm also both born and made, as far as I can tell. It doesn't sound like she can offer any insight, and I'm hesitant to share any more information with her than I have to.

"So really," Alex says, her voice losing some of the supplication she's imbued it with so far, so that Mathilde looks at her sharply. "You have no idea how Evgeny will turn out if he does fully develop his *hexen* powers, so you don't really know if he'll be dangerous at all."

Mathilde shakes her head. "We may not be certain of the result, but do you think a Reborn with the mind powers of a *hexen*, or a *hexen* with the speed and strength and bloodlust of a vampire can be anything but dangerous?"

"I'd be inclined to agree with you," I say, making both witches look at me in surprise. "A lot of nice people turn into complete dicks when they become vamps. Or gain witch abilities. But Evgeny's not one of them."

I know it's not logical. Logically, Ev should be *more* likely to turn into an asshat. Absolute power corrupting absolutely, and all that. But I know him. And I can't explain how I can possibly be certain, but I know that no matter how powerful he becomes, he'll always be the sweet, loving man I know.

"Let's hope you are right, *fuchs*," says Mathilde. "But that won't help him if someone else can control him."

"If you can't tell us what terrible thing he'll become," says Alex, losing the nice-girl attitude entirely, "Will you at least tell us who else is after him? Can't we all pool our resources against *them*? Aren't they the real danger? Or are you just speculating that someone *might* try to control him?"

Mathilde rubs her temples. "You are a willful child," she says. "But then so was I once, according to my teachers. The strongest of us always are." She stands suddenly. "I need a good, strong cup of tea." And she walks into the kitchen.

Alex clenches her fists in frustration, so I squeeze her shoulder, and she sighs.

When Mathilde comes back, she says, "I don't know who it is."

"Who what is?" says Alex. "The … whoever you think is trying to control Evgeny?"

"I haven't noticed anyone but you *hexen* trying to take over him," I say.

"No one?" asks Mathilde, eyebrows raised and eyes glittering.

I sit back. "Well, Charleston, but he was trying to use Ev as a living filter for *hexen* blood for his own use. And Charleston's dead."

"Indeed," says Mathilde. "But there were others behind his research, were there not?"

"The vamp council," I say. "But no one really knows who they are. Plus they didn't direct his research, they just allowed it."

"As far as you know, and probably as far as Charleston knew," says Mathilde.

"So you think other vamps are going to make a try for Evgeny again, to use him in some kind of plan to take over the world." I think of the pocketwatches and their line of poetry. Something about coming out of the shadows.

Mathilde shakes her head. "No, not the vampires. Or not *only* the vampires."

"So you don't know that, either."

"I know that you, *fuchs*, and Alexandra are stronger together than apart, and that you can only both fulfill your potential by a familiar binding."

"So I can live out my days as a fox?" I can't help a little snarl that curls my lip.

"I won't do it," says Alex.

"You may not have a choice, if you really must battle this foe," says Mathilde.

For a while we sit while the older witch makes tea and then we sit looking at each other, holding our cups as if they're the only thing keeping the world together.

I sip mine and I have to admit that Mathilde makes a very fine cup of tea.

"So now what?" says Alex.

Mathilde shrugs. "I suppose if we can't kill the abomination, then we shall have to work together, for the preservation of us all."

"And how do we figure out who this supposed enemy is?"

"You won't need to," says Mathilde, "He'll make himself known sooner or later. Likely sooner, if I sensed correctly that your Reborn friend's *hexen* powers are awakening. It's why we tried to destroy him now instead of waiting until we were more recovered from our captivity."

"So, what, we wait until Ev gets attacked again?" I say.

Mathilde shrugs.

"And then what?"

"Then we gather and strike back," she says.

"How?"

"Much the same way we acted against your friend. Only we pray that all of us together are strong enough."

"We use Rasputin's ashes?" I ask.

"Rasputin?" says Mathilde. "Is that who you think they are?"

"Aren't they?"

"I have always believed it was Alexei, the Romanov, in that bottle. But

I suppose it could be the evil monk."

"You don't know that, either?'

"Contrary to popular belief about Books of Shadows and all that nonsense, *hexen* seldom write anything down. It makes us vulnerable." Mathilde sips her tea and closes her eyes. "Sadly, it also means a lot of information gets lost or distorted and has to be relearned, rediscovered."

"Is that why you make new witches figure out so much on their own?" says Alex. "Because you don't actually know?"

"It's good practice," says Mathilde. "You'll spend your life trying to find out things that have been lost, attempting to re-invent processes and techniques for yourself. It seems a good way to prepare by making you practice with the few things we *can* actually teach you."

Chapter Eighteen

We leave Mathilde with her headache and head back to the loft, where Alex drops me off but doesn't come in. She says she has some errands, and some things she wants to try that require solitude, I figure maybe she's got some witch technique for finding out information. Or maybe she's just got a good idea for an internet search, and I don't have a computer.

I don't stop at Magne's to see if he's home, because I want to pass on what I've learned to Evgeny and see what he's found out. But I can tell as soon as I open the door that he's asleep. It's his breathing. It always sounds quietest when he's asleep, so quiet that most people would look at him and assume he's dead.

He stirs, murmurs something, and settles again. He's probably aware on some level that it's me. I bet if it *wasn't* me that he'd be awake and listening in an instant, and most people who are not me wouldn't even be aware of the change.

I think about waking him, but decide there's no real urgency. No one's trying to take him over just now, and hell, they might not ever. The witches could be wrong about the shadowy person or group that may or may not involve the vampire council, whoever *they* are.

Right now, Evgeny can probably use sleep more that anything, and really so can I. I wonder briefly if there might be some leftovers in the fridge, but I'm not quite hungry enough to look, so I peel off most of my clothes, and let my tail come back into existence – that's a peculiar feeling for sure, but I feel better once it's there. It's hard to believe that only a few days ago I couldn't wait to get rid of it. Then I climb into bed, navigate around the piles of books, and snuggle next to Evgeny under the quilt.

He murmurs again and turns to spoon against me, but doesn't wake. And that feels so nice I fall asleep immediately.

I'm expecting to dream about my ancestor again, and the dream is lucid enough that I wonder again if these dreams are some kind of ancestral memory, or if they're just my brain making up a distant past for me because I have no remembered past of my own.

But this dream is different. I'm not the *hexenfuchs*. At first, I'm not sure who I am. I'm a young woman and the family I live with is not my birth family. Or not my birth *parents* anyway; they seem to be some sort of cousins. They're kind, but I make them nervous.

From the odd looks they give me, I wonder what I look like, if I have some kind of deformity, but I don't pass by any reflective surfaces and the dream isn't so lucid that I can go looking for a mirror. I am self-aware, but the events are not mine to change.

And those events seem to consist of sending me off to the forest with a small bundle of belongings.

Like the younger sister in a fairy tale, I wander under immense trees, aimless. But I recognize them eventually, though the woman whose life I am observing does not. It is the forest near the witch's house. Rose-Perle's house.

Soon, I am at her front door, looking up the ladder and wondering if I should climb up and knock.

But I don't have to, because I hear the witch's voice behind me, and turn. "Sigrún," she says. My name, the name of the woman I inhabit in the dream. Where have I heard that name?

I expect an old woman, but Rose-Perle has not changed at all. Perhaps no time has passed between the last dream and this one.

But no. "You've grown," she says, and I realize whose role I play, and where I heard the name Sigrún. The child of the *hexenfuchs* and the young man with no voice. The child who was too large to be born, who killed her mother coming into the world. She must be about nineteen now. Again, I wonder what I – what she – looks like. Does she appear half-fox, furred and slit-pupiled?

"You must be Frau Holz."

Holz. Right, because Rose-Perle is Alex's ancestor, and her family passed their surname from mother to daughter.

"Rose-Perle," the witch says.

A thrill goes through me when she tells me her name, like the way I felt the first time Alex kissed me.

The dream skips forward as Sigrún settles in to Rose-Perle's house. Each time the witch leaves on an errand, she gives Sigrún lessons to complete. Not lessons in witchcraft, exactly, but things to help her use her fox powers. I try to remember them, so I can use them myself when I wake, but they slip away from me.

Each time, Sigrún hurries through the lesson, then climbs the trees around the house, thins branches, until one day, the house is in the sun at midday. And I think of the hexenfuchs, who thought the witch might smile again, if she lived in sunlight instead of in gloom.

Then Sigrún digs a garden. She doesn't plant it, she just readies it. And waits for Rose-Perle to notice.

The witch says nothing, only sends me, Sigrún, on errands away from the house more often. She does not bind me as a familiar, but she almost treats me as one. Almost, but not quite.

One day when I return to the house, there are things sprouting in the garden, and soon it's lush with herbs and flowers. Still Rose-Perle does not comment, but one evening at supper she tucks an orange lily behind my ear and kisses me on the lips. That night, I do not go to my cot by the fire, but climb into the loft to Rose-Perle's bed.

She shows me how it feels to be touched, shows me how to touch her, and we spend the night stroking bare skin, teasing nipples, and sliding fingers through wet folds until we're both panting. Then she ducks beneath the covers and applies her tongue and I feel like I'm dissolving in the air from waves of pleasure until I have to cry out. And I do the same for her, discover she is sweet and her voice like a bell as she climaxes.

I wake then, from the dream, moist between the legs and wanting sex, but Evgeny is still asleep and I'm really only half awake, so I roll over and drift off again.

I dream of forest once more, but a different forest, and the warm contentment I felt in Rose-Perle's house is gone. Here there is an edge. Uneasiness.

I can feel others in the woods around me, but I can't see them. I try to smell them, but I can only smell faint scents of earth and trees. This must not be my dream any more than the dream of Rose-Perle was. This is even *less* my dream than that one. But whose?

The forest reminds me of the dream of blood and danger that Alex told me about. I had forgotten all about that, and I wonder now if it could have anything to do with the danger Mathilde believes will come if Evgeny is allowed to live.

But the only person I've ever shared dreams with before – that I know of – is Evgeny. I've looked in on his dreams and he has shared mine, mostly unintentionally.

Would a male body feel different to dream in than a female body? I try to remember what it was like to share Evgeny's perspective before. Then whomever I'm inhabiting in this dream moves and he's definitely male – the center of balance is different, and I can tell I've got no breasts and things are definitely different between the legs. *That* feels even weirder than suddenly sprouting a tail.

Evgeny, then. The fear I feel isn't his, but he can sense it. Someone nearby is terrified. Someone Evgeny has a strong connection to. Me? Can I feel my own fear through Evgeny? And is this a prophetic dream or just a nightmare? Before I can determine anything else, I wake up.

I lie in the dark, staring up at the ceiling. Next to me, Evgeny is awake, too.

"Was that your dream," I say softly, even though I know it must have been.

"I know where we need to go," he says. "To find the answers."

I reach out and find his hand. "That was not a good place to be," I say.

"No," he says. "Not a good place at all, but that's where it will end. It's where we'll face one last enemy and find out what they want from me." He squeezes my fingers. "Of course, it's a trap."

I hear the faint whirr of the elevator as we're sitting at the table talking about what little Evgeny has discovered about *others* with a genetic heritage who become infected by a symbiont.

"Does he do that so I'll know he's home?" I say.

"Does who do what?"

Sometimes I forget my hearing is better than Ev's, just as my night-sight and sense of smell are. But when he's in full-on vamp mode, he doesn't seem to need heightened senses. He just *moves* and somehow doesn't bump into anything.

I tilt my head in the general direction of the elevator and Evgeny is silent, listening.

"The elevator," he says. "I suppose he might. Or else he's very lazy." Ev says that last bit louder, so Magne can hear him clearly as he comes in the door after the briefest of knocks.

He's got food, so I don't complain.

"Next round of take-out's on you guys," he says, depositing a large greasy bucket of chicken and an equally greasy paper bag on the table.

I resist making a comment about our differences in food preferences and just agree. I'm thinking I'd like Thai next time. Or sushi. Definitely sushi.

We fill him in on Mathilde's insistence, and Papa Vamp's books correlation, that genetic *others* die when infected with an *otherly* symbiont, unless they're infected before the genes kick in, in which case they *might* live, but the symbiont prevents the genetic *otherness* from developing.

Magne nods and swallows a bite of chicken. "That's about what everyone told me," he says when his mouth is clear. "You can't have both and it's usually death to make the attempt." But he frowns. "I talked to my granddad, though."

I try to imagine what Magne's grandfather might look like. Like Magne, but grey-haired and a little bent? Or do weres age slowly like vamps do? And witches, apparently, if my dream is any indication of reality. In that case, they might look like brothers.

I snag another piece of chicken. My human side isn't impressed by the grease, but the fox half doesn't mind. Evgeny picks at a container of potato salad between sips from a mug full of warmed blood.

"What did he say, and why are you frowning?" I say.

"He brought up the word *koldun* again. I told him the witches insist they're just charismatic men who convince witches to do their dirty work, but Granddad seems to think that's a later meaning for the word."

Evgeny pushes the salad aside and gets up to get a book, brings it back to the table, flipping pages. "I read something like that somewhere, but it didn't say much." The book says *Russian Fairy Tales* on the cover, and sports a beautiful illustration of Baba Yaga's chicken-legged house. It reminds me of Rose-Perle's house on stilts.

"Granddad says in the old stories a *koldun* is a sorcerer. Always male, like a *hexen* is always female. Always evil."

"And they have real powers?" The one constant I've had when investigating the world of the *others* since I woke up into it that autumn night, is that magic – honest-to-goodness making the impossible happen magic – isn't real.

Then I turned into a fox, but I could still pretend it was only a more elaborate version of a were transformation, which is more a rearrangement of parts than an actual change of shape. But if sorcery is real, then maybe … maybe *I'm* magic, too?

Magne shrugs. "Could be they really are just male witches, with the same kind of mental abilities. Granddad seemed to think it was more than that, but he also said he'd never heard of anyone actually meeting a *koldun*."

Evgeny finds what he's looking for in the book. It's a story about a sorcerer whose evil plans are foiled by a plucky young heroine. He shakes his head after reading it aloud. "This basically says the same thing. Nasty man who seems to be more or less a really strong witch."

"With control over the dead," I say. "But what does this have to do with *others* that are both born and made?"

"Nothing, really," says Magne. "It's just something Granddad thought of while we were talking."

Evgeny drums his fingers on the pages of the book, still open to the page with a picture of a man in traditional Russian garb. The sorcerer has a long beard and scary-intense eyes. "Why did the *hexen* pretend to be a *koldun* when they took me over?" he says.

I catch the sound of the elevator again. Probably Alex. I wonder how she's adapting to having nocturnal friends.

"Alex is here," I say, and then there's a knock. I call out for her to come in. She's brought coffee from an expensive coffee shop in four big cardboard cups.

"It's kind of a wake up and dessert in one," she says. And I smell chocolate, caramel, salt, and whipped cream. I hope Magne's and mine aren't real cream.

"We're all going to need exercise after this," Magne says. He wiggles his eyebrows suggestively, and Alex laughs.

We give her the condensed version of what we've discussed and she says, "I assumed the witches used a *koldun* because of the jar. The ashes. They created the illusion of a male presence to hide behind."

"Alexei Romanov would be, what, your grandfather? Great-grandfather?" says Magne, after taking a big sip of his caramel mocha, sans cream. Alex remembered and it makes me smile.

Evgeny shrugs. "I suppose. My dad never said anything about him. I assume he didn't know."

"So the ashes could be your granddad."

"Or a creepy monk," I say.

"Or a *koldun*," says Alex.

"Except we still don't know if they're real, and if they're real what they are, exactly, and what they can do." I contemplate another piece of chicken. My fox nature is urging me to stuff my belly and then sleep, but that doesn't seem very practical just now.

"What was that you said about the dead?" says Evgeny.

"Just that your fairytale" – I tap the book – "has the sorcerer in the story controlling the dead."

"And in vampire folklore, we're supposed to be dead," he says.

"So maybe the sorcerer, the *koldun*, has the power to control vamps? Is that what you're thinking?" I sip my coffee. It's too sweet, but it's good. The coarse salt sprinkled over the caramel-drizzle is a nice touch.

Evgeny shakes his head. "I don't know what to think. We just don't have enough information. I feel like we're thinking in circles."

"So now what?"

We stare at each other for a while. Then Evgeny says, "We find the forest in my dream."

"Are you sure?" I don't like it. He said he knows it's a trap, but he's determined to walk into it anyway.

Of course, Magne and Alex don't know what we're talking about, so we tell them.

Magne says, "You sure it wasn't just a regular dream. You know, like most people have?"

Evgeny blushes slightly. "It could have been," he says.

"No," says Alex. "It sounds too much like my dream. And that one was definitely not just a nightmare."

"I've been having way too many non-normal dreams lately," I say. "Why can't I just have one of those ones where I'm being chased and I can't quite escape no matter how fast I am, and just as the bad guy is about to catch me, I wake up? That would be a nice change."

Evgeny smiles. "I could go for one of the naked in high school dreams, myself."

"You people are lunatics," says Magne. "And as a werewolf, I know a thing or two about the moon and crazy people."

The joking takes the edge off the tension that's gathered, but it doesn't last.

"Okay," I say. "So we go to wherever this forest is, assuming we can find it. And we walk into the trap our hypothetical enemies have set. And then what? We reason with them? Whoever they are?"

Magne snorts. "I don't think there's going to be any reasoning."

I look across the table at Alex. She's playing with a quartz crystal on a leather thong. "You don't have to come," I say, touching her lightly on the back of her hand. "It's not your fight."

She glances up, startled. "It *is* my fight," she says. "Mathilde thinks that whomever this enemy is, they're a threat to all *others*."

"Only if they gain control over Evgeny."

"Maybe," she says. "But friends don't back out on each other." She puts the quartz back in her pocket. "I'm in, and I'll bring as many other *hexen* as I can." She grins, suddenly, and it lights up her face. "That's one of the things I spent today doing. Calling and emailing all the witches I could get Mathilde to give me contact info for. Some of them wouldn't talk to me, but four or five said they'd try to be there when we need them."

"And I've got a handful of wolves and even a couple bloodsuckers to back me up," says Magne.

"So we just need to find this place," I say. "This forest."

"I know where it is," says Evgeny. "That dream … it wasn't a nightmare *or* a prophetic dream. It was a … a sort of communication. And he wanted to use a place he was sure I would recognize." He's looking right in my eyes as he says it, and I realize he thinks I should know the place, too. But I know I've never been there, unless it was before I lost my memories.

But then I remember. We shared a dream once before, in which Evgeny was with his ex-boyfriend. An ex who had taken him camping and raped him. To be fair, the boyfriend had thought Evgeny *liked* it that way. I had never been sure if Ev knew I'd looked in on that dream. The dream hadn't included the worst parts of Evgeny's memories, but he did tell me about that later, because he said he wanted me to know all about him, good and bad, happy and unhappy.

"That's a ways away," I say.

"Not so far," he says. "It's just our past … where I used to live." He won't even say the name of the city. He left to get away from a lover he was crazy about even when the relationship was damaging, and I know he doesn't like thinking about it. "A couple hours by car," he says.

"No big," says Alex. "I can drive the four of us."

"And the *hexen* and weres?"

"They'll have to make their own way," says Magne.

"So when do we do this?"

"Now?" says Evgeny.

"And when daylight comes?" I say. "Where will you hide?"

He glances at the bedcurtains. "Can we make a tent?"

Magne follows his gaze. "I have an *actual* tent. We can rig those curtains over it to make it light-tight."

"That'll take time," I say. "And we've already spent a good part of the night talking."

Evgeny frowns. "Sooner is better," he says.

"And rushing in is folly," says Magne. "We'll spend the rest of tonight prepping. We don't know how long this will take. Then we alert our forces." He glances at Alex, who nods. "And leave at nightfall tomorrow."

"Right," I say. "So what do we take?"

We make lists, gather supplies, make more lists of things to fetch or buy when the shops open in the morning. Evgeny cooks for us – when this is over, I'm definitely going to buy an actual stove, maybe even with an oven. There's plenty of room, anyway.

While Magne and Ev are occupied with the tent, Alex approaches me and says, "Can I talk to you?" She looks at the men, then back to me.

"We can go up to the roof," I say.

Outside, the city casts its dim, reddish glow, and a few stars manage to shine through it. We stand near the edge of the roof, looking out across the industrial wasteland of warehouses and run-down shops. It's not a great neighborhood I live in, but it's oddly private.

"I was thinking about what Mathilde told us," she says. "About you and me being stronger together."

I get a weird feeling in the pit of my stomach. "If I become your familiar," I say.

She nods and takes the quartz out of her pocket and looks at it. "Yeah," she says.

I wonder if I should start backing away from her.

Maybe she senses my uneasiness, because she looks away from the stone in her hand and smiles her lopsided smile. "I'm not going to do it," she says. "To bind you. At least, not unless …" She looks away again, seeming to search the night for the right words.

"But I thought just in case, we should be prepared." She holds up the crystal, lets it hang on the cord so it twists gently in the air, catching the light from a streetlamp and reflecting it in flashes. "I made this," she says. "And I put the binding into it. So if something happens, if one of us needs extra strength…" She stops.

I reach out and take the hand holding the stone in mine. "If it means *your* life or death," I say, "I'll do it. But I don't want to be trapped as a witch's familiar forever."

"I know," she says. "I'm trying to find out if there's a way to reverse the binding, in case we need to use it." She looks right into my eyes and says, "But if it was *your* life or death, I'd sooner bind you than lose you."

For a long time, we stare at each other, her endlessly deep brown eyes full of emotions I can't begin to name, but jealousy does not seem to be among them.

"Tell me how it works," I say.

Chapter Nineteen

I decide it's better not to tell Evgeny about the crystal with Alex's familiar-binding spell. I don't like keeping things from him, so I'm uneasy about it, but if I tell him, he'll only fret. And waste time trying to convince me to toss the stone away.

I don't intend to use it. At least, I hope like hell I don't find myself in a position where I need to subject myself to Alex's will to save her life. Not that I think she'd abuse the situation. It's just the principle of it. I'm a free creature, making my own decisions, and there aren't many things that would induce me to give up that freedom.

At daybreak, Evgeny retreats to Magne's place, where there's an inside room with no window he can shelter in, and Magne, Alex and I divide up the list of purchases between us. It's mostly food and weapons, the first in case we end up camping out for a while, and the second in case our enemy is something we can fight with brute force.

I can tell Alex doesn't like that, and I don't really, either. But if it means saving our lives, I'll kill just about anyone.

Then we sleep. Alex takes my bed, while I crawl in with Evgeny. I'm tempted to get naked and spend the day in pleasant distraction. And I'd hate if something went terribly wrong and we didn't take this last opportunity for intimacy.

But maybe my crazy sex drive is finally slowing down – maybe I've manifested enough of my fox-woman nature to keep it under control instead of constantly being subjected to my raging hormones. Because practical considerations win out: we don't know what we'll be facing, so we should sleep while we can.

Luckily, my fox nature also lets me fall asleep quickly, even plagued by doubts. I tuck myself into a ball against Evgeny's back and close my eyes.

If I dream, I don't recall, so when Magne taps on the door I wake refreshed. Evgeny looks better, too. There's hardly time for a good long hug before we're packing Alex's station wagon. We don't even have coffee until we pass a drive-through place.

Magne seems to want to talk, but the rest of us are quiet, watching the dim scenery go by, mile after mile, so eventually he gives up, leans back in the front passenger seat, and goes to sleep. He snores, too, but not loudly.

From my seat in the back, I can see Alex has a too-tight grip on the wheel.

"You okay?" I ask.

"I'm scared," she says. "We have no idea what to expect."

"You can still opt out," I say. "Just drop us off in the general vicinity and go home."

She glances at me in the rearview mirror and shakes her head. "No way. Ever since I had that dream, I knew I had to …" She hesitates, flicks another look in the rearview, but at Evgeny, not me. "To protect you," she says.

"Perhaps," says Evgeny. "It would help to relate any details you can remember from your dream. We can compare notes."

"Okay," she says. She describes trees, a mix of tall hardwoods and smaller, scruffier spruce. I half expect to be caught up in her memories again, but maybe she doesn't want to use her abilities when driving. Come to think of it, it's probably best she doesn't, if sharing her memories like that affects her the way it affected me last time.

"It's pretty vague," she says. "We were there, me and Su, for sure. Su was running and I think… I think I was trying to reach her. I sensed danger."

"Danger to Su?" says Evgeny. His voice is soft, but there's steel in it.

He really doesn't like when I'm threatened. I've wondered, before, if it's a sign of the depth of his caring, or if there's a streak of possessiveness in him. Not that it would be unusual for a guy to guard his girlfriend jealously.

"Danger in general," says Alex. "But yes, especially to Su I think." She navigates the car around an ancient VW Rabbit that's toiling up the hill, her hands sure on the wheel and the gearshift. Her competence with the car is a contrast to the uncertainty and strain in her voice.

"There are vampires and werewolves and other witches," she says. "But in the dream I couldn't tell which ones were helping me and which ones were a threat. And there's something very cold that brushes my mind now and again."

"Like a consciousness?" asks Evgeny.

"Yes. Like someone searching. And every time I feel it, I'm so relieved it's not me it's looking for."

"I think I felt it in my dream, also," says Evgeny. "Though I didn't notice it so much as an intelligence." He reaches for my hand and twines his fingers with mine, like he's trying to reassure himself that I'm still there.

"In my dream I also felt others around me, and fear." He looks at me. "You were afraid, Su. And I couldn't find you."

"So why are both of you dreaming about me in danger?" I say. "I thought this whole thing was about Evgeny."

"Perhaps it is because you are what we share," says Evgeny.

"It's true," says Alex. "I knew Evgeny existed when I had the dream, but that was all. You're the one I was connected to." She looks at me in the mirror again. I can't see her mouth, but the way her eyes crinkle at the corners, she must be smiling.

"And I was not much concerned with Alex or the other *hexen*," says Evgeny.

"Still," I say. "If Evgeny is the big danger, you'd think he'd be more important in the dreams."

"Unless," says Magne, head still tilted back against the seat and voice clear like maybe he was never asleep at all. Or else he wakes up better than most people. "Both dreams were meant to entrap the dreamer, by targeting what the dreamer cares most about."

"That still doesn't make any sense," I say. "If Evgeny's the target, why lure Alex to this place?"

"Maybe Evgeny's not the target,' says Magne. "Maybe you are."

But that doesn't make sense either, so we fall into silence and our own thoughts again. I stare at the stars, bright against the dark sky now that we're out of the city. If Evgeny didn't have to worry about being caught in the sun, we could go camping. I've thought about moving to the country, and I'd definitely like to visit it now and then. I wonder if Alex likes camping.

We're driving through hills, mountains almost, that are covered with forest. This time of year the hardwoods are bare of leaves, but it's been a mild winter, so there's no snow on the ground. It's probably lovely country, but even my eyes can't make much of it in the dark.

"There was blood in my dream, too," says Alex, suddenly. "I don't know whose. I can't even picture it really. But it was there."

No one answers. What can you say to that, anyway? And soon we're turning off on a back road, and Evgeny has to pay careful attention so he can tell Alex where to turn, and all her concentration is on driving.

"I hope the others can find us," I say.

"I told the wolves to keep watch for stray vamps and witches," says Magne.

And then we're stopped and the car falls silent. We sit like no one knows what to do now that we're here – wherever here is – and Alex doesn't even take her hands off the steering wheel for a moment.

Then Magne stretches and says, "Well, I don't know about you guys, but I have to take a wicked piss," and he gets out of the car and disappears into the dark. A moment later I can hear a stream of liquid and his long sigh of relief. There are times I wish my hearing was not so good.

The rest of us get out, too, one by one, and stretch. We decide to set up camp next to the car as a sort of base of operations.

"I'm going to scout around a bit," says Magne. He strips off his shirt, completely unconcerned about getting naked in front of us. I watch him from the corner of my eye as I help Evgeny with the tent. He may not be my type, exactly, but he is fine to look at.

I'm stupidly relieved when the sight of him naked doesn't make me horny. Not long ago just about anyone not completely repulsive made me want to fuck. But maybe Evgeny's careful attention has made a difference.

Before he changes, Magne does step back into the shadows, out of the light of our lanterns, but not completely out of sight. I guess he's more shy about changing than about being starkers.

When his joints begin to reconfigure, I can't help but stare in fascination. He's shown me small things, like changing a hand into a paw, but I've never seen a whole were transformation.

"Just can't get enough of me, can you?" he says, teasing, when he notices me gawping. Then Evgeny turns to look, too. And Alex. Sadly for Magne, the only one of us who's available has no interest in his manly attributes.

It takes a few minutes – which is somehow both more time and less than I expected. I suppose I was thinking of the movies, where a were is either instantly a full-on wolf between one eyeblink and the next, or else he undergoes a long, excruciating change with lots of cracking bone and stretching skin.

From what I can see of Magne's transformation – which is a lot more than either Alex or Evgeny can see, thanks to my fox eyes – it's neither one nor the other. Magne's compared a were's change to a transformer robot, and in a weird sort of way, that's exactly what is looks like.

Take one very hairy, very muscular man, add joints you never noticed before, fold other joints in ways they'd never bend in a human, and eventually you get something that looks like a not-quite-hairy-enough wolf. Only really big. In the dark, through human eyes, he looks enough like a wolf that most people wouldn't know the difference.

And I was right about the tail. It does kind of telescope out of the end of his spine.

On all fours, he grins at me with a mouth elongated from its human shape, but still having all of its human mobility. "Still find me sexy?" he says, then he leaps away into the dark and I find myself wondering, absurdly, if his penis retreats inside him like a dog's.

So maybe my hormones aren't completely under control yet.

"Wow," says Alex. "That was so weird."

"Rather different from your change," says Evgeny. "Much less elegant."

"Maybe I should scout, too," I say, once the camp is set up as much as it can be.

"If you're the one in danger," says Evgeny, "you should stay close."

He doesn't tell me what to do – I think he knows that approach is sure to backfire. And, I think he doesn't actually want a girlfriend who always does what she's told.

"I just hate waiting," I say. "I like *doing*."

Evgeny gets a mischievous look on his face. *I like doing you*, he looks like he might say. But he doesn't. He doesn't want to make Alex feel uncomfortable, maybe.

Then I hear something in the woods. For a moment I can't move, but then it comes again, far off. A howl. Then another, in a slightly different direction.

Alex stands up alert, but she's not listening to the same thing I'm listening to. Her ears couldn't possibly catch the distant wolf song.

"The weres are here," I say quietly.

"And the *hexen*," says Alex. They must have contacted her mentally somehow.

I look around at Evgeny and he's perfectly still, head cocked like he's listening, too.

"Do you hear them, Ev?" I say.

It takes so long for him to answer than I start to wonder if he's even heard me. Then he says, "The werewolves are coming closer, and the witches, too."

"Any vampires?" asks Alex.

Evgeny shakes his head. "I can't tell. They don't have any abilities of the mind, not anything long-distance at least. And they don't tend to talk in howls like werewolves."

I wonder if vamps do have any sort of long-distance communication. They have vamp-speak, which is so high-pitched it's almost inaudible to humans, and carries a lot farther than regular speech – it may be the source of the idea that vampires can turn into bats.

But it doesn't carry as far as a howl, and it's not very loud. I guess vamps don't tend to be social, so they don't need to keep in contact the way weres do.

So I widen my senses to see what I can find out. I close my eyes and listen, and I inhale deeply. That brings me nothing besides more were-howls – coming closer as Evgeny said – and distant crackling of brush that is probably witches making their way through the woods by flashlight.

Then I kind of *feel* around me. I can't explain it, exactly, but it's like the forest is alive and I can read it. Or it speaks to me. Or ... There aren't any analogies that work, but I can tell a lot more by letting the forest reveal itself, if that makes any sense.

And there are the werewolves, half a dozen, including Magne. I can even tell which one is him, and that four of the others are male and one female.

Five *hexen* – Mathilde is not there, but I'm pretty sure that the curly-haired witch who detests the very idea of Evgeny *is*. I can't tell if she's here to help or if she has another agenda. No, wait, Mathilde *is* here, she's just following more slowly behind the others and there's a strange sparky sort of presence clinging to her. A familiar, maybe?

And I realize there are smaller creatures all around the witches. Several cats, two dogs, a ferret, even an owl.

I concentrate, breathe, *feel*. "Two vamps,' I say. "They're staying back. I think they're wondering why they're even here."

So our forces have gathered, and are making their way towards us, but what of our enemy? I have no sense of anything antagonistic out there. Did he lure us here to get us out of the way for some other purpose? I can't think what that could be.

I open my eyes and Alex and Evgeny are both looking at me like I've sprouted horns. Though come to think of it, that might not be so strange on someone who fairly recently grew a tail.

"What?" I say.

"You *are* amazing," says Evgeny.

"You always say that," I say. Though actually I think the word he used last time was "magnificent." It's almost enough to give a girl an ego.

"Wow," says Alex.

"But no sign of our enemy, whoever or whatever it may be?"

I shake my head. "No big bad, only a few wolves." That sounded funnier in my head, so I'm not surprised when my friends don't laugh. At least they smile.

"How far away are the others?" asks Alex.

"They'll be here within the hour," I say. "Sooner for the weres, because they travel faster."

"We must be missing something," says Evgeny.

"You're sure this is the place?"

"This is as near as we can get with the car," he says.

"But this isn't exactly where your dream was? Maybe we need to go there."

"I'm not sure exactly where the dream was. It was dark." He grins at his joke, but no one's in the mood to laugh, I guess.

"The place I … where I was reminded of, where I was supposed to recognize … I think … that's a bit of a hike from here. But not too far." He stares off into the trees. "I hoped that if we got close, the enemy would reveal himself."

"Maybe we need to get closer to spring the trap," I say.

He nods.

"And maybe we should tell our backup to hang back, so they don't end up in the trap with us."

He nods again. "Can you contact the witches?" he asks Alex. "Have them relay the message?"

"I can try," she says. "She sits on the hood of the car and stares into the night, eyes unfocussed.

Evgeny steps close to me, puts his arms around me, and kisses the top of my head. "I wish I could keep you safe," he says.

"Not without caging me," I say.

"I know." He nuzzles my ear. "I would never do that, my beautiful, wild love."

"I'm tough," I say. "And I'm stronger now."

"Yes," he says. "Even more powerful than when you broke me out of Charleston's prison."

"I'm your night in shining armor," I say. "Or furry armor, maybe."

"Which makes me the damsel in distress, I suppose," he says, and chuckles. "I'm glad I had you to rescue me."

"Any time," I say.

"I love you," he says. "I can't believe how much."

"Hey," I say. "Don't go all mushy on me. We'll kick the ass of this bad guy and be home before the sun rises."

"I hope you're right."

"Of course I'm right," I say.

"Still," he says. "I love you and I'm never going to stop telling you so."

"Good," I say. "I rather enjoy being loved." I pull away enough to kiss the end of his nose. "I love you, too, and I intend to demonstrate exactly how much as soon as we get home."

He gives me a sweet, slow kiss, and then we break apart as Alex gets up from the car. "I think they got the message," she says. "So now do we hike into the deep, dark woods?" She's trying to keep things light, but reminding us how dark it is under the trees without even the wan moonlight to help us out was maybe not the best choice.

"Get your flashlights," says Evgeny.

"You get your flashlight," I say. "I don't need one."

And as Alex stoops to her pack for a torch, I feel something shift in the forest. There is another presence there, waiting. It doesn't *feel* evil, but it doesn't seem friendly, either.

"Can you feel it?" I say.

Alex straightens. "What?" she says. Whatever look is on my face it makes her eyes go wide and she looks around us as if expecting a bad guy to step out of the shadows at any time.

"Is it close?" she whispers.

"No," I say. "But not far, either."

Then I look at Evgeny. He's gone utterly vamp-still. He might as well be a statue. Though his metabolism is slow, as all vamps' are, Evgeny has always seemed more alive to me than other Reborn. Unlike them, he still has unconscious twitches and gestures. He even snores in his sleep sometimes, just a little.

But now he seems inanimate. I can't feel even the faintest hint of warmth in his skin when I touch his hand, and he doesn't even respond to the pressure of my fingers. I feel no pulse and hear no sound of breaths.

"Evgeny?" I say, my voice so hushed I wonder if I've made any sound. "Ev?"

Then his gaze shifts to look at me, just an abrupt quick movement of his eyes. "He's here," he says, his voice higher-pitched than usual, halfway to vamp-speak.

"Are you okay?"

"He's calling me," he says.

"Can you resist?"

"It's not a summons, it's a request."

"Can you tell what he wants?"

He shakes his head, a sudden, staccato movement, then he's still again.

"What do you want to do?"

"I'll meet him, as planned," he says. "Find out what he wants. Fight if I must."

"Okay," I say. "Let's go then."

He blinks, the first human gesture since I sensed the presence.

"It will be faster if I go alone," he says. "Be safe."

Then he's gone so fast I almost don't see him move. My hand no longer holds his and I'm whirling around to see his shadow vanish under the trees.

"Fuck," I say.

"Is he under the enemy's control?" says Magne's voice. He's back, but the rest of the weres are still out in the forest.

"No," I say. "He's trying to play the fucking hero."

"So let's follow," he says.

"Keep Alex safe," I say. And then I leave them behind.

Chapter Twenty

I SHOULDN'T BE ABLE to follow Evgeny. I mean, normally it'd be no big deal. I'd just follow his lingering scent or listen for the faint sounds he makes passing through the trees. But now things are different.

Not long after I first met Evgeny, I found out he was as far beyond other vampires as vamps are beyond humanity in terms of speed and strength. He could do things no other vamp could, even when he was so newborn he hadn't regained his human memories.

But then we learned he'd been fed on vamps and weres and especially *hexen* since the day his parent vamp had killed and revived him. Cannibalism strengthens vamps, and feeding on *others* can give the drinker some of that *other's* abilities. *Hexen* blood is especially potent, but also extremely toxic, which is why Evgeny was kidnapped – being a genetic witch before he was made a vampire seems to have given him the ability to drink witch blood and not die. And not only that, it could pass on some abilities to anyone who then fed on *him*.

And when he seemed to be slowing down some, losing some strength, as the witch blood worked its way through his system, it seemed to confirm the idea that it was what had made him so unnaturally fast and strong. Unnatural even for a vamp, that is.

But now I think we have confirmation that his genetic witch abilities are manifesting, and they've not only given him *hexen* powers, but boosted his vamp strengths, too.

So by the time I rush after him, leaving Alex and Magne behind with the car, he's already so far away I can't smell him, or hear him. He's fast and silent. And deadly. He moves almost instantly.

I head in the direction he took, but I have no trail to follow. So I try that thing where I listen to the forest again, and I locate him, not so far away, but moving very fast. But I can't seem to listen, to feel the woods around me, and pay attention to where I'm walking at the same time. I'm too stuck in the need – the human need – to be aware of my limbs and my head and my feet so I don't brain myself on a branch, or trip.

I stop, stand still, and try to put myself in the same frame of mind I use when I practice kung fu. To move without conscious thought, to respond without pondering. I hold onto that as I start walking again, winding around trees and outcrops of rock. Then I gradually extend my senses outwards again, and look, and smell, and keep walking.

Then I speed up a little, still holding myself in a sort of bubble of non-thought. And I try again to feel the forest around me, and the things in it. I smile when my awareness finds a fox in the darkness. She watches me curiously, and seems to know I'm kin in some way.

And suddenly, my awareness of the woods is like an extension of my own senses and I can feel everything in it as if it touches my own skin. But that's not something a human mind was ever meant to encompass and my consciousness expands, somehow, to compensate. And then I realize I'm not walking upright any more. I'm trotting along on four fox legs, and I have no idea if I left a puddle of clothes behind or if they somehow vanished into nothingness when I changed.

Now *I'm* fast. In this shape I can be faster, even, than Evgeny in full vampire mode. And I know exactly where he is. I'll reach him in minutes.

But I can also feel that other presence, the one I assumed was our enemy. It's old. Unbelievably old. As old, maybe, as human fear of the dark. And it's cold. Just being aware of it makes me shiver where the mid-winter temperature did not.

Unlike every other living thing around me – down to the insects, I suspect, if I concentrated – I can't tell if the presence is male or female.

Maybe it's neither, or both, or somewhere in between. Or maybe it's so old the question has become irrelevant for it.

Then, just at the edge of my senses, far off where the witches and the weres wait until they're needed, there's something else. Something not so old, but much more dark. It's similarly sexless, but not in the same way. This other thing is tentative, flickering, shifting from male to female, like it may be a collective rather than a singular thing. But a collective of what? As I try to feel it out, it flickers and vanishes.

I've almost reached Evgeny when the first presence, the very old one, turns its attention to me. I suddenly understand what Alex meant when she said that every time it brushed her mind she was thankful she wasn't the one it was looking for.

I want to hide under a rock and wait for morning, and then creep away with my tail between my legs and never leave the safety of the city again.

The presence smells of the grave, of fates worse than death, and as it notices me, that second presence flickers into being again, attracts its attention for the barest moment. That collective thing tastes like wasted potential and impotent rage. And fear, pain, and loss. It vanishes again as the terrible old thing turns its attention that way.

Evgeny has almost reached it and I imagine I can see its plan for him. Whatever that plan is, it can't be a good thing. It turns its notice back to me, and I give it pause. Its attention on me makes me cower on the ground. I don't know when I stopped running towards Evgeny, but now I'm belly to the ground and like an animal, I piss myself in fear.

I am the bait, I think. Evgeny will feel my fear and he will come. And Alex will come. And *it*, that ancient thing, will have a vampire that can feed on witches and grow stronger, and it will have a witch to feed him. And Magne, a werewolf, will be an appetizer.

And I will be dessert.

I hear whimpering and realize it's me. And that makes me angry. I've been rendered powerless by nothing, by a mere touch of an old mind. I've been made so afraid I piss myself in terror, so fearful my friends will run to my rescue without thought for their own safety.

By a disembodied mind that doesn't even have the manners to

introduce itself.

That pisses me off. And I have always drawn strength from anger. Not long ago, getting mad was the only way I could draw on my fox nature. I had to come so close to dying I went beyond fear to right ticked off. I called that feeling Angry Su, and that's when I could access my more-than-human strength and speed. It's how I could survive attacks by vamps – who thought I smelled tasty – before I was even as strong as they were.

Now I *am* stronger. It's not something I said just to make Evgeny feel better. I can draw consciously, more and more, on my *hexenfuchs* abilities, and on the powers the three fox women gave me when they saved my life. I don't have to be angry to be strong.

But anger, it seems, still gives me a boost. Being pissed off is what now lets me stand up, step away from the puddle of urine I left on the leaves, stop whimpering, and growl.

The presence seems amused. And then it's gone. Well, not gone from the forest, but gone from my mind. I still feel it out there, but it's muffled, more an absence than a being.

"Goddammit," I say, and startle myself. I forgot I could use human speech in fox shape.

I hesitate now, between following after Evgeny again, and going back to reassure Magne and Alex.

They're not far behind me, but Evgeny's closer, so I head for him again. But I notice, too, that the *hexen* and the weres are closer, and the other strange presence is sparking in and out of my awareness again, stronger now that the old thing has withdrawn. Maybe they didn't get Alex's message after all, or maybe their idea of hanging back is to come closer more slowly. I'm starting to think we shouldn't have asked for their help. If any of them is hurt, I don't know how I'll forgive myself.

When I find Evgeny, it's by almost tripping on him. He's splayed out on his face on the forest floor, like he was running back towards me and tripped and fell and just didn't get up.

He's vamp cold and I'm convinced he's really dead. Not vamp-seeming-dead, but completely and irrevocably dead. The only thing that gives me hope is that he doesn't smell of decay. After staving off aging for so long, once death actually arrives, the vamp symbiont seems to kick the process of decomposition into overdrive.

I have to take human shape to roll him over. Before I do, I think very carefully about how my ancestor pulled leaves around her into the seeming of a dress. Only I think about my own clothes, and returning them from wherever they disappeared to. And when my human shape comes back, so do my clothes. Just like that.

Pretty soon, I'm going to have to let go of my stubborn belief that magic isn't really real.

I lean over Evgeny and press my ear to his chest. I can't hear anything over my own harsh breathing. So I sit back, concentrate, practice the breathing exercises my kung fu teacher taught me, until I can inhale and exhale smoothly and silently. Then I bend over Evgeny again and listen. I hold my breath.

And finally, a faint thump … thump of his vamp-slow heart. His chest rises, just barely. I relax, then, head pillowed on his chest.

"Su?" he says, after a moment. "You were afraid."

"I was terrified," I say. "But I'm okay now. It's moved off. It's not paying attention to me any more."

"Did I faint?" he says. My head slides into his lap as he sits up and he blinks down at me. "I was running to you, and it … it sort of *looked* at me, and then you were lying on me."

"You saw it?" I say.

"No. I mean … No. It didn't look at me, really. Not physically. But it … it *noticed* me."

"What is it?" I say.

He strokes my hair, my face, looking down at me like he hasn't seen me in weeks.

"I don't know," he says. "But if I had to guess, I'd say it was a very, very old vampire."

"I didn't know they had power like that," I say. "Mental power, I mean."

"Me, neither," he says. "But I don't think … it didn't actually seem like it was trying to *hurt* me."

"No," I say. "Me, neither. But just having it aware of me scared the crap out of me." Well, the piss, anyway.

He makes an affirmative gesture with one hand. "But I still don't know what it *wants*," he says.

"And if it wants to take you over, why leave you here?"

"Because it is not I who wants to take you over," says a new voice. "That intent belongs to something else, something not a thinking creature like you or I."

I sit up abruptly, get to my feet, Evgeny next to me. We stand a little apart, to give each other room to fight if need be.

I didn't hear or feel or smell this person approach, but when he steps into view, I can sense him, and I feel my knees go weak. I know him now, and he is that old, cold, terrifying presence. I think he must be keeping his presence muffled somehow, because I'm not overwhelmed as I was before, just very, very on edge.

"You shouldn't let yourself get so distracted," he says. He stops a non-threatening distance away.

I inhale, trying not to be too obvious. He smells human, but his skin is cool, and there's a faint tang, almost undetectable even to me, that says "vampire." And a whiff of grave dirt. He's still, but he's mastered the art of imitating humans, so it almost doesn't look wrong.

"Who are you?" says Evgeny.

The vamp ignores the question. "So you're the prodigy Charleston tried so hard to keep a secret from us."

He's focused on Evgeny, so I guess he doesn't know yet what I am. Maybe he doesn't even know I'm anything more than human. He's just far enough away that a vamp wouldn't be able to make out his features clearly, but I have a fox's night vision, so I can see him quite well.

He's not handsome, but not ugly either, and there's a certain aristocratic look to his features that some people would find attractive. His eyes look old, but his face is barely lined. Vamps tend to get shriveled, desiccated-looking as they age, rather than loose and wrinkly, and if they feed regularly and get their heart rate up with sex fairly often, they age very, very slowly anyway. This one doesn't look shriveled, but he does have an almost waxy look to his flesh that could mean great age. I don't really have enough experience with old vamps to say for sure.

"Who are you?" says Evgeny again.

"Let's just say I represent the elders," he says.

"What do you want?" says Evgeny.

"What do we all want?" the vamp says. "Long life; beautiful, skilled lovers; tasty things to eat." His gaze turns to me briefly, then away. Good, he's dismissed me as a potential meal, and nothing more.

I hate being underestimated, but in a fight, it's an advantage.

It's Evgeny's turn to say nothing, and the other vamp sighs. "I wanted to meet the newborn who stirred up so much trouble for us. Charleston may have been a pain in the ass, but he was useful."

"I object to being imprisoned," says Evgeny.

"Indeed, so do we all." The vamp contemplates Evgeny. He doesn't move, but he has a look on his face that seems just about right for accompanying a thoughtful beard stroke.

Then he turns his head sharply, as if he hears something and the moonlight picks out his features in greater relief. He looks Asian. His age seems to have smoothed his face into something generic, but in this lighting, at this angle, there's a distinctly Japanese cast to his features.

For some reason, vamps, like witches, don't tend to come in many colors. At least witches have their Germanic heritage as an excuse. Vamps can be made from all colors of human. But aside from this guy, Charleston was the only person of color I've met among the Reborn. I wonder if vamps are as racist as the humans they're made from.

He stares into the trees for long enough that it occurs to me to wonder what's attracted his attention, so I let my own awareness drift that way. And I realize there are other vamps out there besides the two Magne recruited. They hang back, out of normal hearing range, and it's not them that got the old vamp's attention. It's that other presence.

"What is it, that fearful thing?" I ask. And the vamp turns his attention back to us.

"It's an old thing, aware, but not quite sentient. Not exactly." The vamp frowns, too smooth to be a real human gesture.

"It's something like a ghost, a collection of old sorrows and wrongdoings, of the results of unfair slaughter. The haunting of a mass grave, perhaps."

His eyes catch a gleam of moonlight and flare orange briefly. His voice is uninflected, as if his own words draw no emotion from him.

"Why have you brought it here?" says Evgeny.

"I?" says the vamp. "No, neither I nor the council set this thing free." He looks at me now, lets a cold smile touch his lips, and I think maybe he hasn't underestimated me after all.

"No," he says. "This thing to drive humans mad with fear was roused by your *hexen* friends." He says *hexen* with contempt, though not with as much disgust as witches say "Reborn."

And now it's my turn to stare. The witches had awakened that other presence? But I remember the puzzle of the male consciousness masking their attempts to take over Evgeny, and I shiver.

"Why?" I say. My voice comes out more timid than I'd like, though in retrospect it might be good to reinforce his underestimation of me.

He lets his smile grow, but there is no more warmth in it than in the winter night air. "They feared it, feared possessing the artifact in which it was caged." He shifts his gaze to Evgeny. "And they feared what I and the elders might make of this Reborn ... savant." He looks back to me. "They believed they could destroy both in one move. They believed they could transfer the demon – for that's what they think it is – from its former prison to a new prison of their making in this boy's mind. And then, they thought they could make him walk out into the sun and that both Reborn and demon would perish together."

I don't want to believe anything this vamp says, but it does make sense. It accounts for the singular presence we felt, masking the witches, and more than that, it accounts for the malevolence and the need for domination, for sexual manipulation. I don't want to trust him, but I believe him.

Evgeny is not so sure.

"Why couldn't they leave well enough alone?"

"Because witches must meddle," the vamp says. "It is in their nature. Like it is in the nature of all women."

This guy is super old, so maybe he can't help it if he believes shit like that. He was probably born in an era when women were property, too. But if he's lived this long, and been at *all* observant, and at *all* willing to rise above his childhood brainwashing, he should know better than to say that something is *anyone's* nature.

I resolve to be more open-minded about all *others* from now on, and to not assume anyone will be any one way just because of what they are. I especially don't want to place limits on myself because I'm a fox, or a woman, or half-Asian, or half-Euro, or because I like a lot of sex.

I really want to tell him to fuck off.

But Evgeny beats me to it. "As it is in your nature to assume you are superior because you're Reborn?" he says. Alas, it doesn't work.

"I *am* superior," says the vamp. "You were born of a noble house, as I was. Better humans make better Reborn. And Reborn make better rulers." He turns his mental presence towards us, unmasks it a crack and I tremble. *That* makes a better argument for superiority than idiotic statements about nobility. But really, how does a Reborn make a better ruler? What kind of ruler can only come out at night?

But I say, "A friend of mine told me the vamp symbiont" – I deliberately don't use their preferred term for themselves – "and the were symbiont split off ages ago and with the vamp version the progeny has to be nearly dead before the symbiont can take them over, because it's weaker."

He blinks at me. Then a smile touches his mouth again and this time I think it might be a little bit real. "You are more that you seem, half breed," he says. I wonder if he's referring to me being Euro-Asian, or human-*hexenfuchs*. Or *hexenfuchs*-Asian fox woman. Then his smile becomes something more like a sneer as he says, "It's unfortunate my descendants have so degenerated."

It takes a moment to sink in, but I think he's saying he became a vampire *before* the vamp and were lines split. That would make him ... I try to remember if Magne ever said *when* that happened. He must be several centuries old, at least. Contrary to a lot of pop culture, there aren't many vamps that old. In fact, a century is enough, so Liam said, to make a person a genuine elder.

Which I suppose made Liam himself an elder, if the photograph we found really *was* his wife.

"Why are you here?" says Evgeny. "If not to set loose or to capture the ... presence. The demon."

"To meet *you*, as I said. As for the demon, that's something you have to deal with, since it was loosed for you. Like it or not, it's connected to you."

"How do I stop it?"

The vamp shrugs. "It was trapped, last time, in the mind of a young man, as the witches sought to trap it in your mind."

"A young man?"

"A child is left behind," says the vamp. It's the last bit of Evgeny's dad's saying. "Then the boy was burned alive. Well, after he had passed on his genes. His bloodline was too valuable to let die." The vamp looks at Evgeny closely, head tipped slightly to one side. "A pity it only lasted another few generations, only to stop with you." He sighs. "And that is the worst tragedy of the degeneration of the Reborn. At least the wolf-curs can still produce offspring."

"I have to die to contain it?"

"I only said that's how it was done last time. You will have to find your own way." He looks amused, the vamp. "But burning yourself in the sun may not leave enough of your substance intact to create a prison for it. If you survive, I would very much like to meet you again."

He sounds like he's making something resembling a closing statement, but he still doesn't move. He just stands and looks at Evgeny. Then he smiles again. "I do have such hopes for you. It's fortunate Charleston didn't ruin you with his experiments."

Ev's nostrils flare, but if he has any thoughts he doesn't voice them.

"Now, you'd better hurry," says the vamp. "Your friends are catching up, and they might make a nice snack for the demon-ghost."

He takes a step away, and almost without thinking, I'm in his way. He raises an eyebrow.

"What do we call you?" I say. "I mean, we can't just refer to you as 'that really old vamp we met in the woods'."

"You are a cheeky child," he says. "Too bad you're not mine to punish."

I hardly think I'm a child at 26, but I guess compared to him my grandmother – if I could remember who she was – would be a child.

"Call me Karasu," he says.

"Raven," I say.

"You know Japanese. Hmmm." Then he bends close, to speak into my ear, and low so Evgeny can't hear. "Beware of witches," he says. "Beware of cages." Then he slips past me. "And never turn your back on a *koldun*." He looks at Evgeny, tilts his head as if to indicate the younger vamp, and then he's gone, as silently and as suddenly as he arrived.

And before I can even think to *start* deciphering what he said, the screaming starts.

Chapter Twenty-One

MY FIRST THOUGHT is for Alex, but it doesn't sound like her voice. One of the other *hexen*, then. Then there's a shriek that *does* sound like Alex, followed by a string of profanity from Magne.

I step towards the sound and Evgeny puts a hand on my arm to stop me.

"Alex and Magne," I say.

"I couldn't tell who it was," he says, dropping his hand.

They're not far off and we reach them quickly. Magne is staring at something and Alex is facing half-away from whatever he's looking at, hands clamped over her mouth, eyes squeezed shut.

I can smell her fear, and I can smell blood.

I step around a tree and turn to see what Magne's looking at, and I almost puke. I have a strong stomach, thanks to my fox nature, but what I see spread out on the ground and in the lowest branches of a stunted maple tree isn't just gruesome, it's something from a nightmare.

One of the *hexen* – I think – lies sprawled on the ground. It's difficult to even tell from looking that she's female, but I can smell it, faint beneath the blood and terror. Her skin is lacerated, almost flayed, and her entrails decorate the branches above her like a garland on a Christmas tree.

"Jesus," says Evgeny.

"I should never have called them," gasps Alex. "I should never have asked for their help." Her voice is just the sane side of hysteria.

"You couldn't have known," I say.

"It seems the witches are responsible for this," says Evgeny, gesturing at the mess that was recently a human life. "It seems the enemy we face is an old terror *they* unleashed."

There's no time, really, to explain, but I think we owe Alex something. So I grab her shoulders, make her look at me and give her the short version. Then I tell her, "If you lose it on me, I'm going to ask Magne to take you home." I wonder if I should ask anyway. The thought of Alex lying flayed on the forest floor makes me feel faint.

"Don't you dare," she says. She glares at me, pulling strength from somewhere. "We're in this together."

I nod. "Good." Then I turn to Magne. "Can you get your weres and your vamp friends out of here? I don't see how they can help, and I'd rather not have anyone else killed.

He nods. He's still in wolf-shape, but somehow that human motion doesn't seem odd anymore. "And the *hexen*?" he asks.

I look at Alex. "This is as much their problem as ours," I say.

"Are you sure it was them?" she says.

I look at Evgeny. "No," I say. "But it makes sense."

"I believe I know what that bottle of ashes was," he says. He's looking off in the gloom, trying to locate the demon, I think. My own senses withdrew from their view of the forest when we met the old vamp, and I can't muster enough calm to expand them again. But there's another scream, far off, and Ev's off in pursuit of it without a word.

"Dammit, Evgeny," I yell after him. "Don't do anything stupid."

Magne's gone, too, off to round up his buddies and get them out of here.

"How about we try to find Mathilde?" I say. "It seems your mentor left a few things out last time we spoke to her, but she deserves a warning about what she's unleashed."

Alex nods sharply and lets her eyes go unfocused. Then they clear and she points, not quite the direction Evgeny headed. "That way."

I wonder how the hell we're ever going to find our way out of these woods once the night is over – assuming we're still alive. Even with a fox's sense of direction, I'm getting confused.

I take Alex's hand. "Leave the flashlight off," I say, "and keep close. If we can avoid being noticed, that would probably be a good thing."

"Right," says Alex. She snaps off her light, then follows me, letting me guide her through the dark with just my hand on hers. "Don't walk me into a tree," she says.

I laugh to make her feel better, but I'm not really feeling it.

For a human, a forest at night is full of terrors, even without a demon lurking in the darkness. Even if it was entirely empty of other animals, it would still be a fearful place. It's hard to appreciate beauty when you can't see it, if your primary means of experiencing the world is visual.

So I know Alex is being brave, just by allowing me to take her into the depths of the woods without a light. Hell, even with a light, she'd be brave.

But for me, this could almost be a wonderful jaunt. The air is clean and crisp and smells like rich soil and forest. Even the almost cat-piss stench of spruce is marvelous. And there are sounds all around, from rustling leaves to insect chirps. And I can see a lot, too: sinuous tree-shapes and an owl gliding on silent wings.

At least, it would be wonderful if it weren't for the demon. And the blood and the fear and the killing. Oh, and the ancient vamp whose very notice is terrifying.

"This thing," says Alex, keeping her voice low. "This demon … How could it tear Stephanie apart like that? I thought it was disembodied."

Stephanie, I guess, was the dead witch. I'm surprised that Alex looked closely enough to identify her. I probably shouldn't be, though. Wanting to know who to mourn later seems exactly like something Alex would do. Respecting the dead enough to put a name to her, so she's not just an anonymous corpse.

But that's a good point. How *could* the demon do any physical damage?

"Maybe it possessed someone," I say.

I feel Alex's shiver through our joined hands. "How terrible for whomever was possessed," she says. "To wake up with that on your conscience."

"Let's hope he doesn't remember later," I say. Then I reach back and gently place my fingers on her lips to quiet her, because I know she won't be able to see a gesture, and I can hear voices ahead.

We slow down, creep closer until we see faint, flickering light through the trees. I sniff. Hot wax. Someone's burning candles.

As we approach, the voices resolve into words. The names of goddesses. It's the same chant the witches used to try to take over Evgeny. I pick out three, no four, distinct voices, and one of them, the one that speaks commandingly over the chant of the others, is Mathilde.

If there are four *hexen* here, and one is dead, that leaves one unaccounted for, which is probably the scream Evgeny went after.

We stop outside the reach of the light. Three witches sit around Mathilde, and around them is a ragged circle of candles. Mathilde stands, holding her bottle of ashes up.

"Return to your prison, I command you," she says. "Enter the *koldun*. Fulfill your purpose and return to him. Return!"

The other three stare up at her, hope and terror in their eyes.

"Return as you were summoned forth to do, and rest again."

I let go of Alex's hand and step into the candlelight. "That won't work," I say. "You can't stuff the genie back into the bottle."

Mathilde looks at me, something like hatred in her voice. "This would not be necessary if you hadn't interfered in the first place," she says. "And prevented us from destroying it then."

"That wouldn't have worked, either," I say. "It needs a physical prison. That's why the ashes. No corpse for it to reanimate, but still a physical prison. But without the ashes, it would be free again."

She sneers at me, but doesn't answer. I feel Alex move closer, hear the leaves crackle as she moves to stand at my shoulder.

"There wouldn't have been enough left of Evgeny to hold the demon," I say. "If you walked him out into the sun." I'm kind of making this shit up as I go, but all of my guesses are reasonable and logical. I might actually be right.

"What do you know?" Mathilde says.

"We know you've been afraid of the bottle of ashes for a very long time," says Alex. "But we don't know why you decided to try to destroy it now."

"And we don't know why you're so afraid of it," I add.

"This hardly seems the time or place for telling folk tales," says Mathilde.

"So try telling the truth," I say.

"If we know more," says Alex, "we might be able to help defeat it."

Mathilde looks like she'd rather spit on us than tell us anything, but she finally begins to talk. "In this bottle," she says, "Are the ashes of a young man. A man who could have been the founder of a new line of *hexen*, both male and female, and stronger than any of us have ever been."

"Alexei Romanov," I say.

"Just so. His protector, an evil monk with aspirations to sorcery, used the boy's power to raise a demon."

"Rasputin," I say. "The *koldun*."

"He thought he was a *koldun*," spits Mathilde. "But he was nothing without Alexei."

"Whatever. So he roused a demon."

"He could not have done it without Alexei, and when he realized the danger he had raised up, he could not defeat it without Alexei. The boy become the demon's cage. But he could not fully contain it, and so it controlled him. And he became an evil man, so the monk burned him alive and placed the ashes in this jar to act as the demon's new prison. So it was passed down to Alexei's son, and eventually came into my hands."

"And you felt compelled to let the demon out again," I say.

She gives me a cold stare. "When that Reborn – Charleston – gathered together and imprisoned us, he revealed the existence of the abomination."

"His name is Evgeny," says Alex, which is just what I was about to say. It surprises me a little that she would stand up for him.

"He was one like Alexei, but corrupted by vampire filth," Mathilde says. "And when it became apparent that he might actually manifest his heritage, despite the taint he had been given – "

"How did you know that?"

"Someone has been keeping an eye on you," says Mathilde smugly. She looks at Alex.

Alex steps closer to me, puts her hand on my arm. "I didn't know what they planned," she says. "I – I was making sure you were okay, anyway. I suppose I said a thing or two."

I step suddenly away from her. "You were spying on me?" I look around at her and she's flushed, embarrassed, but she faces me without flinching.

"I needed to know you were safe. After those dreams. I – " She reaches out a hand but doesn't touch me. "I'm sorry. If I'd known what the plan was for him, I never would have said anything."

I look back to Mathilde. I'm furious. Furious at Alex for watching me and never letting me know she was there. Furious at Mathilde for using her.

"So, what?" I say to Mathilde. "You decided Evgeny was too offensive to live and to capture him with your demon and then destroy them both?"

"We would have succeeded, then, and we can still succeed now. You brought him here, and you brought Alexandra here. As Alexandra's familiar, you will give her the power to bind the demon to … *Evgeny*. Being what he is, that binding will be so complete that his destruction will mean the demon's final end."

Everything goes still and cold inside me. I *was* the bait. But not for that ancient, scary vamp we met earlier. For Mathilde and her pet demon.

"You will *not* succeed," says a new voice. Male, guttural, and colder than my frozen insides. I shiver.

A werewolf steps into the flickering light, eyes glowing green. He's big, though not as big as Magne, and he's not old enough, I guess, to be able to become fully wolf-like yet. He looks like a cheesy B-movie monster, but there's nothing funny about him.

His claws and face are stained with blood, black in the forest gloom.

"I like this body," he says. "But it's weak. Too weak."

Mathilde steps back from him, but to her credit, she doesn't run. Two of the other witches do flee, and the were is on one of them before any of us can react. I'm not quick enough to stop him from snapping her neck, but at least I can prevent him from violating her corpse.

I kick him in the head as he crouches over her and he turns, rises. His cock stands proud, incongruously smooth-skinned against his hairy belly. I slip a dagger out of my boot – why didn't I bring my silver-tipped stake? Oh, right, because since the thing where I freed all those vamps and weres from Charleston, I haven't needed to defend myself from them, so I got out of the habit of carrying it. Bad idea.

The were laughs at me, so I cut his throat for him.

I do it without thinking, and after, I stare at him. "Shit," I say. I'm not really a violent person. I've killed only when I have to and it's obvious that the were was not himself, but was possessed by the demon.

Alex has bent over the dead witch, and she looks up suddenly. I expect her to say something about me and killing, but she doesn't. "It's still in him, trying to reanimate the... body," she says.

"Can it do that?"

"It cannot," says Mathilde. "But it will seek a new host."

"At a guess, I say, "It needs a vamp or a were."

"Why do you say that?" says Alex. She gets up, very deliberately not looking at the were, or at the bloody knife in my hand.

"Evgeny's story said the evil sorcerer could command the dead. Maybe it was by using this ... whatever it is we're calling a demon. And weres have a similar symbiont to vamps. They used to be one and the same. So I figured – "

"The demon is limited to a specific type of host," says Mathilde. "But there is a hole in your theory. It possessed Alexei, and Alexei was a witch."

"But did it *choose* to possess Alexei?" I say. "Or was it bound somehow? That could make a difference, couldn't it?"

"It hasn't tried to possess any of us," says Alex.

Mathilde scowls. "We must get it into your ... *Evgeny*." I notice the emphasis she keeps putting on his name, like she's humoring me by using it, but like it tastes like slime.

"Can we bind it, now that it's trapped in the werewolf?" It's the other witch, the one who didn't run. She's the tall dark-skinned woman I remember from Charleston's. The only Black – or other non-white – *hexen* I've seen.

"If we had a crematorium," says Mathilde. "And even then it could jump free now that the host is dead." She looks at me, a gloating expression on her face. "You did exactly what it wished. Freed it to find a new body."

"It's gone now," Alex says.

"Damn," I say.

"Either we let it take your witch-vampire," says Mathilde, "and finish as I planned, or we convince it to return to its former prison." She holds up the bottle of ashes. I want to smack them out of her hands, send the jar flying to smash against a tree, but I refrain.

"I think," says Alex, hesitantly. We all turn to look at her. "I think it has to be trapped the way the monk trapped it, or it will just keep jumping from body to body as its host dies." She looks at me apologetically.

"You mean Evgeny has to trap it in his mind?" I don't look at Mathilde. I don't want to see her face when she realizes we may have to go with her plan after all.

"Yes." Alex's voice is almost a whisper.

"That's what I was afraid of." I think about what the old vamp Karasu told Evgeny. Once it's in his mind, maybe he can find some way to deal with it besides letting it control him, or letting us burn him alive. Assuming there would be enough left of him to serve as a prison, or assuming Mathilde is right and it would be so tightly bound to him it would be destroyed along with him. I have my doubts about both of those things.

There's a short sharp scream somewhere nearby, and we all draw closer together and turn to face it.

"I guess it's found a new host," I say. I should be more horrified. People have died tonight who didn't need to. *Too many* people have died over this idiocy.

"And it had found one of my sisters," says Mathilde. She sounds tired, and sick, like maybe the horrible thing she brought about is finally sinking in. Why couldn't she have just left the stupid bottle corked?

"Stay close together," I say. "I'm going to find Evgeny."

I hope the latest witch victim keeps the demon busy enough for me to find Ev. If he's following the screams, he should be on his way already. And so should Magne. Fuck, I hope the demon's new host isn't Magne.

I'm barely out of the candlelight when I see Ev. And when I put my hand on his shoulder, he turns and starts and the look on his face would have sent me into fits of laughter, under other circumstances.

"It took over one of Magne's weres," I say, keeping my voice as low as I can. "That's how it was able to tear the witch apart."

"It's in a vampire now," he says. "And it seems to be more comfortable."

"You know you're the only one who can stop it." I lace my fingers into his.

"Yes."

"Can you do it without losing yourself? It nearly had you before."

He's quiet, looking off to where there are wet noises and the coppery scent of blood. "I don't know," he finally says. "But I have no choice."

"I wish I could help you," I say.

He turns then, and puts his free hand on my face. "I love you Su. Whatever happens, remember that." Then he's gone.

I follow more slowly, using all my *hexenfuchs* stealth to step silently between the trees until I'm watching Evgeny face the other vampire over the body of a witch. No, not a body. Somehow, she's still alive.

She moans. Her face is streaming blood and I think she has broken bones, from the way she lies crookedly on the forest floor. She tries feebly to crawl away.

The vamp, now hosting the demon, looks down at her, then up at Evgeny. He gestures. "Share my feast, brother."

"You are no brother of mine," says Evgeny.

The demon sneers, and makes to bend over the witch again. Evgeny gets there first, snatches her bodily away. She tries to scream.

"Poor thing," says Evgeny. He puts her down again, bends over her, and twists her head sharply to one side. There's a loud crack and she goes still and quiet. "She would not have recovered from those wounds," he says.

"I didn't intend her to recover," says the demon. "I intended her to suffer, and then die." But I'm pretty sure Evgeny was talking to me, even though he can't know for sure I'm here. He knows me pretty well, and he knows I would follow him.

"You will not make anyone suffer ever again," says Evgeny.

The demon laughs. "Do you know how a *koldun* is made? Has anyone bothered to tell you?"

"No one seems to know if they even exist."

"I will tell you."

It occurs to me that this demon is far more self-aware than it ought to be if what Karasu told us about it is accurate. Maybe it's a side effect of possessing a sentient body, but it seems to have a personality that a collection of ghosts and memories shouldn't have. Whether it's the focussing power of a body, or something else, it also certainly makes it more dangerous than we thought, and we already thought it was pretty bad news.

"Tell me," says Ev.

I glance up at the sky, but too many branches obscure my view. How close is it to sunrise? How long have we been chasing around through these trees, and how far are we from camp? Does Evgeny have time to converse when he should be … doing whatever it is he has to do to trap this thing? But I guess that's the problem. He doesn't know *what* he's supposed to do, and maybe something it says will help him figure it out.

"Three things make a *koldun*," says the demon. "A real *koldun*, not those no-power manipulators-of-witches who like to use that name for themselves."

"What three things?"

The demon watches Evgeny watch it. It stands immobile, only its eyes following Ev as he steps slowly around, away from the body of the witch, to put me at his back.

"First, a rare male witch."

"Why not a woman?"

The demon shrugs. The movement looks natural, like it's normal for a demon to shrug where it would be unnatural for a vampire. Like it's *used* to being in a human shape. That, more than anything, makes me nervous. Shouldn't it be used to being disembodied and trapped in a jar?

"Perhaps it is only tradition," it says. "But women have always had less power, socially, so why not use all the varieties of power available?"

If it weren't for the harsh voice and the malevolent aura this thing is putting out, he'd sound like a political science teacher I had once. And damn, but I want to pause and explore the not-quite-memory of taking a political science class. But this is not exactly the time or place.

"Second," says the demon. "A Reborn to infuse the witch with his blood."

"Which, more often than not, kills the witch," says Evgeny. He's still now, as still as the demon, but rather than stiff, he looks relaxed.

"Maybe *that* is why it takes a male witch," says the demon. "Perhaps they have something even more unique than their sex. Perhaps they can survive the process."

Evgeny could drink *hexen* blood and not die, as a vamp. It's not such a stretch the same genetic inheritance could let his *hexen* nature survive rebirth. And it's not impossible that both of those things could be tied to the Y chromosome, the way *hexen* abilities are usually tied to the double X.

"And the third thing?" says Evgeny.

"Patience," the demon says. "The new vampire-witch must survive being reborn. Tradition says that if they don't kill their maker in the process, they should take his life once they are able."

"My maker didn't die making me."

"No, but I'd wager you killed him later."

I get a chill in my guts again, colder even than the frost crackling on the dead leaves.

"I didn't," says Evgeny. "A friend did."

"Curious," says the demon. "But he's dead, anyway."

"Is that the third thing?"

"Third," says the demon. "When the witch-vampire's powers have begun to awaken" – he gestures at Evgeny – "then he must allow himself to be possessed by a demon born of the slaughter of innocents."

"Alexei was a *koldun*?"

"Your grandsire was weak in the end. He could not contain me, so now he is a part of me. Perhaps it is because he didn't kill *his* maker, either." It grins, and I realize *that's* what makes the demon seem male, and whole, and sentient. Alexei Romanov didn't just give his ashes to make a prison, he gave his consciousness to the demon.

Then Evgeny moves. Between one eyeblink and the next, he's got the demon-ridden vampire by the throat.

"Then try me," he says, and I'm glad he's got his back to me so I don't have to see him rip the vamp's throat out with his teeth.

Chapter Twenty-Two

TIME SEEMS FROZEN as I stare between the branches at Evgeny's back. The sounds of sucking seem to go on far too long, and then Ev drops the body of the vampire who was but recently demon-ridden. He straightens.

"Su?"

"I'm here." I stay where I am, still hidden from Evgeny, and he doesn't turn to look for me.

"I think it escaped."

I reached out with my senses, try to feel the forest around me again, now that I'm not moving. The chill confusion of the demon is still close by. It hovers around Evgeny like an aura.

"No," I say. "It's right by you."

"I don't know how to do this."

"I think…" I hesitate to voice the thought that occurs. I hate the idea of destiny, of our futures being chosen for us, but … "I think maybe this is what you were born for."

"You mean what I was *made* for." His words are bitter, his voice hard.

"Maybe. But you don't have to let it define you, any more than you let the vamp symbiont define you."

Then he flings his head back, a painful-looking snap, and his hands reach out as if for something to hold on to.

"Su?" he says again, and now his voice is soft, strained, like he might be crying.

"I'm still here."

"It hurts," he says. He falls to his knees.

The frigid, sparking aura that is the demon has condensed around Evgeny's head. I remember the look in the werewolf's eyes when the demon possessed it. I didn't even really see the were when I cut his throat, only the evil inside. And now that thing is crawling into my boyfriend.

It contracts suddenly and though it's not actually visible except to my mind's eye, it's like a blinding pinpoint of light, stabbing into Evgeny's head. Then it's gone.

And he screams. I can't describe it, but it's the worst sound I've ever heard. It tears at my heart, batters my eardrums, and it must be ripping Evgeny's throat raw.

I find myself yelling, "Stop. Ev, stop it!" And it goes on and on until I close the distance between us, step around in front of him, and slap him sharply across the face.

He rocks back, sways in place, eyes closed. Then he opens his eyes and I can't get away fast enough. His eyes are not the crazy intense blue they should be, but blank white, pupils like black pits. It is not Evgeny looking back at me.

I run. For I don't know how long I run mindlessly and only my fox nature keeps me from smacking into trees. Finally, stumbling into the shallows of a lake stops me, brings me back to myself.

I stand up to my knees in water and lake weed, brace my hands on my thighs, and pant to catch my breath.

"Fuck," I say, when I have enough wind to speak. "Goddammit," I yell at the sky.

The sky. I have enough presence of mind to note that there are no signs of dawn yet. I check the stars, but I guess I never got in the habit of noticing how they move, because I can't tell the time from their position. I was hoping it would turn out the be one of those things I was good at, before.

I can see the constellation Orion, though, half-visible above the trees, and it gives me comfort. I don't know why, but seeing Orion bright in the sky always makes me feel better. Maybe that's part of why I like winter better than summer.

I turn around and splash back out of the lake. "Shit," I say, but softly. Evgeny needed me, and I ran away. And I can't even explain why. The touch of Karasu's ancient vamp mind make me cower and soil myself – and damn but I'm glad I was in fox shape when that happened – but even he didn't make me run blindly away. And it's not like I haven't faced this demon before. But now, loose in Ev's head, it's like it went from being a vague, disordered presence to a focused evil. I'd bet it would even give Karasu pause.

If I hadn't run, could I have helped Evgeny contain it? Probably not, but just being there for him might have given him courage, or at least encouragement.

Damn.

I sit on a log by the lakeshore, and have to shift position because of a knot poking me in the ass. No, not a bump on the log, but something in my pocket. I pull it out. Alex's crystal.

I wonder. But there's only one way to find out. I get up and start walking back the way I came. Then I remember how Ev screamed when the demon entered his mind and I run.

Maybe I get turned around somewhere in the trees, because I find the witches before I find Evgeny. They're all huddled together behind Magne, like he's protecting them, though he could easily become a host for the demon and kill them all.

They stare at me when I appear between the trees.

"Where's Ev?" says Magne.

"What was that screaming?" says Alex.

"No time," I say. I turn to Alex and hold out the quartz.

"I can't think when he looks at me," I say. "The demon has become something even more terrible inside Evgeny."

"Of course," says Mathilde, contemptuously. "It was born from terror. It *is* terror."

I ignore her. "I need…" I'm not even sure what to ask for. "I need to be able to reach out to it."

Alex looks from me to the stone and back. "It terrifies me, too," she says.

"What do you have in mind?" says Magne.

"To go into Evgeny's mind, like I did when I drove it … when I drove the witches out.

"To do what you did before?"

I shake my head. "Before, the demon was still weak, it was still controlled by the witches, and I only had to drive them out and it went too. Now it's on its own, and it's in there by invitation. Evgeny's invitation. And even if I could drive it out, we'd just be back where we started."

"So," says Alex, thoughtfully, "You want to join your power with mine. To enter Evgeny's mind together and help him contain the demon?"

"Yes," I say.

"It would mean binding yourself to me, as my familiar," she reminds me. Her voice is gentle, apologetic. I don't think she wants to bind me any more than I want to be bound.

Mathilde laughs. "I told you she'd come begging to you eventually."

Alex glares at her, then turns back to me. "You really want to do this?" she says, putting a hand on my shoulder.

"I don't *want* to," I say. "But it's Evgeny. I have to do *something*. I can't let him be taken over by that thing."

Alex nods.

"That filthy creature must mean a great deal to you," says Mathilde. "Though you're hardly more than an animal yourself."

"You really are a hateful woman, Mathilde," says the other witch. She steps around to the other side of Magne, not seeming to be bothered by his near-wolf shape at all. "I don't know why I never saw that before."

Magne looks at her and smiles, and despite the unsettling look the expression gives his face, she smiles back.

"He means everything to me," I say. Enough to give up my freedom? If I had time to think about it, I might not think so. I value my freedom pretty highly, and if any man ever demanded I give it up, or even asked outright, I'd leave him with hardly a thought. But Evgeny hasn't asked, would never ask. And that's why I'd do it for him.

And there's also the fact that a lot more people could die if I don't.

"Okay," says Alex. Then, "When this is over, I promise we'll find a way to undo the binding."

Mathilde snorts at that, but no one pays her any attention.

"Just do it," I say.

So Alex takes the quartz from me and I bow my head so she can slip the thong around my neck. The stone settles in the hollow of my throat, cold from the night air, but it quickly warms.

She touches it with her fingertip and it beings to glow. She tilts my head up with the same finger under my chin so I have to look into her eyes. For the first time, I notice that her dark brown irises are ringed with violet. You'd think I might have noticed before.

I feel like my mind is falling into hers, and then something tightens like a leash, except it's not physical. My first instinct is to fight it, and I think I might even be strong enough to break it.

"That's the familiar binding," says Alex, and I can't tell if she's speaking out loud, or in my head. I force myself to relax, to let the leash pull snug. I might be able to get used to it, I suppose, but I don't like it now.

Then Alex has to kneel to keep looking me in the eyes, and I hear the gasps of the two other witches and I realize I've taken fox shape.

"You *are* strong," says Alex. "There's more in you than just the *hexenfuchs* ancestry."

Did I never tell her about the fox women and their gifts? Surely I did, but maybe she didn't know what I meant, that I'm also both born and made *other*.

"I don't know if you even need me to do this," she says.

"I need you. I need you to keep the terror at bay."

She nods. "Let's do it, then."

Evgeny is still where I left him when I ran off, kneeling on the forest floor, hands clenched, head tilted back. We approach him cautiously, but he doesn't move.

We circle around, and his eyes are closed. The chill feeling is still in the air, but it's bearable, just.

"He's fighting it," says Alex. "But it's weakening him."

"How do we do this?" I say, and Alex looks startled. I must have been speaking to her with my mind until now, and she's surprised at the human voice coming from my fox mouth.

Alex crouches next to me, in front of Evgeny, then reaches out and touches his forehead. His head snaps forward and his eyes open. They are blue, but clouded, as if with a film of age.

"I can't do it," he says. "It's too strong."

"Because I killed your parent vamp when you should have?" I ask.

His eyes go white and I fight the terror that floods me, struggle to remain sitting calmly in front of him. I can feel Alex fighting off the fear, too, and her presence is enough to give me strength.

"Clever beast," the demon says. "If he had killed his papa and drank his blood I could not hope to resist him. That was Alexei's failing, too. But now, I will take his body and wear it for my own and the first thing I will do with it is violate you in every way I can think of. And your little witch, too."

"No," I say, and I'm surprised at how firm my voice is. Then I stare deep into its eyes and use them to enter Evgeny's mind, pulling Alex after me.

"Su?" I hear his voice.

"Ev?"

"You shouldn't be here, Su," he says. "It will take you, too, and I could never forgive myself."

"It will *not* take me," I say. "Or you. Or Alex."

"Three against one," says Alex. "I think the odds are in our favor."

But the demon laughs and suddenly Evgeny's head is filled with light, liquid-nitrogen cold and retina-searing bright.

"I will be free at last," the demon says. "With a body and a thinking mind. The world will cower before me."

I feel for Alex and she's there beside me, strong and warm. The light she sheds here in Evgeny's mind is green, like the plants she loves. I draw her close to me, but my light is red and hot and together we make something murky. But that's not right. That's not how light combines.

I feel for Evgeny and he's harder to find, blocked out by the demon's flare. But I locate him, draw him to me, and he's cool, but not cold, and glowing softly blue. I almost laugh. Red, green, blue. Together we make pure white light, as bright as the demon, but warm and alive – Ev's cool balancing my hot – where the demon is cold and dead.

"You cannot defeat me," it says. "You cannot destroy me."

"We don't have to destroy you," I say. "We only have to contain you."

It laughs. "Not you," says the demon. "Only him. Only he can contain me." And a beam of white light like an icicle spears through the blue glow of Evgeny's thoughts.

The blue wavers, flickers, and together Alex and I reach out and strengthen him.

"Go get that creep," I tell Evgeny. "Use our strength and bind that thing so tight it can't even wiggle."

"Yeah," says Alex. Then she adds, "It said it was going to violate Su."

For a moment, Evgeny does nothing. Then he says, "You should not have threatened her," and his tone sends a thrill – a good, hot one – through me.

Then he's moving. Well, not actually moving, since inside his head we're all blobs of light, but he *seems* to be moving, pulling me and Alex along with him, circling around and around the demon-glow, caging it in soft white until that's all that's visible.

Then, as the sphere of light encloses it, the demon starts to ... sort of dissolve. It remains where it is, inside the bubble, but its own sharp glare fades and seems to disintegrate into multiple points of light like fireflies.

And each little glow, as it brushes against the light walling it in, gives up its story.

A peasant woman, baby torn from her arms, falls beneath a soldier's sword, living just long enough to see her sister raped and tossed into a pit of corpses.

A young man, slender and pretty, held down by one burly soldier while a line of others take their turn to violate him. When death comes, it's a mercy, but what remains after is fear and pain.

A small child, too little to waste a bullet or blade on, is tossed alive into the pit, to be smothered as more bodies are piled in on top of him.

A little girl hiding, witnessing every death, every rape, every beating, but thanking God the soldiers haven't found her. But they do find her, when they set fire to the barn and she must run or burn. She wishes, as she lies broken and dying, that she had chosen to burn.

One by one the stories of the slaughtered, the ghost-memories that make up the substance of the demon, brush up against the light, as if trying to extinguish themselves. Their stories flicker through our thoughts until I want to run from them, to flee. Until I want to abandon Evgeny just so I don't have to *see* any more.

"Be strong, Su," says Alex. Her voice sounds stricken, but also solid, and because of her I can hold on. "We're the only ones who will remember them, now."

"Born of the slaughter of innocents," says Evgeny. His voice is also filled with sorrow. "The old vampire wasn't exaggerating."

How long it goes on, I have no idea, but there must be more than a hundred of them, dumped somewhere in a mass grave, unmourned because anyone who would know to mourn them dies with them.

So many lives, so much fear and pain.

"Was it deliberate?" I say. "Did someone do this to create the demon on purpose, or was it accidental?"

"Oh, gods, I hope it wasn't deliberate," says Alex. "It's horrifying enough as it is, but if someone made this happen just to create a demon…" She doesn't have to say any more.

The abruptly, it stops. The firefly lights of the ghosts cluster together, centered in the glowing bubble in Evgeny's mind, and we three can be still.

"Can we set them free, somehow?" I say. "Lay them to rest?"

"Like showing them the way to the other side?" says Alex.

"They're not ghosts," says Evgeny. "Not really. They're more like memories. The distilled fear and pain and humiliation of all those people. But the people themselves, their souls, if there is such a thing, I think those are long gone."

"So we leave them here?" I say.

"For now," says Evgeny. "I suppose we do."

I wake up in darkness. It's not so complete I can't see, and it smells like my bed in the loft, but it's the wrong shape.

Then I remember that Evgeny and Magne made the curtains into a tent, so Ev would have a place to shelter if we were gone through the night.

I lie still and listen and breathe. Close by, I smell Evgeny, hear his faint sleeping breaths. I put out my hand and touch his chest. He mumbles, but doesn't wake.

Outside, I hear crackling. A campfire. And I smell meat roasting. My stomach grumbles. There's a snort, and a sneeze. Magne.

I sit up and have to feel around to find the tent opening. As I pull the flap aside, Magne says, "Careful, sun's up out here." So I slither out of the smallest opening I can make, then close the tent up again.

"Alex?" I say.

"Asleep in the back of the car."

I stand up and glance in the station wagon's window and there she is. Eyes bruised purple, but sleeping peacefully.

"What about the witches?"

"The cold biddy took the enchanting Cara away with her, but not before I got her phone number." He grins.

"You got Mathilde's number?" I say, pretending to be serious. I have to duck the fir cone he flings at my head.

"Cara's number, you sly vixen," he says.

"Hmm," I say. "Aren't there any girl weres?"

"Plenty," he says. "But I'm not racist. Or speciesist. As long as she's human-shaped most of the time, and sentient. And not evil."

That make me laugh, which feels unbelievably good after the night I've just had. We've just had.

I sit next to Magne and take the hot dog he hands me. I'm so hungry I barely taste it. The second one I eat slowly, and I'm pleased to discover Magne's not one of those men who eats cheap, gross hot dogs. These are real smokies, big and spicy. Roasted on a stick over a campfire, they're the most delicious thing I can imagine right now.

"Your werewolves?" I finally ask around a mouthful.

"One dead," he says.

I'd forgotten that. I *did* that.

"Not your fault," he says. "Also one vamp dead. The rest got out safely. A friend is taking care of the … remains. The witches, too." He glances at the car. "He'll tell me where they're buried, so Alex can visit the graves if she wants to. But it would be best not to go too often. Just in case someone gets suspicious."

I nod and we sit side by side, waiting for darkness, so we can wake Evgeny and go home.

HEIR of WITCHES

read on for a preview of book three of the *Fictive Kin* series

Chapter One

I WAKE SUDDENLY, and I can't breathe. There's something wrapped around my throat, pulling tight, tugging at me, choking off my air.

When I sit up in the darkness behind the bedcurtains, I'm gasping in great sucking lungsfull and even though the feeling of choking is now a lingering memory I still feel like I can't get enough oxygen.

I turn to talk to Evgeny, expecting him to be awake, concerned. But then I remember he's not here. He took a part-time nightshift job at the mall to pay the rent, and his apartment is closer to the job than mine. That's important when you catch fire in sunlight, being able to get home quickly and on time.

It occurs to me that one of us should have asked the other to move in by now, since we spend most of our time together, anyway. Except it's good to be able to have solitude when you need it. I crack the curtain and sunlight floods in. He'll be home now, asleep, safe behind his double-insulated blinds. I wonder why I didn't stay at his place.

I yawn and stretch, feeling fatigue like a throbbing behind my eyes. Oh, right, I stayed home because I haven't been sleeping well and I thought I might sleep better without a beautiful young man sharing my bed.

I put my hand to my throat. I have enough experience with weird dreams to know that they aren't always meaningless picture-shows dredged up by an active imagination, and they aren't always just metaphorical.

I need to talk to Alex.

A couple of months ago, I needed her help … Well, Evgeny needed *our* help to stop a … the witches called it a demon, but it wasn't, exactly. But Ev had to trap it in his own head and for various reasons he wasn't quite strong enough.

And the demon-ghost-thing – an evil presence born from the slaughter of innocents, actually – terrified me. It was something that made even a super-old, super-strong vampire nervous, and he's a guy who so freaked me out the mere touch of his mind is the only thing ever to have made me piss myself. Literally. I was in the shape of a fox at the time, so it wasn't as messy as it could have been, but still. Anyway, the whole story is complicated, but I couldn't help Evgeny on my own. I needed Alex.

The only way for me and Alex to pool our powers (I dislike that word, but I can't think of another that fits) was for her to bind me with a familiar spell. Because Alex is a witch. And you know how witches are supposed to have cats for familiars? Some of them do, but legend says foxes make the best familiars, and *hexenfuchs* are supposed to be especially good. But they're rare. And I'm not explaining very well.

One of my ancestors, as impossible as it may seem, was a *hexenfuchs*, a witch-fox. And I had just learned how to take fox shape, and to keep this short, I'll just say that to help my boyfriend trap the demon, I allowed a witch to bind me to her will, as her familiar.

So, yeah, I'm Su, and I turn into a fox and let one of my closest friends make me her slave.

When Alex did the binding, it was like being leashed with an invisible rope made of her energy. And that's what I've been dreaming about. We haven't been able to find a way to reverse or break the binding, short of one of us dying, so lately we've just sort of ignored it. It's not like Alex would ever order me around.

But now my sex life is suffering, because I know that if she wants to, Alex can feel what I feel, see what I see, hear what I hear. And if *she* chooses, I can listen in on her. If she chooses.

The only thing keeping me from total paranoia about getting naked with Evgeny is that Alex is a lesbian, so she's not going to be interested in what it feels like to sleep with him. But still, knowing she *can* look in makes it hard to relax, you know? I *think* I would know if she were watching, but I'm not certain.

Also, a year and a bit ago, Alex and I were lovers, on track to having a really great long-term relationship, and now we're still negotiating the current terms of our friendship. So sex is a bit of a touchy topic.

Lately, it's been getting worse. Not the sex. Well, that too, but I mean the feeling of being *leashed*. Of being watched, controlled.

I don't think Alex is doing anything differently. I don't think she's actually watching in on me or trying to make me do things. But I wonder if her developing witch abilities are somehow unconsciously draining me, draining my powers.

So I need to talk to her. Really talk, not the catching up and chatting about life in general that we do every couple of weeks over coffee. The problem is, I can't just call her up, because the last time I saw her, she was all giddy about a road trip she was planning with her new love interest. So I expect her to be out of contact. But if I really need to get in touch with her, I can borrow Evgeny's cellphone, or Magne's, and leave her a message.

When I feel a little more awake, I crawl out of bed and put the kettle on – green tea, because I'm essentially nocturnal these days and I plan to go back to sleep soon. Then I dig around in a drawer and find the bit of paper with Alex's number on it. I have her home phone number memorized – she insists on keeping a landline as well as a cell, says it's a witch thing. Something to do with physical phone lines relaying more non-verbal information, whatever that means.

But her cell number is new. She got the phone just before she left, with the idea that even if roaming charges are ridiculously high, at least she'd have it for emergencies.

Then, number in one hand and tea in the other, I sit on the couch and realize I can't call her anyway, not yet, so I might as well have stayed in bed. I not only don't have a cellphone, I don't have any sort of phone. Or an internet connection. My neighbor and good friend Magne likes to tease me about it, asking if I'd like him to disconnect my electricity, too, or my plumbing. I tell him let me ease into this whole being connected thing. It's only been a few months since I bought a microwave and mere weeks since

I added a secondhand stove so I don't have to cook on a hotplate.

I put Alex's number on the table and glare at it as I sip my tea. My tail starts to twitch in annoyance – I can make it vanish, but since I learned to change shape I find I'm most comfortable, most *myself*, I guess, when I'm in human form with a big bushy fox tail. Fox-tailed girl, that's me. It's weird, but I like it. I have slit-pupiled fox eyes, too, unless I deliberately make them look human.

By the time I get to the bottom of my tea, I'm forced to acknowledge that I'm not going to be able to sleep until I call Alex. So I pad down the hall to the elevator and take it down to Magne's floor. It's only one level and it would actually be faster to take the stairs, but we got into the habit of taking the elevator as a way of letting each other know when we're coming and going. So we can look out for each other. We both have better-than-human hearing – Magne's a werewolf – but our building is a converted warehouse and nearly soundproof. Doors are impossible even for me to hear from one floor up, but we can both hear the hum and feel the vibration of the elevator's ancient motor.

It's still morning and Magne's almost as nocturnal as I am, especially this close to the full moon, so I'm not all that surprised he doesn't answer. Either he's not home, or he's got company and he's ignoring me.

I don't remember hearing him come home, but I was asleep and might have missed it. Anyway, Magne, like Alex, has a new woman friend, and he hasn't been around as much as usual either.

So I'm feeling a bit abandoned when I plod back to my loft, via the stairs this time. Alex is on a road trip with her girlfriend, Magne is probably at *his* girlfriend's place, and my boyfriend is at his own place. It makes me grumpy, and I hate feeling sorry for myself.

So I vanish my tail, make my eyes look properly human, and get dressed in clothes I can actually be seen in public in. Then I go out to catch the bus to Evgeny's place.

It feels strange to be out during the day. I've gotten so used to being one of those things that goes bump in the night that I forgot how nice it can be to see things in colour. Because not only does the darkness reduce the world to shades of grey, but even in daylight my fox eyes don't see the same range of colour as my human eyes.

I find myself mesmerized by the movement of light through the leaves of the tired old oak that grows near one side of my building. They're not fully unfurled yet, those leaves, since spring is still new – so new it could snow and not be entirely unseasonal – but they're open enough that I can see the tracery of veins inside their delicate surfaces.

And the sky. It's smudged with the dingy, dusty taint of the city, but it's still glorious. Evgeny's eyes are nearly that colour when he's happy. Thinking of Ev happy makes me smile and I laugh out loud.

I realize, too late, that it probably makes me seem like a madwoman, but then I realize that I don't care. As it turns out, there's no one on the street to see me anyway. One of the benefits of living in a largely industrial part of town is that I don't have many neighbors. There are a couple of other warehouses converted to flats and studios, but most of them are rented by vamps and weres and other *others* for the same reasons I live here. It's not a pretty neighbourhood, but it's quiet, and it's close enough to the river and several parks that there's room to run.

I sit on the bus stop bench and tilt my face up to the sun, feel it soak into my skin. My fox nature wants to curl up in the heat and take a nap, but my human side is energized by the light.

One of the disadvantages of living where I do is the shitty bus service. They do come here, but only at considerable intervals. So I finally decide to walk, at least to somewhere busier where I can get a bus that goes where I want to go without having to transfer. I stand up, stretch, and head towards downtown via the park.

It was there I killed Ev's papa vamp, which sort of resulted in him gaining his freedom – it definitely ended up with me feeling obligated to help him.

I should point out that I don't go around killing vampires willy-nilly. They're sentient, thinking beings and have as much right to exist as I do. And hell, Ev's a vamp himself. But when they try to make me into a snack, I don't hesitate to fight back.

Killing Papa Vamp also sort of indirectly resulted in Evgeny needing my help with the demon-ghost evil thing he's now got trapped inside his head. It's a long story, and complicated, and I'm not even sure I know how all the connections worked.

But this is where I staked the nasty old prick, when he decided he wanted to feed me to his progeny – after raping me, of course. You can understand, I hope, that I was rather anxious that neither of those things happen. And here, too, is where Ev and I fought off a gang of vamps – who call themselves "Reborn" by the way – who were trying to capture him. Actually, Evgeny did most of the fighting, though I was not exactly a pushover.

I have a lot of memories here, good and bad, but they're all recent, because something over a year ago, a year and a half nearly, I was attacked, violated, and left for dead in a formal Japanese garden outside of town. I woke up in this park, with no memories of my past.

Since then, I've gained a few memories back – a trio of ancient fox women helped with that – but a lot of my life is still a blank. It used to bother me, but since I learned more about my fox nature I've started to care less and less about who I used to be. I am who I am now, and that's what matters, right?

Still, there are times when knowing my past would really come in handy. Like when a good-looking guy, dusky-skinned, late 30s or not much older, with Ben Franklin specs and dressed like an academic in jeans and a sports jacket grabs my arm as I pass by and says, "Panya? My God, where have you been?" And hugs me.

My first instinct is to shove him away and pretend I don't know who the fuck he is. Hell, I wouldn't have to pretend, because I *don't* know who he is. But he knows who I am. Or who I used to be. And he smells – just barely – like magic.

My full name is Panya Su Fuchs, and since I woke up on a park bench – one not far from where I'm being hugged by a stranger – I've called myself Su. Of the two given names on my expired driver's license, it felt the most like me. But I learned when the fox women gave me back a night of my memory, when I remembered loving Alex, that I used to be called Panya. Sometimes Alex still calls me Panya by accident, because that's how she knew me first.

I force myself not to kick this guy in the nuts – I know kung fu, but gonad-crushing is easier from this close up – and I just stand still. After a brief moment he steps back. He looks confused, and I feel kind of bad.

"Um," I say. Yeah, I'm not exactly eloquent. I spend too much time in my own head, I guess.

"Panya?" says the man. He's got a trace of an accent. Indian, maybe. How did I know him? "Are you all right?"

Then this thing happens that sometimes does. It's like déjà vu, only much, much stronger. And it usually brings some fragment of lost memory with it. This man at a podium, giving a lecture. There's a map behind him, showing the Middle East.

I'm dizzy suddenly, and when I put out my hand to catch my balance, he's there, one hand in mine, one at my elbow, leading me to a bench, helping me sit.

"Dr Pradip?" I say. Then I remember another day, an office, he's leading me to a chair just like he lead me to the bench. I've had some devastating news. What was it?

"John," he says. "Have we become strangers?" He touches my hair and I know that touch, intimately. I turn my face against his hand, and remember the heat of his skin, his mouth.

Oh, fuck. This man was my political science professor, and then my lover. I get up and I'm ten steps away before I stop myself, turn back.

"I'm sorry," I say.

"No," he says. "I'm sorry. I shouldn't have… I never explained to you why I… why I broke things off."

"Things are complicated right now," I say. I try to remember more about him, about me, but forcing the déjà vu only makes it recede faster. Another moment, and it's gone. My head is clear and I have a few more facts about my life, but otherwise everything is back to normal.

"Okay," he says. "But I feel I owe you an explanation. Perhaps I could buy you lunch?"

I hesitate. I want to leave, quickly, and not deal with this fragment of my past. I don't want the woman I used to be to intrude any more on my life now. But one thing I've learned in the last year is that you never know when a bit of information is going to be useful. And I've also learned that the past has a habit of catching up to you, whether you want it to or not.

And my past might just hold the answers to how exactly my fox nature fits with my human side. Plus there's that faint whiff of what I think of as the smell of magic, which is more likely the scent of *otherness*, that clings to him like a faded cologne. It's so tenuous I don't think *he's other*, but he's been around someone who is.

So I nod, and take his business card, shake his hand, let him kiss me chastely on the cheek, and walk away.

I make it out of sight around a bend in the path before dizziness hits me again, so hard I fall to my knees on the pathway. This time, it's not déjà vu that does it. It's Alex's familiar binding, and it feels so much like strangling I think I actually black out for a few seconds.

As soon as I fight off panic, as soon as I can breathe again, I walk straight to a bus stop and get on the first bus heading in the general direction of Evgeny's place.

When I get there, I fumble so much with the key that by the time I get the door open Ev's awake, blinking at me from beyond the reach of sunlight through the doorway.

"Su?" he says. "What's wrong?"

I don't cry much. I don't like how helpless it makes me feel. But when I've got the door closed again, I can feel hot tears streaming down my face.

Evgeny puts his arms around me, strokes my hair, and murmurs nice things into my ear until the tears stop. He doesn't ask me to explain, he just waits, holding me until I'm ready to talk. I tell him about the familiar binding and how it's started choking me, about the nightmares of strangling, and even about meeting my professor – my ex-lover – in the park.

He puts his hand on my face, and his touch, unlike John Pradip's, is cool. He's a vampire, so his circulation is slow, so slow he can appear dead, though he's very much alive. But it makes his body temperature cooler than human.

"Is there anything I can do?" he asks.

I scrub my face with both hands. "How are your witch abilities?" I say. Because Ev, though made a vampire, was born a witch, maybe the only male witch currently alive. It shouldn't be possible for him to be both witch and vamp – it should have killed him to be made Reborn – but Ev's not exactly a run-of-the-mill guy.

He shrugs. "I've been practicing. I'm not even sure what I'm supposed to be capable of."

"Can you block my mind from… from outside influences?" I'm not even sure I really want to ask him this; I don't like anyone meddling with my mind, but better Ev than anyone else. Usually my fox powers are enough to keep witches and other manipulators-of-thoughts away.

"From Alex?" he says. "Is that what you want?"

Alex, because of the familiar binding, is the one person I can't block. Not anymore. I nod.

"I can try," he says.

"Do it," I say. "Please." And then I kiss him, push my mouth against his, slide my tongue between his teeth, press myself against him until I feel his breath quicken and the heat of his body increase as his metabolism picks up from arousal. I can smell his desire and my own response to it.

And something eases in my head, a tension I was hardly aware of.

He pulls away to say, "I don't think I can keep her out if she really wants to force the issue."

Then I drop to my knees for the second time that day, tug down his pyjama bottoms, and render him incapable of saying anything else by applying my mouth to his erection.

About the Author

NICOLE SILVER LIVES like a hermit on the edge of the woods, but haunts used bookstores like a wraith. She fully expected to be found someday as a mummified old corpse crushed under a toppled to-be-read pile, but the rise of e-books has made that somewhat less likely, though the books will always outnumber even the dustbunnies. Nic will read just about anything, including the instructions on the back of medicine bottles, but has a particular fondness for good stories with a hint of magic. She writes dark, sexy urban fantasy, and sometimes dreams in black and white.

Made in the USA
Columbia, SC
05 April 2023

7ef2cfb6-2352-4dd9-a956-7e7072147aa2R01